"This is strictly business, Jussy..." Sam said.

Strictly business. Jussy's smile was wry. So much for daydreams. She came to her feet. "I'll think about your proposition, and let you know tomorrow."

Sam got up, too, and held out his hand to her.

After some hesitation, Jussy took it. She expected a jolt of electricity at his touch, and steeled herself for it. But what followed turned out to be something worse: a seductive warmth that spread like slow fire throughout her body, and was impossible to ignore.

I could desire this man.

The thought came from nowhere, taking Jussy unawares, embarrassing her.

Oh, Lord, suppose he noticed?

The door closed behind him. *Strictly business...*

Dear Reader,

Special Edition's lineup for August will definitely make this a memorable summer of romance! Our THAT SPECIAL WOMAN! title for this month is *The Bride Price* by reader favorite Ginna Gray. Wyatt Sommersby has his work cut out for him when he tries to convince the freedom-loving Maggie Muldoon to accept his proposal of marriage.

Concluding the new trilogy MAN, WOMAN AND CHILD this month is *Nobody's Child* by Pat Warren. Don't miss the final installment of this innovative series. Also in August, we have three veteran authors bringing you three wonderful new stories. In *Scarlet Woman* by Barbara Faith, reunited lovers face their past and once again surrender to their passion. *What She Did on Her Summer Vacation* is Tracy Sinclair's story of a young woman on holiday who finds herself an instant nanny to two adorable kids—and the object of a young aristocrat's affections. Ruth Wind's *The Last Chance Ranch* is the emotional story of one woman's second chance at life when she reclaims her child. Finally, August introduces *New York Times* bestseller Ellen Tanner Marsh to Silhouette **Special Edition**. She brings her popular and unique style to her first story for us, *A Family of Her Own*. This passionate and heartwarming tale is one you won't want to miss.

This summer of love and romance isn't over yet! I hope you enjoy each and every story to come!

Sincerely,

Tara Gavin, Senior Editor

Please address questions and book requests to:
Silhouette Reader Service
U.S.: 3010 Walden Ave., P.O. Box 1325, Buffalo, NY 14269
Canadian: P.O. Box 609, Fort Erie, Ont. L2A 5X3

ELLEN
TANNER MARSH
A FAMILY OF HER OWN

Silhouette®

SPECIAL EDITION®

Published by Silhouette Books
America's Publisher of Contemporary Romance

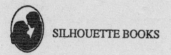

SILHOUETTE BOOKS

ISBN 0-373-09978-9

A FAMILY OF HER OWN

***ELLEN TANNER MARSH*'s**

love of animals almost cost her readers the pleasure of experiencing her immensely popular romances. However, Ellen's dream of becoming a veterinarian was superseded by her desire to write. So, after college, she took her pen and molded her ideas and notes into full-length stories. Her combination of steamy prose and fastidious historical research eventually landed her on the *New York Times* bestseller list with her very first novel, *Reap the Savage Wind*. She now has over three million books in print, is translated into four languages and is the recipient of a *Romantic Times* Lifetime Achievement Award.

When Ellen is not at her word processor, she is showing her brindled Great Dane, raising birds and keeping the grass cut on the family's four-acre property. She is married to her high-school sweetheart and lives with him and her two young sons, Zachary and Nicholas, in the South Carolina low country.

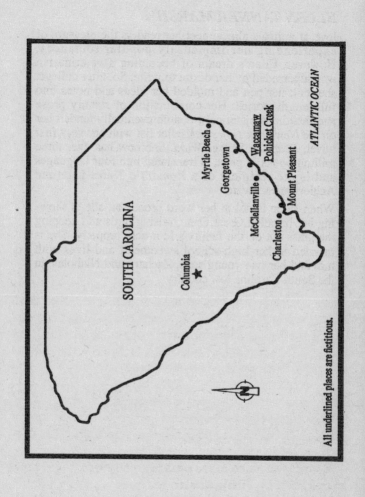

SOUTH CAROLINA

Columbia ★

ATLANTIC OCEAN

Myrtle Beach •

Georgetown •

Waccamaw
Pohicket Creek

McClellanville •

Charleston •

Mount Pleasant

All underlined places are fictitious.

Chapter One

The funeral was over. Driving out of the churchyard, Jussy Waring turned left into the pouring rain. Her black dress was soaking, and her hair hung in damp auburn ringlets down her back. She was actually shivering with the cold. Spring in the South Carolina low country was late this year.

The road was lined with towering oaks. Skeins of Spanish moss hung from the branches, making a tunnel for the car. The wet pavement hissed beneath the tires. Next to Jussy on the front seat, the little girl with the curly blond hair stuck her thumb in her mouth and fell asleep.

Poor thing, Jussy thought, reaching over to caress her. It couldn't be easy losing your mother, even if you didn't remember much about her.

Thunder rumbled in the distance, and the little girl murmured fretfully. Jussy caressed her again.

"It's okay, Ash. Go back to sleep."

Reassured, the child quieted. Jussy glanced down at her with a sudden sense of helplessness. How on earth was she ever going to replace the mother Ashley had lost?

Ashley Waring was barely five years old. For the last few months of her young life she had rarely seen her mother. Caroline had been the one who had insisted that Ashley stay away from the hospital once her illness worsened.

Jussy had understood and respected her sister-in-law's wish. Grim hospital scenes should never be the last memories anyone had of their mother.

But four months were a long time in the life of a five-year-old. Over the last few weeks, Ashley had pretty much stopped asking questions, stopped mentioning Caroline's name, stopped wondering when her mother would be coming home.

Everyone Jussy consulted about this had assured her it was normal. Caroline had been sick for so long that a high-spirited child like Ashley couldn't help but focus her attentions elsewhere. And Jussy had certainly gone out of her way to make her niece feel happy and secure from the moment Caroline had brought her to the Warings' big plantation house on Pohicket Creek.

Tears burned the back of Jussy's eyes as she remembered that day. Nearly a year had passed since then, a long, difficult, disheartening year in which Ashley had been the only brightness in Jussy's life. Caroline's decline had been hard on all of them, but as her primary care giver, Jussy had borne the brunt of it. There had been endless trips to Charleston for surgery and chemotherapy, and days on end when her sister-in-law had needed constant watching because she was strung out on painkillers and too weak to get out of bed. Worst of all had been the endless worry about money, because Caroline's insurance had paid for only so much and, after her second operation, had darn near refused to pay anything at all.

Things would have been so much easier if Jussy's brother had agreed to help his ex-wife just a little. Only he hadn't. None of the bills Jussy stubbornly mailed to Los Angeles were ever taken care of, and few of the endless calls she made to his answering machine were returned. Whenever Gerald did call, he rarely asked about Ashley and never about Caroline.

The creep hadn't even shown up for her funeral.

Now it was all on Jussy's shoulders. Caroline had been awarded full custody of Ashley, and she had named Jussy Ashley's guardian.

All at once Jussy became aware that her hands were shaking. She gripped the steering wheel tighter. The windshield wipers could barely keep up with the downpour.

I should have accepted Reverend Mac's offer of a ride home, Jussy thought despairingly. *I'm exhausted, and it's impossible to see through this rain.*

Up ahead the trees parted, revealing a dilapidated country store with a faded sign reading Reid's Grocery. A battered pickup truck stood at the curb.

Jussy's heart swelled with relief. Because Caroline's funeral had been private, Ella Reid hadn't shut down her store to attend, and Jussy could already envision her standing behind the counter with a big pot of coffee steaming at her elbow.

"Let's stop a minute," she told the sleeping child, although Ashley didn't stir.

Parking the Ford right in front, where she would know instantly if the child woke up, Jussy locked the doors and hurried inside. Only in a peaceful town like Waccamaw, where she knew everyone and everyone knew her, would she ever dream of doing such a thing.

It was Friday afternoon, and Reid's was empty. March was always a slow month in this isolated part of the South Carolina low country. The tourists were down in Florida enjoying the late-winter sunshine and wouldn't be arriving in any real numbers until next month, when the weather warmed and the azaleas in Charleston's historic gardens began to bloom.

Actually, Jussy was relieved to find Ella alone. At the moment she didn't feel like talking to anyone. Over her head the paddle fans turned, circulating the musty smell of scrubbed wood, detergent and ripening apples. Fluorescent lights glowed on the pockmarked counter where Ella, an overweight woman in a faded print dress, stood leafing through the morning paper. Rows of canned goods clogged the shelves behind her, competing for space with oil funnels, flannel underwear, wrenches, fishing tackle and camouflage caps.

Ella's expression brightened as she saw Jussy come in. "Hey, honey! I was hopin' you'd stop by. Lord a mercy, can you believe this rain?"

Shaking her head, Jussy slid onto one of the stools. Ella's chatter warmed her, and she was glad she'd come in.

"You're wet to the bone," Ella clucked. "Let me pour you some coffee. How 'bout a sandwich?"

"Thanks, I'm not hungry. And I've got Ashley in the car. She's sleeping."

Ella craned to look out the window. "Poor darlin'. Funeral's over, I take it. How'd she do?"

Jussy smiled faintly. She scarcely remembered that, once upon a time, she had smiled much more brightly and far more often. "She did a lot of fidgeting. Wanted to know if we could watch a video when we got home."

"D'you think she realized they was buryin' her mama?"

Jussy's smile faded. "I discussed it with her, but I'm not really sure. You know she never says much about it. By the way, can you keep an eye on her for me? I'd like to freshen up."

Ella nodded, and Jussy went to the back of the store, where the ladies' room was located.

In the washroom, she did her best to dry her hair and sodden dress. It was hopeless. With a sigh, she tossed away the paper towels and glanced into the mirror. Hers was a pretty face with a wide mouth and unusual, violet-colored eyes, but at the moment tired, and much too pale. So pale, in fact, that the freckles dusting her upturned nose were more noticeable than ever before. Maybe she should have put on powder and a little eyeliner before heading out to the churchyard.

As if she'd had the time or the inclination! Jussy scoffed at her reflection. Maybe that's what happened when you nursed somebody through a terminal illness like ovarian cancer. You neglected everybody else, especially yourself.

"Don't think about it now," she told herself aloud. But it was hard not to feel depressed. The weather only made matters worse, and Jussy hated the thought of going home to the big, chilly house she shared with Ashley. She knew that she was going to have to light a fire to warm up the high-ceilinged rooms, because it was too expensive to run the inefficient, old oil furnace. The thought of shoveling ashes and toting in firewood—which would be soaking wet and impossible to light—made her feel more discouraged than ever.

Oh, why hadn't Gerald come?

Until the very last minute, Jussy had been hoping he would. After all, how difficult could it be to catch a flight from Los Angeles? Never mind that Gerald and Caroline had been divorced ever since Ashley was born. Surely he owed his daughter the courtesy of showing up at her mother's funeral!

And what about Ashley? Jussy wondered, working herself easily into a bona fide fury. Wasn't it time Gerald decided to take some real responsibility for his daughter's welfare?

But that particular thought served instantly to douse the fires of her anger. The question of Ashley's fate had been tormenting her for months. What if Gerald wanted his daughter back now that Caroline was gone? What if he insisted that Jussy bring her out to California? Ashley was happy here in South Carolina, and the big old house, cold, damp and dilapidated though it might be, was home to her now.

When Caroline had still been strong enough, she and Jussy had gone to family court, where the judge had awarded full custody of Ashley during an emotional hearing. Everyone had agreed that Ashley would suffer the least if she wasn't uprooted again following her mother's death. Furthermore, Jussy loved the child, and Ashley returned that love. How would she react to moving in with a father she had rarely seen and whom she scarcely knew?

The subject had come up a time or two during Gerald's infrequent phone calls. He had assured both Caroline and Jussy that he had no intention of challenging the judge's decision and sending for Ashley when the time came.

"She's better off with you, Juss," he always said. "You're a better mother to her than Caroline ever was. And don't worry about the house, either. Stay as long as you need to. When the time comes, I'll be there to take care of it, or I'll send someone who will."

Jussy, bristling at the unfair attack on her sister-in-law, hadn't trusted herself to reply.

But now that much-dreaded time had finally come. Caroline was gone, and Ashley's future had to be decided. Jussy wanted more than anything to offer the little girl a permanent home on Pohicket Creek. True, Gerald legally owned the house, after having inherited it when their father died, but he had never returned to live there and had let it stand empty and neglected until Jussy moved back. Now, there was no reason Jussy couldn't go on living there with Ashley. But would Gerald agree?

"Everything's going to be fine," she said aloud, but her reflection in the mirror didn't seem too convinced.

Back at the counter, Jussy found that Ella had cut her a slab of pound cake. Perched on the bar stool, she did her best to eat it while the shopkeeper looked on, frowning.

"You're too skinny," Ella complained.

"I know."

"Why don't I come over Sunday and cook for you? The store'll be closed and I ain't got no plans."

"That'd be great," Jussy said immediately. During the last year, she had learned the painful lesson of swallowing one's pride and accepting help whenever it was offered.

Ella had cooked for them often after Caroline's situation grew critical and Jussy had to be away at the hospital so much. Besides, Ella's meals were heavenly compared to the few, awful dishes Jussy knew how to fix.

"I'll come over straight from church," Ella said now. "If I close out the register tomorrow night, I won't have to come in at all on Sunday."

The fact that her store was closed on Sundays by law reminded Ella of something else. "Hey, you hear about them fellers got arrested for drinkin' on Tod Slater's front porch last night?"

Jussy swallowed a mouthful of coffee before answering. "Sure did."

Nobody in town had been able to talk about anything else. In fact, even Reverend Mac and the pallbearers had discussed it while heading back to their cars after the service. Blue laws were blue laws, and apparently Waccamaw's spanking-new police chief saw no reason to ignore them even though folks had been strolling around town with open beer cans for as long as Jussy could remember.

"If you ask me—" Ella began, only to be interrupted by the tinkling of the bell over the door.

Ella and Jussy exchanged looks of surprise. Experience told them not to expect a stranger at two-thirty on a damp afternoon in late March. But that's exactly who came in: a broad-shouldered stranger with deep blue eyes, hair the color of harvested wheat and a face that was almost too rugged to be called handsome—but not quite. He was deeply tanned, which complemented his rough good looks equally as well as the pinstripe shirt and navy blue cable-knit sweater that spanned his broad shoulders. His shoes were brand-new, although they looked comfortably worn in, the way expensive shoes always do.

Ella's eyes fairly bulged at the sight of such a prime specimen of manhood. She might be divorced and glad of it, but men this tall and good-looking didn't wander into Waccamaw just any day of the week.

"Howdy," she said warmly. "Can I help ya?"

"I hope so." The stranger's voice was deep and sexy and decidedly un-Southern. "I'm looking for a town called Waccamaw."

Ella beamed. "This here's it."

"You're kidding."

"'Fraid not. Most folks passin' through miss it altogether."

Which wasn't surprising. Not counting Reid's store, with its single gas pump, there wasn't much to Waccamaw, South

Carolina, beyond the laundromat and a sorry-looking secondhand store as well as a few old bungalows and Victorian houses lining the only road.

Of course, one could always add Manigaults' Seafood over near the docks, but since it was never officially open, maybe it didn't count. If you were lucky, you could sometimes catch George Manigault or one of his sons sorting oysters or unloading a truckful of ice out back, but that was about the extent of it.

"You lookin' for someplace in particular?" Ella asked curiously.

"Not here in town, no. A little place on the water... Hmm. I forgot the name. Hold on a minute."

Lifting a hip as he spoke, the stranger dug into his back pocket. Both Jussy and Ella watched with interest as he pulled out a soft leather billfold.

"Here it is." Unfolding a piece of paper, he smoothed it between tanned, well-shaped fingers. "There's supposed to be a little place around here called Pohicket Creek. Ever hear of it?"

"Sure have." Ella jabbed a finger at Jussy. "Ask Jussy what you wanna know. She lives there."

For the first time, the stranger seemed to realize that he and Ella weren't alone. Turning, he looked down at Jussy, and the moment his blue eyes clashed with hers, she could understand why Ella had been blushing like a chinaberry ever since he'd walked in.

She was mortified to feel a blush rising to her own cheeks, but what could she do? She wasn't used to handsome males like this, just fishermen and homespun, good ol' boys like George and his sons.

"C-can I help you?" she squeaked.

"I'm looking for Gerald Waring's place. It's somewhere along the marsh on Pohicket Creek. Do you know how to get there?"

Jussy could feel her mouth dropping open. "I'm—I'm Jussy Waring, Gerald's sister," she stammered. "Do I know you?"

"I seriously doubt it. My name's Sam Baker. Gerald gave me this address and asked me to come."

Tears of relief suddenly surged to Jussy's eyes. She had the wild urge to clasp her hands to her heart and whoop out loud. Oh, thank the Lord, Gerald had come through for her after all! Why, he'd actually sent someone to represent him at the funeral and take care of the mountain of legal work involving Caroline's medical bills, her insurance, the settlement of her estate and, most of all, the welfare of her daughter!

"I'm afraid you've missed the funeral," she said shakily, not sure if she was going to burst out laughing or succumb to a good cry. "We've just come from church. Ashley was with me, but I left her out in the car. She fell asleep."

Sam Baker frowned. "Ashley?"

"Yes, Gerald's daughter. My niece."

Sam had been putting his billfold back in his pocket. Now he froze.

The expression on his face brought a horrible suspicion to Jussy's mind. "Didn't—didn't he tell you about her?"

"No, Ms. Waring, he didn't. I was led to believe there was no one left in his family."

"No one? I—I don't understand."

He gestured impatiently. "I was aware he had a sister, of course, but not a daughter. Good God, not a daughter!" He scrubbed his hands over his eyes. "When he called yesterday he said that his wife had died and there was no one left. He insisted this was a good time to come."

"But you missed the funeral! And if you didn't know about Ashley, then why are you here?"

"I came because of the house."

Jussy stared at him blankly.

"The house on Pohicket Creek," Sam Baker said, as though that was perfectly obvious.

"The—the house?" Jussy knew she sounded like an idiot, but she couldn't help it. "What about it?"

"I suppose you wouldn't know that, either." He sounded frustrated, impatient. "Now that Gerald's wife is gone, it belongs to me. I've come to put it up for sale."

Chapter Two

Sam Baker's rental car was a brand-new Lincoln that smelled voluptuously of leather. Tossing his briefcase and raincoat onto the back seat to make room, he barely gave Jussy time to slam the door before backing out of the parking lot at the side of Reid's store.

"Which way?" he demanded, switching on the windshield wipers.

"That way." Jussy pointed to an intersection of two country lanes ahead.

Sam took the right-hand turn. Immediately the clapboard houses and sorry-looking stores of Waccamaw were left behind. Dense vegetation surrounded them: scrub pine, stunted oaks, an occasional palmetto.

Out on the highway, a diner appeared through the rain. Sam parked near the door and both of them sprinted inside. In a private booth way in the back, Sam ordered two coffees while Jussy slid reluctantly into her seat.

It was Ella who had suggested that the two of them go elsewhere to talk. She had closed the store and taken Ashley home with her for the night, looking equally as shocked as Jussy had.

Well, who wouldn't be shocked? Jussy felt as if someone had knocked the wind right out of her. She wanted to scream curses at Sam Baker, grab him by the collar and demand an explanation, and then boot him clear back to Los Angeles or wherever it was he had come from.

Instead, she slid silently into the booth while he took his time peeling off his damp sweater.

Twisting her fingers together, she hid them in her lap so that he wouldn't see how much they were shaking. Not until he was sitting across from her did she speak, forcing herself to sound curt and to the point.

"What did you mean when you said you own my house?"

Sam scowled at her. "I understand it's your brother's house."

"Legally, yes. It was left to him when my father died. But I moved back about a year ago."

"Well, I was led to believe that no one lived there anymore. Gerald told me his mother had died a number of years ago and that his sister—you, I presume—was attending college out of state. He said you had no intention of making a claim on the place."

Jussy's chin tipped to a stubborn angle. "I'm afraid you've been misled about that, too, Mr. Baker. I moved back home with Gerald's ex-wife and daughter shortly after Caroline was diagnosed with ovarian cancer. It was my idea, and Gerald was all for it. Caroline had been living in Atlanta and didn't have anyone to take care of her. I was finishing up my doctorate at the University of Georgia, and I put my studies on hold when Caroline got sick."

The waitress brought coffee. Both of them were silent until she had gone. Then Jussy frowned.

"Didn't Gerald tell you any of this?"

"I'm sorry, Ms. Waring, he didn't." Sam sounded cold. "I was told Gerald's ex-wife had been diagnosed with cancer and that she'd recently passed away, but not that she'd been living in the house here in Waccamaw. When Gerald asked me for a loan, he mentioned nothing about it."

"A loan?" Jussy's brow furrowed. "Are you a banker?"

For the first time since he'd walked into Ella Reid's store, Sam Baker looked flustered. "Actually, no. I'm a marine architect."

"Oh? I wasn't aware that architects made loans."

"They don't usually," Sam said, scowling at her. Sassy, wasn't she? And far from unattractive, even though she was all eyes and pointed chin and thin as a rail. "I only did it to help out a friend."

A friend? Jussy found it difficult to imagine a man as obviously well educated and cosmopolitan as Sam Baker having anything in common with her brother, Gerald, whose idea of a good time was drinking beer on the front porch and picking off the chickens in the yard with a BB gun. About the only thing they had in common was their age. Gerald was thirty-two. Sam Baker looked to be about the same.

"Have you known my brother long?"

"Ten, maybe fifteen years. My folks owned a summer house in Maine, down the road from your father's."

Ah. So that was it. That explained why he knew her brother so well and still didn't have an inkling about Ashley.

John Owen Waring, Jussy's father, had been an artist of some renown. For most of his life he had spent his summers in Maine, painting the wildlife and local scenery and running a successful gallery from his studio. Jussy had never been to Maine, because her mother had hated the chilly weather and preferred packing her children off to Atlanta whenever John Owen was gone.

Not until she grew up herself did Jussy come to realize how vital such lengthy separations had been for her highly incompatible parents. Maybe that was why she had never made the trip herself after her mother died, even though she knew that Gerald had visited their father in Maine often after he quit high school and left home.

"So you met my brother in Maine," she said carefully. "And he asked you for money."

Sam nodded. "About a year ago he told me his wife had been diagnosed with inoperable cancer. Since he didn't have health insurance, he asked if I'd lend him enough money to cover his debts."

Jussy stared at him in disbelief. "You don't mean Caroline's debts!"

"Of course I do. He had stacks of medical bills to show me."

"Oh, did he?" Jussy's eyes sparked with fury. "Did he also happen to mention that most of those bills had already been paid? Back in the early days, *I* settled all of Caroline's bills, Mr. Baker. Until the money ran out. Then I had no choice but to pass the rest along to Gerald, only he never took care of any of them."

"Then what did he do with my money?"

"I don't know." Jussy's voice throbbed. "But I have a pretty good idea. Last fall he wrote to tell us that he'd opened a restaurant in Los Angeles. It didn't last long—half a year at most, which didn't surprise me or Caroline. Gerald never had a head for business, to put it mildly. Besides, he's a high school dropout from Pohicket Creek, and as lousy a cook as I am!" By now her voice was shaking. What could Gerald possibly understand about California nouvelle cuisine?"

Sam didn't answer. He just sat there looking stunned.

A long silence fell. Outside, the rain drummed against the glass. A truck loaded with logs bound for the paper mill in Georgetown whooshed past on the highway. Up near the cash register, the waitress lit a cigarette and admired her brightly polished nails.

"I really had no idea," he said at last.

From the tone of his voice it was obvious that he hadn't. Jussy might have felt sorry for him if she hadn't been so furious.

She sipped her coffee and looked down at her own hands, wondering how on earth she could sit there so calmly when she felt like exploding inside. Oh, wouldn't it feel good to give vent to a full-fledged temper tantrum, run screaming down the aisle and throw every last dish up there on the counter at Sam Baker's gorgeous head?

Too bad it wasn't possible. She was simply too tired. Tired and drained and utterly defeated. Wordlessly, she leaned her head against the padded seat and closed her eyes.

Watching her, Sam expelled his breath in an unsteady rush. What a mess! He'd known Gerald Waring for years, and there had never been anything about the man to indicate that he was capable of doing something so underhanded to his own flesh and blood!

Frowning, he looked again at Jussy. Gerald's easy manner, his slow charm and handsome looks were evident in his younger sister, despite the fact that she seemed on the verge of bursting into tears. If he could only convince himself that she was lying... But no way. Anyone could see that her anger and shock were genuine.

"I'm truly sorry about this, Ms. Waring," he said at last. He kept his voice even, if only to give her the chance to regain her composure. "I really had no idea that you or any-one else was still living in that house. When your brother came to Boston last week, he never once mentioned—"

Jussy's eyes snapped open. They were the most unusual color Sam had ever seen. Violet, maybe, or purple, and fringed all around with long, sexy lashes. Smoky bedroom eyes, though at the moment they were angry enough to slay him with a glance. "Gerald was in *Boston* last week?"

"Yes, to deliver the deed and the house key. My attorney took care of the paperwork. I thought... Ms. Waring? What's wrong?"

"I called him last week," Jussy said through clenched teeth. "I told him Caroline wasn't... that there didn't seem to be much time left. I asked him if he would please come home. To be there for the funeral. Instead, he went to Boston to see you...." Her voice trailed away in disbelief. She swallowed hard.

Sam picked up his cup, but the coffee was cold. "Well," he said, grimacing, "I guess we'd better take a look at the house. If you don't mind, that is."

Mind? Why should I mind? Jussy wanted to shout at him. Come right in and make yourself at home, Mr. Baker! Ashley and I will be glad to move out now that you own the place. Hope you don't object to our staying in the toolshed for a while, though, because we've got nowhere else to live!

Thin lipped with fury, she slid out of the booth. "Would you mind picking up the check, Mr. Baker? I happen to be a little short on cash."

And off she marched down the aisle, chin tipped at an angle that warned the world that Sam Baker had taken on a lot more than he'd bargained for with Gerald Waring's baby sister.

The tension in the car as they drove away from the diner was thick enough to cut with a knife. Jussy sat with her face averted, but her clenched jaw and set expression told their own story.

Sam kept stealing glances at her, wanting to ease the awful tension between them but not quite knowing how.

"Have you lived hereabouts long?" he asked at last.

"All my life. There've been Warings on Pohicket Creek since the early 1700s."

That figured.

"There's Pohicket Creek up ahead," Jussy added, straightening in her seat.

Through the slapping windshield wipers, Sam saw that the heavy woods had given way to level grass dotted with oak trees. Their enormous, spreading limbs were festooned with Spanish moss. Beyond them the marsh began, gray in the rain, crisscrossed with shallow creeks. The tide was out and the oyster banks lay exposed to the downpour. The smell of the sea, of salty mud and marine life, was strong.

Ahead of them the trees parted suddenly to reveal a ramshackle house with a sagging front porch and unadorned windows.

"Is that your place?" Sam asked, unable to hide his dismay.

For the first time since he'd walked into Reid's Store, he saw Jussy smile in genuine amusement. Instantly her tired face was transformed, giving her a vibrant beauty that left him staring.

"No. That's Jasper Oley's place. He's our only neighbor."

"It's pretty remote out here, isn't it?" Sam observed, hiding his relief.

"That's what we like about it," Jussy replied pointedly.

Ka-whump!

The county road had ended without warning and now the Lincoln lurched into a pothole deep enough to crack its axles. Since Sam stood six foot three in his socks, the steep plunge slammed him up against the car's headliner. Grabbing his head, he clamped his mouth shut to keep from cursing.

"Sorry," Jussy said sheepishly. "I forgot to tell you that the road ends."

Sam glared at her. He had no idea if she'd done that on purpose or not.

"And this is my place," Jussy added, with an unmistakable emphasis on the last two words.

The sandy road took a sharp curve to the right and ended in an oyster-shell driveway. A patch of lawn, still brown from the winter, lay between the road and the house, with another patch stretching beyond it to the marsh. Oleanders and camellias grew everywhere, as did mounds of towering azaleas, which were showing their first tentative buds. There was a pretty carriage house with a slate roof and gingerbread trim tucked between the side yard and the woods beyond, but Sam didn't notice. All he had eyes for was the house.

The Waring house was a prime example of fine Southern architecture gone badly to seed. Built more than a hundred and fifty years ago in the plantation style, it boasted wide porches running along the length of each story, with a crumbling chimney on either end. There were rows of tall windows intended to capture the hot summer breezes, but half of them were missing their screens and shutters. Sweeping columns with peeling paint supported the front portico, which had a floor of crumbling brick.

Although it must have been very beautiful once, the house was shabby now. Lichen covered the old slate roof. The brick walk needed weeding, and it was doubtful that the shrubs had been pruned in years.

As Sam looked, his earlier daydreams of a lovely Southern mansion faded to nothing. So did his plans, which had consisted of making a quick inspection of the house before turning it over to the real-estate agent Gerald had recommended. He had wanted to see a For Sale sign appear on the lawn as fast as possible. But who on earth was going to shell out for this dump?

In grim silence he parked the car and cut the engine.

The rain had tapered off, so there was no need to hurry, but Jussy's steps quickened as she went up the walk. She had to fight the urge to slam the door in Sam Baker's face, even though she knew that doing so would never make him go away.

Sam followed much more slowly. Pausing on the front porch, he peered at the ceiling high overhead. Paint was peeling from the tongue-and-groove boards, and a swallow's nest hung from a crossbeam. Mud wasps were building their own nests nearby. Once again Sam got the impression of sad neglect wherever he looked. With a sigh, he opened the screen door to follow Jussy inside.

As he did so, he was overwhelmed by an explosion of noise so loud that his briefcase literally dropped from his grasp. Voices, all of them sharply abrasive, set up such a deafening clamor that he had to clap his hands over his ears.

"Mama! Mama!"

"Hello, pretty!"

"Where have you been?"

"Let me out! Let me out!"

Sam froze in disbelief. What in hell was going on in there? Did she have more children or something? Could kids really make so much noise? And why on earth did she keep them locked up?

Jussy appeared from somewhere inside to hold the screen door for him. "Come in, Mr. Baker!" she shouted. "Sorry about the racket! I was going to move them down to the carriage house, but didn't have the time!''

Them?

Sam stepped hesitantly inside, then turned to take a look. His eyes widened. "Parrots?" he shouted back at her. "You keep parrots in here?"

The sound of his voice must have startled them, because all of them fell silent as if on cue. It would have been extremely comical, if Sam hadn't been so shocked. As it was, all he could do was stand there and stare.

Numerous pairs of beady eyes regarded him warily from cages set up in what had once been a very formal parlor. Evidence of the room's beauty remained in the high ceiling, with its delicate moldings, its carved cornices, and in the Adam-style fireplace mantel. The floor was made of hand-pegged oak, but the planks had been almost completely covered with ugly linoleum.

The parrots, and there must have been at least a dozen of them, represented nearly every color of the rainbow. There were green ones and blue ones, brilliant yellows and grays, a scarlet one with deep blue wings and a number of white ones that Sam, with his limited knowledge of exotic birds, nonetheless recognized as cockatoos.

"Are all of these yours?" he demanded incredulously.

"Some of them. The rest are for sale."

"For sale?"

"Yes. I breed them."

Sam's brows shot up. "In here?"

"No, down in the aviary. It's behind the carriage house. Like I said, I was planning to move them, but there hasn't been time."

"Does the zoning board allow you to live in a house full of parrots?"

"The zoning board? Really, Mr. Baker! This is Pohicket Creek!"

"I see," said Sam, who didn't.

Silence fell between them. They stood looking at each other across the narrow hall, Jussy feeling smugly in control for the first time since Sam Baker had walked into Ella's store. Hopefully her parrots would drive him so mad that he'd hightail it right back to Boston!

But Sam didn't seem to be ready for that yet. Instead he set his briefcase down by the stairs and looked at her. "Would you mind showing me around?"

Of course she would, but Jussy wasn't about to let him know that. In silence she led him up the creaking stairs, which were old and worn and in dire need of paint. High overhead, the plaster ceiling was cracked, and the once-grand chandelier lacked most of its bulbs.

For the first time in her life, Jussy was glad that the house was so shabby. And that her housekeeping skills were nothing short of Neanderthal. If Sam Baker thought he had inherited a prime piece of real estate, he was sadly mistaken.

Still, she did feel a need to defend the place, if only because Sam was looking around him with an expression that was nothing short of horrified.

"I was planning to buy the house from Gerald once I got back on my feet. Fix it up a little, you know?"

But that would never happen now. Jussy had inherited little more than a thousand dollars when her father died, while Gerald had gotten the house. And she had spent every penny of that on college tuition.

Sam didn't say anything. He just grunted.

The stairwell opened onto a long corridor brightened by windows on either end. Here, the plaster was flaking off in huge chunks, and a radiator thumped brokenly somewhere behind the peeling wallpaper.

"This was my mother's room," Jussy said reluctantly, opening the last door on the left. "It has a view of the marsh, which she loved. She died ten years ago, the year I graduated from high school. Caroline stayed here, too, whenever she was well enough to be home."

Grimly Sam entered the room ahead of her. To his surprise he found that it had been charmingly restored. The wide-planked oak floor gleamed with polish and the walls were freshly painted in a warm cream color. Puffy curtains graced the windows, which let in a glorious view of the marsh, even on a murky day like this one. The bed was huge, the hand-turned posts on the antique frame topped with carved pineapples. The crisply laundered sheets were a pale, soothing yellow. A matching rug lay on the floor beside the bed, which was flanked by an antique Sheraton dresser that Sam's experienced eye told him was genuine.

"Caroline did all this herself, back when she still had the strength," Jussy explained, watching him. He seemed so out of place in this frilly, feminine room. At any other time she might have taken pleasure in Sam Baker's blatant masculinity, but not here, with Caroline's funeral only hours behind them. "She was an interior decorator back in Atlanta. She had plans for the whole house, but never managed more than this room and Ashley's, and the library."

That was before their money had run out, as well as Caroline's strength, but Jussy wasn't about to tell Sam Baker anything so personal. She watched him suspiciously as he wandered over to inspect the paintings hanging along the walls. All of them were views of the marsh from various rooms in the house.

"These are outstanding," he said. "Did your father paint them?"

Jussy nodded. Wordlessly, she brushed past him to open a narrow door in the corner. "This room has a private bath. Not all of them do."

To Sam's surprise, the bath, too, had been meticulously restored. A white pedestal sink stood on a floor of gleaming black-and-white tile. Tasteful floral wallpaper started where the chair rail left off and reached clear to the eleven-foot ceiling, which had been sponge painted a pale, charming blue. There was a modern shower-bath combination, with plump towels folded over the brass bars. A block of hand-milled, French soap lay on the shelf above the sink along with several neatly folded washcloths.

How long had it been since Caroline Waring had used them?

With an explosion of thunder, the rain started up again. Stepping around him, Jussy reached over to pull the bathroom window shut. Sam found himself watching the way her slim hips dipped forward as she leaned over the sill in her short black dress.

"How about coffee?" she asked, turning and almost catching him staring.

"No, thanks," he said, quickly averting his eyes. The dress had a plunging neckline in back, and with her hair done up in a braid, a lot of smooth, golden skin showed. Against his better judgment, Sam found himself longing to touch it, to find out if it was as silky as it looked.

He scowled. "I'd like to see the rest of the house, if that's all right."

"No problem," Jussy said stiffly. "There's plenty left."

And so there was. Sam hadn't been able to grasp the very size of the house from the outside. Jussy led him through a series of bedrooms that opened off numerous landings and corridors by way of confusing twists and turns.

Unfortunately, all of these rooms had the same, sad air of neglect as the front parlor and the hall. Plaster was peeling from most of the walls, the wallpaper itself was faded or stained and the ceilings showed evidence of numerous leaks.

Ashley's bedroom was the last one they visited. Tucked under the eaves and overlooking the carriage house, it was decorated in tea-rose yellow, with countless dolls and stuffed animals lovingly displayed on the canopied bed.

Sam felt like an intruder when he stepped inside. Caroline Waring had obviously worked hard to make her daughter's bedroom a warm and welcoming place. Everything looked so neat and innocent, and the room's young owner unquestionably took great pride in her possessions.

Grimly, Sam followed Jussy down a narrow flight of back stairs to the kitchen. It was the sorriest-looking kitchen he had ever seen. Forty years ago it would have been considered modern, with its enormous enamel sink and gas range, and a linoleum floor worked in a green-and-peach cabbage-rose pattern that was all but faded now.

The cabinets were made of beaded board, as were the walls and soaring ceiling. Nearly every wooden surface was coated with white paint, so glossy that Sam suspected it was marine paint left over from some fishing boat. A few of the cabinets had doors made of glass, revealing interiors crammed with mismatched mixing bowls and utensils. Others were fronted with chicken wire, of all things, and contained small appliances like toasters and mixers that had probably been around since the Second World War. High above in the shadows, a bare bulb glowed feebly and a ceiling fan turned at a painfully labored speed.

The library, at least, was just as lovely as Caroline's room had been. A fresh coat of ivory paint brightened the beaded board wainscoting, and crisp wallpaper in a pleasing masculine pattern stretched to the newly plastered ceiling.

Bookcases of honey-colored pine ran along three of the walls, while the fourth, behind the big oak desk, boasted a walk-in brick fireplace. There was a cosy reading corner across from the desk and a thick Oriental carpet underfoot.

Hands behind his back, Sam strolled along the shelves, scanning the orderly rows of books. There were numerous volumes of Southern history and low-country tales, reams of paperwork bundled into folders, countless books on avian science, of all things, and something called *The Gullah Dialect*.

"Quite a selection," he observed.

"Caroline loved to read," Jussy said quietly, watching him from the door. "That's why she fixed up the library. It's where she spent most of her time when...when she still felt well enough."

Something in her voice made Sam turn to look at her. She was standing in the doorway with the light from the hall falling upon her. He hadn't noticed until now that there were shadows under her magnificent eyes and a strained look around her soft mouth.

All at once it occurred to him that she had to be exhausted. She had just come from a funeral, and here he was expecting her to give him a grand tour of her home—which, as he had casually informed her time and again, wasn't hers any longer.

"Look," he said, "maybe I'd better be going. We can talk tomorrow."

Jussy didn't bother hiding her relief. Tomorrow, after she'd had a good night's sleep, she'd feel much more confident about tackling the likes of Mr. Sam Baker.

Because fight him she would. If Gerald thought for one minute that he could turn his own daughter out onto the streets while Jussy merely stood by and watched, he had another think coming! And so did Sam Baker!

"I'll show you to the door." Her voice was cool.

"Thanks. Do you mind telling me how to get to the nearest hotel?"

Jussy frowned. "Most of the better ones are south of here in Mount Pleasant, just this side of the river from Charleston."

"How far is that?"

"Thirty, maybe forty miles."

"Forty miles?" Sam was visibly startled.

"You could head north to Myrtle Beach, but that's just about as far."

Great. On the front porch, Sam watched the rain coming down in torrents. It was a tropical downpour, vastly different from the rainstorms up in Boston. He could barely see his car, parked at the end of the walk. The wind howled and lightning seared the sky. Thunder rumbled an ominous warning.

"It's a real squall," Jussy observed, peering over his shoulder. "I guess you'd better stay until it blows over."

"I don't want to put you out."

Her smile was tinged with irony. "Oh, you won't. I'll be busy feeding my parrots."

"Mind if I tag along?"

She did, but knew better than to say so. "I've got to get out of this dress first." Her voice was cool. "Why don't you wait in the living room? I'll be right down."

Without another word, she vanished up the stairs.

Sam watched her go, wondering if she knew that her willowy legs could easily match anything he'd ever seen in Boston.

Not that he cared. As far as he was concerned, the less he saw of Jussy Waring, the better!

Chapter Three

When Jussy returned, she was wearing a pair of faded jeans and a man's flannel shirt with the sleeves rolled past her elbows. She had pinned her hair in a no-nonsense ponytail and removed the sedate gold earrings she had worn to the funeral.

Gone was the air of subdued glamour about her, but the jeans and ponytail gave her a fresh, sexy look that took Sam by surprise. He couldn't help watching her as she paused on the bottom step to peer out the window. He had never really cared much for freckles and whiskey-colored hair, but maybe that was because he'd never met a woman whom they seemed to suit so incredibly well.

"It's still coming down in buckets, isn't it?" he said.

Jussy nodded without speaking. She had secretly been hoping that he would vanish into thin air the moment she went upstairs.

"I hope you don't mind that I made myself at home," he added, indicating his sweater, which he'd taken off and hung over a chair to dry.

"Hey, it's your house now, isn't it?" Jussy asked with a toss of her head.

Sam scowled at her. Tough as nails, wasn't she? He wondered if she would still sound so indifferent when he informed her that he intended to sell this ugly white elephant right out from under her upturned nose.

Okay, so maybe she didn't exactly deserve to be turned out on the street, but he couldn't afford to be sentimental. He hadn't built a highly successful architectural firm by letting his emotions get in the way of reason, and he wasn't about to start now.

On the other hand, Sam had the distinct feeling that this slim, pansy-eyed woman was going to fight him tooth and nail to save her brother's house. He knew that he had no choice but to take her on, because he couldn't simply walk away from the money he'd lent to Gerald.

It wasn't a cheerful thought. Sam disliked complications. His own life was unfailingly orderly and manageable. He owned a highly successful and well-respected company, lived in a tidy apartment in a restored warehouse along the Boston waterfront and boasted a circle of worldly and supportive friends—which included a number of very obliging ladies who were always ready to take in a play, a symphony, a long weekend on Martha's Vineyard without attaching the dreaded word *commitment* to Sam's invitations.

Neat, orderly, predictable, with no tiresome entanglements. That was Sam Baker's life, and the way he preferred it, thank you very much.

Scowling, he became aware all at once that Jussy had brushed past him and gone into the parlor. Following her, he found her talking softly to her parrots. His presence made them nervous, he guessed, because they stopped their chirping and whistling the moment he appeared in the doorway. Obviously they weren't used to strangers.

Only the big white cockatoo didn't seem to mind. When Sam approached the cage, it lifted the crest on its head and made the most pitiful squawking sounds Sam had ever heard.

"What's his problem?"

Jussy looked up. "That one? He's hungry."

"Really? How can you tell?"

Jussy stared at him. "Isn't it obvious?"

Not to Sam it wasn't, but he wasn't about to admit that to her. "What does he eat?"

"Formula."

"Formula?" Sam's brows rose. "You mean baby food?"

"Sort of. It's a weaning mash I feed my chicks with a spoon. Hand feeding makes a parrot tame. And that makes for a better pet."

"Oh." What else could he say?

The cockatoo squawked again.

"Want to hold him?" Jussy asked.

Sam didn't, but he wasn't about to let her know that. "Sure."

The cockatoo perched on his wrist with the same distrustful expression Sam felt sure was on his own face. The bird weighed a lot for a baby, and that hooked black beak looked pretty sharp. Did parrots bite? Sam had no idea.

"Oops," Jussy said suddenly.

Sam looked down in time to see a big green blob land smack on the toe of his new docksider shoe.

Quickly, Jussy took the bird from him and put it back in its cage. "They're not housebroken," she explained, fetching a roll of paper towels and a spray bottle.

"Here, I'll do that." The last thing Sam wanted was to have her wipe his shoes for him.

Jussy gazed around the room while he cleaned up the mess. The parlor looked like a disaster area. There were seeds and fruit rinds scattered all over the floor, and the scarlet macaw had shredded the block of wood she'd given him as a chew toy. The room had never looked so messy or smelled so much like a pet shop.

So what? She'd be more than glad if it scared Sam Baker away!

Fat chance. Jussy's lips twisted as she stole a glance at him. He was at least a foot taller than she was, and the wall of muscle that spanned his chest told her that he was in outstanding physical shape—not the kind of guy you could scare off easily. What did he do with himself all day, anyway? Work out in a gym? Now that he'd taken off his sweater, Jussy could see the unsettling width of his shoulders and the way his biceps bulged beneath his shirtsleeves.

An odd little shiver fled down her spine. What was it about this man that made a woman aware of him on such a physical level, whether she was interested or not?

And Jussy definitely wasn't interested! If it was up to her, she'd pick him up by the collar and the seat of his pants and toss him clean out the door!

Sam cleared his throat. "Is anything wrong, Ms. Waring?"

Startled, Jussy realized that she'd been caught staring at him. "Nothing," she said quickly. "Nothing at all."

Blushing furiously, she fled to the kitchen and started rummaging through the refrigerator. Crossing to the sink, she savagely tore a head of leafy chard into strips.

"What's that for?" Sam asked, coming up behind her.

"Supper for the parrots," she answered tersely.

"Do they eat that stuff?"

"They love it."

Sam propped his hip against the counter to watch. He was standing so close that Jussy couldn't help becoming aware of the clean scent of his after-shave. For some reason it made her stomach do a strange little flip-flop, which infuriated her. But how on earth could she help it? She wasn't used to men who wore after-shave or cologne. More often than not, the fellows around Waccamaw smelled like fish!

"I thought parrots ate seeds."

"They do, but it's not part of a healthy diet. Fruits and vegetables are better."

"Low fat, high fiber. Just like people, huh?"

Jussy nodded without looking at him.

"And just like people, I bet they prefer the fatty stuff."

Jussy couldn't keep the reluctant smile from curving her lips. Annoyed with herself, she retrieved a carton of eggs from the refrigerator. Keeping her eyes downcast, she cracked several into a bowl.

"Now what?" Sam prodded.

"I'm giving them scrambled eggs tonight, with home-made bran muffins."

"You mean you actually cook for them?"

"Why not? They'd be bored with pellets and raw vege-tables day after day."

"I've got a lot to learn about parrots," Sam observed. *And about her.* He could almost feel the animosity crack-ling from her every time she spoke to him. It was a new ex-perience for him. More often than not, he was the one who had to let the woman know he wasn't interested.

"Do you mind telling me how old you are?" he asked unexpectedly.

"Twenty-eight."

Sam was startled. He had thought her much younger, with those freckles, that perky ponytail, the air of fragile femininity about her. "That's hard to believe."

Jussy shot him an unsmiling look. "Actually, it won't be official until October."

October. His mother's birthday was in October. Sam would have liked to ask the date, but Jussy spun away to pour the eggs into a frying pan. The rigid set of her slim shoulders told him that his questions were unwelcome.

He could feel a wave of frustration rising within him. What on earth was he going to do about Jussy Waring, with her big, wary eyes, and about the fact that she didn't deserve what her brother had done to her—especially after she'd heroically nursed his ex-wife through her final illness?

Sam wasn't blind. He could see perfectly well what kind of toll those difficult months had taken on her. What had Jussy Waring looked like, laughed like, *been like*, before hard work and sorrow and endless cares had put that strain on her pretty face and taken the smile from her eyes?

Twenty-eight. She looked so much younger, so vulnerable, the sort of woman any decent man would want to keep from heartache no matter how hard she was trying to convince him to leave her the hell alone.

Why wasn't she married? Were all the men who lived here in Waccamaw certifiably blind? Or had Jussy chosen to keep them at arm's length and put her own life on hold while she watched over the ending of another's?

"Oh, great."

The eggs had started to burn. Black smoke filled the kitchen, and Jussy quickly jerked the pan from the stove. Fishing out the blackest pieces and discarding them, she divided the rest into a row of small earthenware crocks. After crumbling bran muffins on top of each, she stacked them on a tray.

"I'm going down to the aviary," she said without looking at Sam.

"Let me give you a hand," he offered, as she reached for the strainer of chard.

"Thanks," she said, sounding more annoyed than grateful.

In silence they crossed the lawn and walked down to the carriage house. The rain had stopped briefly, but dark clouds scudded across the sky. Thunder growled in the distance and the wind rippled through the trees.

Sam breathed deeply of the cool, salty air. No one had to tell him that the ocean was near.

The aviary was located a few feet behind the carriage house. Roomy wire flight passages led outside into the backyard through cunning doors that the parrots knew how to work themselves. Freshly raked sand was spread on the ground beneath the mesh floor, and there were tree limbs to climb on and tidy nesting boxes hidden high in the eaves for privacy.

The parrots were hungry and didn't care who knew it. The cockatoos were particularly noisy, shrieking obnoxiously as Jussy drew back the small doors and placed the crocks into their flights. Clambering down the wire mesh with their beaks, they dove into their meals with so much enthusiasm that Sam forgot his dislike of them and couldn't help laughing.

Other parrots were not so brave. Clinging to the backs of their cages, they looked on with wide, frightened eyes as Jussy slid their crocks through the doorway.

"What's wrong with them?" Sam asked.

"These are breeding pairs," Jussy explained. "They're not used to strangers, and they're not tame. In fact, some of them can be downright aggressive."

A lightning bolt seared the sky as Jussy rinsed the empty tray in the sink. "Uh oh. We'd better hurry."

They were halfway across the yard when the sky opened up with a roar. Within seconds they were drenched. A deafening thunderclap exploded overhead and an answering growl, low and ominous, rumbled across the length of the sky and back. The rain pounded harder, hissing through the trees as they raced up the back stairs and into the kitchen.

"Man!" Sam had never experienced such a storm. The wind seemed to shake the very foundations of the house, and the marsh was lost behind a wall of falling water.

Wordlessly Jussy handed him a towel and watched as he dried his hair and dripping face. Water pooled at his feet.

"Maybe you should stay a little longer," she said reluctantly. "It really isn't safe to drive."

Sam's head came up and the towel stilled in his hands. "Are you sure?"

Their eyes met across the room. It was a candid look, the first moment of honesty they'd shared. Jussy had asked him to stay, despite feeling the way she did about him. Was this a glimmer of that famed Southern hospitality Sam had heard so much about? Or had this wet and bedraggled Yankee merely made a sudden impression on Jussy Waring's generous heart?

Yes, darn it, he had, and now it was too late to do anything about it! Standing there in her kitchen, hopelessly wet and windblown, he had touched her in a way that Jussy hadn't expected—or wanted.

"How about supper?" she asked frostily. She'd made her bed, now she might as well lie in it.

"I don't want to put you out—"

Oh, really? But by now Jussy was too hungry and tired to point out the irony of *that* remark. And maybe a taste of her cooking would serve to send him scurrying for the hills.

"No trouble. I'm hungry myself. Making an extra helping won't kill me. Any requests?"

A slow grin lit Sam's ruggedly handsome face. "How about some parrot food?"

Jussy regarded him blankly. "I'm sorry?"

"Those scrambled eggs looked mighty tasty," he clarified, "and I haven't had homemade muffins for a long time."

Before Jussy knew what she was about, she found herself smiling back at him. It was an unaffected smile, the kind she hadn't found inside herself for a long, long time. She had no idea that it lit the violet depths of her eyes and curved her mouth in a wonderfully sexy way.

But Sam did. And he noticed, too, how her flannel shirt clung wetly to her rounded breasts when she turned away to light the stove. Watching her, he found himself wondering how on earth he could ever have mistaken her for an unripe twenty-something.

"Okay, then," Jussy announced, unaware of his darkly masculine look, "one parrot dinner coming up."

"Great."

Pulling up a chair, he settled down to watch her work. He supposed she was nervous, because she nicked herself while cutting up some of the cold ham she fetched from the refrigerator, and almost burned this second batch of scrambled eggs, too. But all the time she kept such a determined scowl on her face that Sam didn't dare offer his help. He had the feeling she'd not be very appreciative if he drew attention to her shaky cooking skills.

So instead he just watched, and later, shared supper with her at the small kitchen table, with its checkered oilcloth and mismatched stools. He had to admit that the shabby kitchen was strangely cosy with the storm raging outside, and he wondered if maybe Jussy wasn't mellowing a little, too. She wasn't scowling at him nearly as much, and once or twice she even answered his questions with a hint of laughter in her soft, Southern voice.

"How about dessert?" she invited when Sam pushed away his plate.

"Hoo boy. I'm not sure I can manage."

"It's pecan pie."

Sam's brows rose. "Homemade?"

Jussy nodded.

He grinned at her. He had a very charming grin, and despite the circumstances between them, Jussy couldn't help returning it.

"Well?" she prodded.

"How can I refuse?"

She heated the pie in the microwave, which was the only nod to modernization in the antiquated kitchen. On top of both their slices she added a big dollop of vanilla ice cream.

When the first bite melted on Sam's tongue, he warned himself to be careful. A fellow could fall in love with a woman for a whole lot less than a pie like this.

"More?" Jussy asked when he laid down his fork and leaned back with a groan.

"Thanks, I've had it. How about help with those dishes?"

"Oh, no," she said quickly, surprised that he'd offered.

Sam consulted his watch. Jussy's eyes followed, noticing the fine golden hairs on the back of his very tanned wrist. "Then I'd better find a motel. I'll be back first thing in the morning. We can talk about the house then."

"Is there any sense in talking?" Jussy asked, sounding defensive once again.

"Jussy..." It was the first time he'd said her name out loud, and she was taken aback by the ease with which it rolled off his tongue.

"What?" she said, stubbornly refusing to meet his gaze, although she could feel it burning through her.

"You know I'd never turn you and Ashley out of your own home."

She tossed her head. "No, I don't know that. Besides, it's your house now, remember? Gerald gave it to you."

Sam took in a huge lungful of air and expelled it slowly. "Let's talk tomorrow, okay?"

"Okay." Jussy stood up and began stacking the dishes. "Can you find your way back to the highway from here?"

"Sure can. I'll call you in the morning. And thanks again for dinner."

"You're welcome. Good night."

In the doorway, Sam ventured a look back, but Jussy was already busy at the sink. Her auburn hair brushed against her slim neck as she scrubbed away at the frying pan. Sam couldn't see her expression because her back was to him, but there was no mistaking the icy stiffness of her shoulders.

With a sigh, he turned and walked out.

Jussy didn't turn around until she heard Sam's car starting up. She had expected to feel a sense of relief as the sound faded into the whisper of the rain, but she was unprepared for the sudden loneliness that pierced her heart. She stood there with the pot in her hand, feeling angry and annoyed and dangerously close to tears. What on earth was the matter with her?

Maybe she just wasn't used to being here in this big old house without Ashley for company. And, of course, the funeral today still colored her every thought and feeling.

The phone rang. Brightening, Jussy hurried to answer it.

"Warings'."

"Howdy, Juss."

Warmth flowed through her. "Hi, Ella. I'm so glad you called. How's Ashley?"

"Snug in bed and sleepin' like a baby. Had a big ole supper of grits and ham steak, and played with my cat before goin' off to take a bath like an angel. Storm scared her a little and I said maybe we should call you, but she said you'd be feeding the parrots, and anyway, she was a big girl now. Of course, I had to agree to let her sleep in my bed. Do you mind?"

"Of course not," Jussy said, smiling.

"How'd ya make out with the Yankee?"

Jussy tensed. "We haven't worked anything out yet. He's coming back in the morning to talk things over." She took a deep breath and confessed, "I'm scared, Ella. He doesn't seem like an ogre, but he does have legal title to Gerald's house. Gerald gave him the deed, and some attorney up in Boston saw that it was recorded good and proper. You know I'd been planning to buy the house back from Gerald once I had the money, but now it's too late."

"Listen, honey." Ella sounded emphatic. "You put all that out of your head this instant and go to bed. You need your sleep so you can think straight tomorrow. Don't fret about Ashley. We're gonna bake cookies in the mornin' and then she's gonna help me put out my bean shoots before I open the store. I'll drop her off on the way, and bring fried chicken along for dinner. Now go on and scoot to bed, hear?"

"Yes, ma'am." Jussy felt a little better. Ella always had a way of making things seem a lot less awful than they were. "Good night, Ella, and thanks."

"'Night, honey, and don't you mention it."

Chapter Four

The first thing Jussy saw when she came downstairs the following morning was Sam Baker's briefcase. He had set it down after her parrots had nearly given him a heart attack yesterday, and had obviously forgotten it.

When Jussy picked it up, the clasps sprang open. Pens and papers went scattering across the floor.

"Oh, great!"

Angrily, Jussy knelt to gather them up. As she stacked the papers into an orderly pile, her eyes fell on the top sheet, which was embossed with a gold letterhead. The words sprang out at her like flashing neon signs:

Baker Portland Incorporated
Coastal Development and Marine Industry Consultants

Startled, she scanned further. Words like *marina, Pohicket Creek* and *environmental impact* leapt out at her.

Jussy's heart went cold. *It couldn't be!*

Slamming the briefcase shut, she stormed into the kitchen.

A developer! Sam Baker was a developer!

The glass carafe nearly shattered as she slammed the lid on the coffeemaker.

Now she understood why he hadn't told her anything about himself when they had talked at dinner last night. He hadn't wanted her to know that he had really come to Pohicket Creek to see if Gerald's property was suitable for development!

Jussy's heart lurched at the thought. A marina on Pohicket Creek where the house now stood? Access roads cut into the woods and fill dirt brought in to bulk up the creekside bordering the Warings' back lawn? Uncaring boat owners dumping their refuse into the pristine water and leaving beer cans in the sand?

No way!

She slammed the frying pan down on the burner.

Oh, she knew all too well what would follow those boat slips and docks! Shops, bars, restaurants, and finally houses and neighborhoods, because who in his right mind would build a marina in the middle of nowhere, without anyplace for the boaters to go once they arrived?

Jussy cracked eggs with bloodthirsty ferocity. Too bad she couldn't do the same to Sam Baker's head!

The Warings owned thirty-six acres of land. That was more than enough for a marina, wasn't it? And even if not, there was always Jasper Oley's place next door, nearly ten times that amount and most of it prime forest, with deepwater frontage! Jasper was an elderly widower who lived on a modest VA pension. Jussy knew he wouldn't hesitate a minute to sell out to some rich Yankee developer for a nice, fat sum, and who in his right mind could blame him?

I had you pegged right all along, Sam Baker, Jussy thought furiously. *And you're making a big mistake if you think I'm going to let you turn Pohicket Creek into some fancy resort, while Ashley loses her home and your company rakes in the profits! I'll stop you! Just see if I don't!*

The rain was still falling when Sam parked his car in front of the rambling brick walk. In the gloomy morning light, the big plantation house looked just as unwelcoming as it had the day before.

Sam had spent a lousy night in a lousy motel room, and his mood only worsened as he knocked continuously on the front door without being admitted. Was Jussy in the aviary or had she simply decided not to let him in?

Scowling, he gave up pounding on the front door and squelched across the lawn to the back porch. Through the half drawn blinds he could make out someone moving around in the kitchen. Lifting his hand to try the knob, he was brought up short by unexpected laughter.

Sam had never heard Jussy laugh like that before. It was a gay and unaffected laugh, both heartwarming and contagious. He reached for the knob again.

"Give me a kiss, gorgeous."

The voice was low and unmistakably masculine—not Jussy's, by any means.

Sam froze.

"Not now," Jussy answered with a giggle. "I'm busy."

"Give me a kiss," the fellow repeated.

Sam stooped to peer beneath the blind. Who on earth was she talking to? He could see her sitting at the kitchen table, the same one where the two of them had shared supper the night before.

"No kisses," Jussy was saying, wagging an admonishing finger.

"Aww, come on. Please?"

What was the matter with this guy? Sam wondered irritably. Didn't he understand the word *no?*

"Please?" The wheedling request came again.

Sam gritted his teeth.

"Well . . . okay."

He heard kissing sounds, loud, wet and extremely obscene. Sam's brows rose to his hairline.

"I love you, Jussy."

"I love you, too, Mr. Binks."

Mr. Binks? Who in hell was that? A boyfriend Jussy hadn't told him about? The garbage man? The meter reader? And why on earth was she being so formal with the guy when they'd just exchanged such a sloppy, personal kiss?

"No more, now," Jussy warned, half laughing, half serious. Sam could almost picture her trying to fend the fellow off. "I've got to clean up before Sam gets here."

"Sam?" The name came out in a deliberately insulting drawl. "Who's Sam?"

Jussy hesitated before answering. "A friend."

"Sam bad! Bad Sam!"

It was too much for the real Sam. Throwing open the kitchen door, he strode inside.

Jussy whirled, caught off guard. "Why, hello. I—I didn't hear you drive up."

Sam made no reply. Scowling, he searched the room for a glimpse of the clod who had dared utter his name so contemptuously.

But there was no one. Only Jussy, with a parrot perched on her shoulder, a smoky gray one with a brilliant red tail that was staring at Sam with an expression almost as startled as Jussy's. If parrots could have expressions, that is.

"Good morning," Jussy said, trying again. She was clearly flustered by the way Sam was standing there in the doorway not speaking, his narrowed gaze searching every corner of her kitchen. He was wearing a navy sweatshirt and gray sweatpants, which made him look much more approachable than the pinstripe shirt and knitted sweater of yesterday. Lace-up hiking boots were on his feet, and he had exchanged the gold Vacheron Constantin on his wrist for a black diving watch. His wheat-colored hair was ruffled from the rain and the wind, and he exuded a glowering maleness that Jussy found very hard to ignore.

"Is anything wrong?" she asked hesitantly.

All of a sudden he was glaring at her with a gaze intense enough to bore holes through her sweatshirt. "Who were you talking to?"

"When?"

"Just now."

Jussy looked around, bewildered. "Why, Mr. Binks, of course."

"Mr. Binks?" Sam repeated.

Jussy went red, misinterpreting the cutting tone of his voice. "Yes, I know. It's a stupid name, but he had it before I got him, and, African greys being what they are, he wouldn't respond to anyth—"

"The parrot?" Sam interrupted disbelievingly. "You're talking about the parrot?"

Jussy stared at him as if he'd lost his mind. "Of course I am! Who else would I be talking to?"

But Sam didn't want to answer that. He felt much too stupid all of a sudden. On the other hand, he couldn't quite believe that the gray bird perched so innocently on Jussy's shoulder was capable of the conversation he had just over-heard. She had to be lying.

Or hiding something from him. A lover, maybe? Once again his suspicious gaze swept the kitchen.

"Mr. Binks has quite a vocabulary," he observed coldly, when he saw that the room was still empty.

"Yes, he does." Jussy turned to set the bird on a T-stand near the back door. The bird perched obligingly, although it never took its eyes off Sam.

For a moment Sam could have sworn that there was animosity in the parrot's beady gaze, but that was utterly ridiculous. Birds weren't capable of feeling emotions like people were!

"Most African greys are outstanding talkers," Jussy was saying, crossing to the sink to wash her hands. "They can mimic people's voices and everyday sounds like telephones, dishwashers, even a cat fight." She threw an affectionate glance at the bird, who was still watching Sam with cold, condemning eyes. "Mr. Binks has fooled me more times than I care to admit by imitating the doorbell, which is really dumb, considering that we don't even have one."

It suddenly dawned on Sam that she was being entirely serious. That Mr. Binks, the gray-colored parrot, really *had* said all those things to her before Sam came in—asking for a kiss and inquiring in that snide, disapproving way who Sam was. Not *what* Sam suddenly realized, but *who,* as though the bird had actually understood that "Sam," rather than being a thing, was the name of a human being.

Ridiculous!

But he couldn't resist strolling closer to the stand to look the parrot over.

The parrot looked back, head up in a watchful stance, his barred gray wings held just a little away from his body as though he was considering fleeing—or striking—the moment Sam came too close. A low growl rumbled in his feathery chest.

"He isn't saying anything now," Sam observed suspiciously. "He's growling."

"Greys usually don't perform in front of strangers. You'll have to sneak up on him if you want to hear him talk."

"Yes," Sam agreed. "I guess I'll have to do that, won't I?"

Jussy threw him a puzzled glance. Why did he sound so guilty all of a sudden?

But Sam wasn't looking at her. He was still looking at Mr. Binks and getting the distinct impression that the parrot was waiting for him to leave, that his presence here in the kitchen was entirely unwelcome.

Oh, great, he thought contemptuously. Now I'm anthropomorphizing just like Jussy! Parrots do *not* have personalities like people!

Behind him, Jussy cleared her throat. "Did you have a good night's sleep?"

"Yes," Sam lied. "How about you?"

She shrugged by way of reply, but Sam, taking a good look at her, thought she looked just as tired today as she had the day before. She was pale, and particularly thin and waiflike in the oversize white sweatshirt she'd slipped on over a pair of black leggings. How was it that she could look so feminine and alluring nonetheless?

Sam turned away quickly, not wanting Jussy to suspect that he was looking at her with pure male interest, although he was.

"Had breakfast yet?" Jussy asked.

"Doughnuts and coffee."

She saw him grimace. "That bad, huh? How about some pancakes?"

"I'd really appreciate that."

"Okay. We can talk while I fix 'em."

It would be easier that way, while her hands were busy and her back was turned. And if she burned the darned things the way she usually did, she'd at least have the excuse that she'd been distracted by the conversation.

Besides, Jussy had a few choice things she wanted to say to Sam Baker of Baker Portland, Inc. herself—things that had been simmering inside her all morning and that she was just barely able to control despite the civility she'd been showing him so far.

"We need to talk," Sam agreed. Pulling out a chair, he flipped it around and straddled it, his arms propped loosely across the back. He looked thoroughly at ease lounging there in her kitchen, and Jussy felt a sudden flash of longing as she watched him. Oh, how much easier it would be to lock horns with a man who wasn't so darned attractive!

"I've been thinking a lot about the loan you made to Gerald," she said curtly, trying to cover up her treacherous feelings with anger. Butter sizzled on the griddle as it heated. "I've decided that I'm going to find some way of paying you back."

Sam looked surprised. "You don't owe me money. Gerald does. Or at least he used to. I own his house now, remember?"

Jussy struggled to keep a grip on her temper. "I know, but I was hoping you'd let me pay you back whatever amount you lent to Gerald. Then you can turn the deed back over to me."

She held her breath as she made the offer. The wire whisk flew through the pancake batter as she tried to appear unconcerned.

"I don't think that's possible," Sam said quietly.

Jussy whirled, bristling. "Why not?"

Sam said softly, "I honestly don't think you have that kind of money."

"Oh? Exactly how much did you lend my brother?"

He named a sum, and for the space of several seconds, Jussy's heart simply stopped beating. Her mind reeled. Why, with that kind of money, she could have hired a private nurse for Caroline, and later, when the end was near, taken her to that lovely hospice near Beaufort that everyone in the oncology department had told her about! She could have paid off all the bills that had mounted with such alarming speed during the last few months, and given Caroline a grand farewell, not yesterday's simple burial!

"I could take out a loan," she whispered, her anger fizzling like ashes.

"You could," Sam agreed slowly. "There's no mortgage on the house."

"Of course there isn't." Now Jussy sounded scornful. "It's been in the family for generations." She stirred the batter again, even though it didn't need it. The recipe was one of her Georgia grandmother's and was usually foolproof, even for Jussy. "What would a mortgage like that cost me?"

Sam leaned back, considering. "Interest rates aren't very good at the moment. Your best bet would be to take out an equity line." He paused, calculating the figures in his head. "Count on four, maybe five hundred dollars a month repayment over fifteen years or so."

Five hundred dollars? Fifteen years? A hopeless tear rolled down Jussy's cheek. Stubbornly she wiped it away and ladled the first of the pancakes onto the griddle.

The kitchen was silent. Outside, rain whispered through the leaves. Mr. Binks preened and muttered to himself on the T-stand near the door.

"I'll just have to forget that, won't I?" Jussy said at last, coldly and matter-of-factly. "I can't pay you back with a loan, Mr. Baker. I make a little money with my aviary, but the exotic-bird business isn't *that* good."

"I wish you'd call me Sam."

What for? she wanted to yell at him. *You're not a friend! You mean the end of my life here in this house, maybe my life together with Ashley! Even though you're awfully hard to dislike, I wish I'd never, ever heard your name to begin with!*

"Jussy..."

Damn it! She'd burned the first batch of pancakes, just as she'd known she would. But at least in the rush to scrape the smoking mess off the griddle, she had time to swallow the aching lump in her throat. She wished Sam wouldn't call her by her first name, either. Not when it came off his tongue like a whispered caress and made goose bumps race up and down her arms.

"Jussy, there are other ways to—"

"Who's that? Who's that?" Mr. Bink's shrill cry startled both of them. Outside, headlights appeared through the rain and a pickup truck pulled to the back door.

"It's Ashley," Jussy said, peering out the window.

"Ashley! Ashley!" screamed Mr. Binks.

Car doors slammed and a little girl's voice could be heard calling Jussy's name.

"That's everything you need to know right there, Mr. Baker," Jussy said coldly, wiping her hands and pointing toward the window. "The one reason I'm not letting you take this house away. It's the only real home Ashley's ever had. I won't deny that we Warings are a mighty dysfunctional family, but Ashley's going to have a normal, happy childhood as far as I'm concerned. And I won't let you stand in the way."

The door burst open and a little girl with two blond pigtails threw herself into Jussy's arms. She was babbling excitedly about everything she had done at Miss Ella's house. Then, still talking, she wriggled free and whirled to greet Mr. Binks, who was squawking loudly for attention. At the same moment she spotted Sam.

"Hello," she said, not the least bit shy. "I'm Ashley. Who are you? Do you like my hair? Miss Ella braided it."

"It's very pretty," Sam said truthfully. She had beautiful blond hair and eyes as huge and expressive as Jussy's, although Ashley's were blue.

"What's your name?" Ashley prodded.

"Sam."

Behind them, Jussy cleared her throat. "Sam is a . . . a friend, honey."

"Oh." Ashley spun away, distracted by Mr. Bink's insistent calls. As Sam watched, horrified, she rushed toward the parrot, screeching its name. To his amazement, Mr. Binks stepped right onto her offered hand and didn't use his beak to deliver the menacing bite Sam expected.

"I love you, Inks."

It was the parrot that spoke, not Ashley.

"Inks?" Sam echoed, catching Jussy's eye.

"He knows I was gonna tell him that," Ashley explained, "but he likes to say it first."

"'Inks' is what he calls himself," Jussy added helpfully.

"He can't say the letter *B* because he don't have any lips," Ashley explained.

Sam couldn't help laughing. He wasn't used to children, but he had to admit that he liked this one.

On the other hand, little Ashley Waring was going to pose an enormous problem for him, seeing that he had come down from Boston to sell the very house she lived in.

Jussy was right; she certainly seemed at home here. The moment Jussy went outside to greet Ella, Ashley pulled a chair to the counter and boldly stuck her finger in the pancake batter. Sam caught her eye and tried to look disapproving, but Ashley just grinned at him, a mischievous grin that revealed missing front teeth.

"Promise you won't tell?"

Sam considered gravely. "No, I guess not."

"Wanna try some?"

"No, thanks." In one easy motion, Sam got to his feet. "Tell your aunt Jussy I'll be back soon."

Ashley looked surprised. "Where ya goin'?"

"Out."

"But it's rainin'!"

"I know. I'll take my umbrella."

"Okay. 'Bye," said Ashley.

"'Bye," answered Sam, and he left the house by way of the front door, before Jussy and Ella came in.

Chapter Five

Where in the heck was Sam?

Jussy paced the house for hours after Ella left, and told herself she wasn't pacing. She tried to come up with a suitable explanation for his abrupt departure, and told herself she wasn't fretting.

But where had he gone? Why had he left through the front door while she and Ella were coming in through the back?

Out, he'd told Ashley. He was going out.

But where? Why?

Ashley claimed he hadn't said. Ashley had thought him nice. She wanted to know if he was coming back.

Jussy couldn't tell her. Part of her hoped he wouldn't. Part of her firmly believed that Sam had gone off somewhere to plot ways of turning every inch of Pohicket Creek into a miniature version of heavily commercialized Myrtle Beach.

But what worried—and annoyed—her the most was the fact that another part of her, one that was dismayingly honest, hoped he would come back again, and soon. If she and Sam Baker had met at another time and under different circumstances...

But that was idiotic! She had a five-year-old to look after, and she was saddled with a mountain of debts. She couldn't let herself become attracted to a well-heeled Bostonian architect who was planning to throw her out of her house and who, for all she knew, could just as easily be married!

The sudden thought made Jussy's stomach curl into a knot. It had never occurred to her to wonder if Sam might be married. She didn't think he wore a ring, but then again, she'd never really bothered to look. And he could always be engaged....

"Stop it!" she said aloud.

"Stop what, Aunt Jussy?" Ashley was standing in the kitchen doorway, her head cocked to one side.

Jussy smiled ruefully. "Nothin', honey. I'm just talking to myself like some senile old lady. Is the movie over?"

"Mmm-hmm. I'm rewinding it. Can I watch another one?"

Jussy hesitated. She didn't approve of too much TV. On the other hand, the rain was still coming down, and Ashley was in one of those rare moods when curling up in front of the set seemed the best thing for her.

"Okay."

She was rewarded with a quick hug and the assurance that Ashley considered herself old enough to switch the videos alone.

Jussy kept herself busy that afternoon by setting the parlor to rights. It was hard, both because she kept fretting about what had happened to Sam and because she had never been the most efficient of housekeepers, to say the very least. After wrestling with the sponge mop and the embarrassingly unfamiliar attachments on the vacuum cleaner, she turned her attention to her parrots. Some of the younger ones were due for hand feedings, while the older ones demanded baths, which Jussy obligingly provided by spraying them lightly with water from a misting bottle, laughing as she watched them preen and flap and roll their eyes in pleasure.

Afterward, she fielded several telephone calls from people interested in purchasing pet birds. Jussy always made certain to interview prospective buyers carefully. Parrots, especially the larger cockatoos and macaws, were notoriously long-lived, and she wanted people to be aware that they were making a commitment for a half century or more whenever they took a bird home.

Besides, a lot of people had the mistaken notion that parrots were nothing more than glamorous pets to be displayed in cages like works of art, when in truth they needed a tremendous amount of interaction with their owners, who soon became the substitute for flocks or even individual mates that these wild creatures by nature sought out in the wild. Even though Jussy's parrots were all hand raised, they rarely remained as tame and sweet when they grew up, a fact most people didn't seem to realize.

Jussy had several parrots, Mr. Binks among them, that had been abandoned by their former owners when these charming, down-covered babies matured into difficult creatures with the minds and manners of spoiled two-year-olds and beaks strong enough to bite hard when they were denied.

Fortunately, all of the phone calls sounded promising, and Jussy made several appointments to show her birds before hanging up. She felt a lot more hopeful after that.

Maybe she didn't have money to repay Sam, but at least she would now be able to put food on the table and pay Ashley's preschool fees for a few more months.

At suppertime, she and Ashley argued good-naturedly over what they were going to eat. Ashley was all too familiar with Jussy's dismal cooking, and the fried chicken Ella had brought with her from home hadn't made it past lunch.

They finally agreed on that faithful old standby, spaghetti noodles with tomato sauce from a jar, and Jussy had just put the water on to boil when Ashley said, "Aunt Jussy, that man's back."

Jussy whirled. Sam was coming up the back steps, his broad shoulders all but blocking out the porch light. Nervously she smoothed back her ponytail and went to open the door.

"Hope I'm not too late," Sam said, scanning the sink for used supper dishes. He smiled when he saw there were none.

"Pizza!" Ashley squealed, clapping her hands. "You brought pizza!"

Sam set the boxes down on the table. "One plain, one pepperoni. They need reheating. It's a long drive from Myrtle Beach."

"You were in Myrtle Beach?" Jussy asked, astonished.

"Yup. I wanted to have a look around."

"What for?" It was inconceivable to Jussy, driving all that way in such nasty weather just to "look around."

"We'll talk later," he said, winking at her.

"Okay."

But it was hard to sit there at the table and control her curiosity. What on earth was the matter with Sam? He was acting almost as bad as Ashley did whenever she was sitting on a bubbling secret.

Thankfully, Ashley made up for Jussy's nervous silence. They didn't have pizza often—not with the cost and the

nearest pizza parlor being more than twenty miles away—
and Ashley kept up a stream of engaging chatter as she polished off nearly as many pieces as Sam did. She was not the
least bit shy around him, and Sam wondered where she had
come by such outgoing charm. Had she learned to laugh so
much from Jussy, before endless work and financial worries had subdued and changed her aunt?

Oh, Sam didn't have to know someone like Jussy Waring
very long to suspect how much she'd changed. Every now
and then he caught glimpses of a woman who truly in-
trigued him. Like last night, when they'd shared such a
companionable dinner, or when they'd laughed together
over the antics of Mr. Binks.

Unfortunately, Jussy's brother, Gerald, had been pretty
much the same—easygoing, charming, impossible to dislike. Sam had never heard him say an unkind word about
anyone or give any indication that he was not a man above
reproach. He had seemed so sincerely distraught over his ex-
wife's medical bills that Sam hadn't hesitated a moment in
making him that loan. After all, he'd known Gerald for
years and Jussy's father almost all his life. And the loan
wasn't an impossible sum for Sam, not after the runaway
success of Baker Portland over the last few years.

Sam sighed heavily. Well, he'd been wrong about Gerald, and now it was Gerald's sister who was paying the price.
Jussy and this golden-haired chatterbox, who seemed to
have very firm opinions about everything, including Sam's
appetite.

"You ain't ate enough yet," she announced when he
groaned and tossed aside an uneaten pizza crust.

"You haven't," Jussy corrected automatically.

"You haven't," Ashley repeated. "You gonna eat that
last piece?"

Sam leaned forward to inspect the contents of the box. "Nope, I can't. Besides, it's got your name on it."

Ashley craned forward. "Where?"

"There? See? *A-S-H-L-E-Y.*"

"Those ain't letters." Ashley giggled. "Those are pepperonis."

"Are you sure?"

Ashley giggled again. Jussy sat with her chin in her hand, a smile playing on her lips as she watched them.

"You better eat it quick," Sam added. "No sunshine tomorrow unless it's all gone."

"Pooh, that's an old wives' tale," Ashley said scornfully, but obliged him anyway.

Later, after she had put Ashley to bed, Jussy went out to the aviary to lock up for the night. When she returned, she found Sam lounging in a rocking chair on the front porch. The moon was peeping through the clouds, and tree frogs shrilled from the woods. Sam was sipping iced tea and looking very relaxed, with his long legs stretched before him and the rocker moving slowly back and forth.

"Y'all pull up a chair," he invited in a passable Southern drawl.

But Jussy propped herself on the porch railing a good distance away with her arms folded in front of her. She didn't want to get too comfortable around Sam Baker. Not when he was probably going to drop another unpleasant bombshell on her.

"So why did you go to Myrtle Beach?" she demanded.

The rocker stopped moving. "I had an idea."

"An idea? Is that why you up and ran out of the house? Because you had an idea?"

"Yup. And because I wanted to look into it before dark. I apologize for leaving without a word, but I didn't want to get tied up talking with Mrs. Reid."

Jussy was glad Sam couldn't see her lips twitching in the dark. He was right: once you got Ella talking, it was impossible to make her stop.

"So what was your idea?" she prodded. "And why Myrtle Beach?"

"I wanted to see how long a drive it was from here. I already know the distance from Charleston. It's way too long, and the Francis Marion National Forest takes up most of the space in between. No motels, no restaurants, nothing. And there's nothing between here and Georgetown, either, while Georgetown, I might add, doesn't have much to recommend it. Steel mills, paper mills, abandoned storefronts..."

"The historic district is pretty."

"Maybe, but that's not my point."

"What is your point, then?"

Sam started the chair rocking again. "I think I know how you can pay off Gerald's debt and keep your house at the same time."

Jussy's breath caught. "How?"

Sam gestured expansively. "It's obvious. Make your house work for you. The place has history and charm, Jussy, and I bet a lot of people would love to spend the night here instead of in Georgetown, or instead of pushing on to Charleston after a long day of driving."

"Spend the night? Here at my house? I don't get you."

"A bed-and-breakfast place, Jussy. You could turn the place into an inn. Lord knows it's big enough."

Jussy stared at him through the dark. All the hope and excitement his words had aroused in her collapsed like ashes. "That's the most ridiculous thing I've ever heard!" Disappointment sharpened her voice, while tears bit the back of her eyes.

The rocking chair dipped madly as Sam got up and crossed over to her. It was dark, so Jussy couldn't see him coming until he took her by the arms. When he spoke, she had to tilt back her head in order to look into his face. She'd never been this close to him before, and she hadn't realized until now just how tall he really was.

"Don't dismiss my suggestion so fast," he urged, gripping her shoulders. "Think it through with me. I'm convinced there's a need for a good hotel between Myrtle Beach and Charleston, and with all the new developments going up along the highway, that need will only get greater over time. Spending nights in an historic house instead of a Holiday Inn is becoming more popular with tourists, too. And yours certainly qualifies."

"With all the peeling paint? The broken plaster and rusty bathroom fixtures? Who in his right mind would want to stay here?"

"I admit it needs a little fixing up."

"A little?" Jussy's voice trembled dangerously. "It would take thousands of dollars that I just don't have! Maybe it's easy for you to talk about spending money like it grew on trees, but that's not the way things work for me. Life is hard for some people, Mr. Baker. They can't depend on quick fixes! And I'm not like Gerald, willing to take money from strangers," she added as Sam opened his mouth to speak.

His hands fell away and for a long moment he didn't say anything. When he did, his face remained averted. "I didn't think we were strangers anymore, Jussy."

She felt the thrill of that clear to her toes, but she forced herself to speak coolly. "No? We only met yesterday."

"True enough, but I've known your family for years."

"My father and brother," Jussy corrected bitterly, "and you've got to admit they're not the best representatives a family can have. And that still doesn't mean you know me.

Why, I'll bet my father never mentioned me once during all the years y'all were together in Maine, did he?''

"No," Sam admitted.

"I'm not surprised," she said stiffly. "He never seemed to know I was alive whenever he was here, either, which was pretty rare, I might add. All winter long he'd be off painting the marshes or visiting friends in Charleston or partying out on Pawleys Island, and in the summer he'd just pack up and leave for Maine without us. I remember the first time I came home from college during semester break." She gave a hard little laugh. "Do you know, he hadn't even realized I'd been gone?"

"I'm sorry," Sam said after a moment. "I had no idea."

"Oh, heck, it doesn't matter," she said with another pained laugh. What mattered was the fact that Sam thought nothing of making such enthusiastic and grandiose plans, and then flying back to Boston, leaving her to manage a bed-and-breakfast alone—when she hadn't the faintest idea how to run such a place to begin with!

"I thought you'd go for the idea." Sam sounded genuinely disappointed.

"Well, I'm sorry. It isn't possible. It would cost a small fortune just to fix the place up."

"I know. But I'm willing to make the investment. An investment, Jussy, not a handout. Since I own this house now, I don't see any reason why I shouldn't develop its full potential. You could stay here and manage the place for me, and provide a stable home for Ashley at the same time. And if the inn is successful, which it should be, you could even pay me back eventually."

"I see. It's a business proposition, then."

Sam frowned. "What else should it be?"

He was right, of course. What else *could* it be? There was no way Sam was going to get his money back simply by putting the run-down house up for sale, so it made perfect sense from a purely financial viewpoint to turn the place into a business that might generate an income of its own.

A business deal. Nothing in Sam's words or manner indicated that he might be moved by other motives.

Like what? Jussy asked herself scathingly. Had she been hoping secretly that he was beginning to like her? That he might even be attracted to her? A wealthy Yankee developer like him? Guess again, Jussy girl!

"I need some time to think about this," she said sullenly. Oh, great. Now she sounded just like Ashley whenever she was sulking about something that hadn't gone her way.

But Sam didn't seem to notice. "I figured you would. Take as long as you need. But it can work, Jussy. I'm convinced of it."

He was certainly making it hard for her to refuse, wasn't he?

"I—I don't know."

"C'mon , Jussy, say you'll give it a try."

He looked so endearing standing there smiling down at her that Jussy felt something long neglected stirring to life inside her. A thread of humor. The desire to flirt with a good-looking man. For the first time in a very long time she wanted to throw caution to the wind and know what it felt like to laugh and joke on equal footing with a male.

"You Yankees sure are persuasive," she said, wagging a finger at him.

Sam understood immediately. Leaning forward, he propped his hand on the porch column next to her head and smiled appreciatively into her eyes. His voice was husky, making her shiver.

"Trust me, we can be very persuasive, ma'am. But that wasn't my best effort at convincing a lovely Southern belle to agree with me. Not by a long shot."

Jussy's heart was beating with a delicious kind of anticipation. Sam was standing much too close, but she couldn't back up even an inch because she was already pressed against the porch railing. He was leaning so near, in fact, that even in the dark she could see every angle of his rugged face and watch the smoky flame that had leapt into his eyes.

"Would you like me to show you what I mean?"

"I—I'm not sure."

It was a lie, but she had no idea if Sam realized that.

Not that it mattered. Already he was leaning even closer, and his other hand, the one that wasn't propped next to her head, was sliding around her waist. Jussy's breath caught as it curved lazily along her back. In one slow, easy motion, he brought her toward him.

"What—what are you doing?" Jussy demanded breathlessly.

He chuckled, a slow, masculine sound that shivered through her blood. She'd never dreamed a man could make her feel so confused with his laughter, with the way he was drawing her closer still, his eyes never leaving hers. His touch was fire and ice at the small of her back, and now his other hand was dropping down to the slim curve of her neck.

"I'm going to kiss you, Jussy," he murmured, even though she'd already guessed that and was trying desperately to decide if she should slip away now or after he kissed her—or if she even wanted to run away at all.

"I—I know," she squeaked.

"I think it's the only way to convince a stubborn Waring like you to make up her mind."

By now they were standing so close that their bodies brushed together lightly, like a whisper. Sam leaned her back against the crook of his arm, his mouth hovering tantalizingly above hers.

Jussy's eyes were as wide and purple as morning glories as she looked back at him. God, the things they did to him.

"Close your eyes," he murmured against her mouth.

"Wh-what?"

"Close your eyes."

Jussy did so, and felt his mouth swoop down to claim her own.

She didn't know what she'd expected. She thought maybe he would grab her wildly or crush her in a fierce embrace, but Sam did neither. He tantalized, tasted and teased, softly, gloriously, as though she were a fragile flower that might break in his grasp.

Jussy's senses reeled. The world tilted out of focus. Sam's lips were parting her own, and now his tongue was seducing hers. She was pressed fully against the length of him as he bent her slightly backward, and she could feel the hammering of his pulse in time with hers.

A spark flickered between them, building into a flame that spread slowly and seductively. Sam could feel the passion stirring within him as Jussy's very bones seemed to melt against him in the heated wonder of their kiss. A warning went off in his brain. He knew he had to end the momentum now, before the gentle flirting he'd begun and Jussy had so sweetly countered changed into something more.

With more willpower than he knew he possessed, he set her firmly away from him. Holding her by the elbows, he looked down at her, glad that her eyes were still closed. It gave him time to take a deep breath and let his own reeling senses swim back into focus.

By the time she opened her eyes, he thought he was ready for her. But once again he'd misjudged her. Granted, she did look as stunned and dazed as he thought she would, but that didn't stop her from seizing the upper hand.

"There's one little problem you've neglected," she told him angrily.

"Oh? What's that?"

"I don't know the first thing about running a bed-and-breakfast."

Sam couldn't help it. He threw back his head and laughed. And had to subdue the urge to sweep her back into his arms and bury his face in the glory of her hair.

"No need to worry about that," he assured her.

"What do you mean?"

"Because I do."

Chapter Six

For the past fifteen years, Sam's parents had owned and run a successful bed-and-breakfast in Maine. After retiring as president of an accounting firm in Boston, Sam's father had enthusiastically converted the family's summer home on Rangeley Lake into an inn. With Sam's help, he had enlarged the lovely cabin into an impressive Adirondack-style lodge, and Jussy was surprised when Sam told her that it stood not far down the lane from the studio where her father had done most of his painting.

"My parents rent out canoes and paddleboats, and have a private fishing dock and swimming area for their guests to enjoy," he explained. "You could do the same here on the creek."

"I don't have a canoe."

"We'll buy one. And once the gardens are restored, you can serve breakfast and tea out on the terrace."

"I don't have a terrace."

"We'll build one."

How ambitious it sounded! And how easy—for a man as worldly and experienced as Sam. To Jussy, who had lived here all her life, not counting the years she'd spent studying in Georgia, it seemed an overwhelming task. The more Sam talked, the more she felt convinced she wasn't up to it.

But she didn't want to tell *him* that.

By now it was long after midnight. The mosquitoes had driven them into the kitchen, where they sat drinking iced tea at the table. Sam had done all the talking, while Jussy had listened, feeling more and more as though she was being plunged into something entirely beyond her control.

On the other hand, Sam made everything sound so incredibly simple.

Maybe because it was.

"You still haven't addressed the biggest problem," she reminded him at last.

"What's that?"

"I don't know the first thing about innkeeping. And it looks as if I'm the one who's going to run the place, doesn't it?"

"And I said earlier that I'd show you, didn't I?"

"How can you?"

Sam had to smile at her anxious expression. This was the Jussy he felt most comfortable with—this charming mix of girl and woman, so uncertain of her own strengths, and unknowingly blessed with so many. Better this wary Jussy than the smiling, teasing stranger who had spun him out of control with a kiss that had gone far beyond anything he had intended!

Sam wondered if she was having just as much trouble putting that kiss out of her thoughts as he was. He wondered if she was thinking about it now, while they sat across the table from each other, their restless gazes falling every-where but on each other.

With an effort, he forced himself back to the subject at hand. "I've got an open flight back to Boston. I'm not ex-pected at work for a couple of weeks. I'd be more than happy to get the restorations started and show you the ropes of running an inn."

Jussy looked down at her hands. There was so much to think about, from the empty despair she'd felt after Caro-line's funeral yesterday to possibilities that were all but overwhelming now. And Sam had said he would stay and help her. He wasn't going to leave just yet.

She tried to ignore the joy that bubbled inside her as she considered this. Could she deny any longer that she was at-tracted to this man, that she enjoyed being with him? That she was still sizzling inside from the heat of his kiss?

"It'll be a partnership, Jussy," Sam asserted. "Strictly business. I'll stay long enough to get you started, and then the rest is up to you."

Strictly business.

Jussy's smile was wry. So much for daydreams. She got to her feet. "I'll think about it and let you know tomor-row."

Sam got up, too, and held out his hand to her.

After some hesitation, Jussy took it. She expected a jolt of electricity at the touch and steeled herself for it. But what followed turned out to be something worse—a seductive warmth that spread like slow fire throughout her body and was impossible to ignore.

I could desire this man.

The thought came from nowhere, taking Jussy un-awares, embarrassing her. Oh, Lord, suppose he noticed?

They shook hands—strictly business—and exchanged a solemn good-night. Jussy kept her eyes averted.

"See you tomorrow," Sam said gruffly.

"I'll be here," she answered. Her voice was unsteady.

The door closed behind him.

Out on the porch, Sam fumbled for his car keys. Strictly business, he thought. What a liar he was!

The small marina that served the needs of Waccamaw village was strictly a working place. No pleasure boats tied up at the sagging pier, just one or two commercial crab boats, an old Boston whaler and Rusty Simmons's battered shrimping trawler, the *Mary C.*

The sandy path leading to the dock was littered with industrial debris. Old discarded ship parts and building supplies, rusted fifty-five-gallon drums, several buoys and a tangle of torn shrimp nets led in a sad trail to the Manigaults' dilapidated warehouse. Out in the marsh and underneath the spreading oaks lay the long-neglected detritus of Hurricane Hugo, a category-four storm that had devastated the area several years earlier.

But nobody really seemed to mind the sorry state of the Waccamaw docks. Most of the villagers were watermen by trade, and all of them felt that the docks reflected their working heritage. Arguably, there was even a certain charm to the rusty anchors and old wooden crates littering the landscape.

Rusty Simmons, as red of face and hair as his name suggested, was smoking a cigarette on the cluttered deck of his trawler when Jussy appeared in the gangway. With both his arms in a cast from fingertips to elbow following a winching accident early last month, it was not an easy task to bring the cigarette to his lips, but Rusty responded with a good-natured grin to Jussy's chiding comment as she joined him on deck.

"No, I ain' gwonna quit," he told her, taking another clumsy drag with his arms sticking out as straight as posts in front of his face. "Jus' 'cause it's harder this way doan' make it less satisfyin'."

Rusty had been born and raised in Waccamaw, but his speech reflected the strange, singsong dialect of Geechee Charlestonese rather than the stereotypical Southern drawl most Northern visitors expected to hear. No one else in Waccamaw was quite as "geechee" as Rusty, but that was part of his charm. Everybody was fond of him, and he was as much a local landmark as the enormous magnolia tree growing in the town square.

Now Rusty indicated a bucket of paint and several brushes propped against the wheelhouse. "Nice dry day, ain' it? I was thinkin' 'boot fixin' up th'wheelhouse."

Sure you were, Jussy thought, trying hard to hide her smile. Rusty was notoriously lazy. He had probably whipped out those supplies the moment he saw her bicycling up the path, in the hopes that she'd lend a hand.

Sure enough, he turned his head and regarded her shrewdly. "Can' figure oot how I'm gwonna paint wi' these casts."

To be honest, Jussy didn't mind the thought of doing a little painting. It would keep her hands busy while she considered everything Sam had proposed to her the night before. She'd slept very little and had had to get up early to drive Ashley to kindergarten. With the sun shining after endless days of rain, she hadn't been able to stand the thought of spending another morning indoors.

"Okay, I'll give you a hand," she agreed now, just as Rusty had known she would.

Pushing back the sleeves of her sweatshirt, she knelt to stir the paint. Without looking, she knew that Rusty hadn't moved from his seat to help her.

Nor would he. As soon as he finished that cigarette and she herself was hard at work, he'd remember something pressing to be done down in the hold of the boat or on the dock below—anything that would prevent him from having to pitch in himself. Those broken arms, Jussy thought with a grin, were the best things that had ever happened to Rusty Simmons.

Sure enough, the moment she dipped her brush into the paint, Rusty mumbled something about inspecting the winches and stumped off to the rear deck. Jussy didn't care. The sun was climbing high above the *Mary C*'s towering nets, and the salty breeze held the wonderful freshness of spring. Gulls wheeled overhead, screaming and squabbling, and a lone osprey hunted far out in the creek. Mullet made plopping sounds in the water as they fed and an air of sleepy peacefulness hung over the day.

Jussy was hard at work on the wheelhouse when Rusty returned. "Well, now, that's lookin' mighty fine," he said approvingly.

"Care to join in?" she teased.

Rusty looked suitably regretful. "Can't. Gotta run over t' store for a few... Oooahh, now who izzat, I wonder?"

Jussy straightened and was startled to see Sam Baker's Lincoln bucking down the sandy road toward them. "Well, I'll be darned."

"Who is it?"

"His name is Sam Baker. He's from Boston."

"Ella tol' me 'bout some Yankee in town. Izzat he?"

Jussy nodded. Furtively, she wiped a streak of paint from her cheek and tried to smooth her windblown hair.

Parking the car, Sam came striding up the sagging pier. Sunlight brightened his wheat-colored hair, and his eyes were hidden behind a pair of very fashionable sunglasses. He was wearing jeans beneath his navy sweatshirt, and Jussy couldn't help noticing how nicely they rode over his hips and muscular thighs. Once again she tried to make some hasty order out of her hair, although the result was far from satisfactory.

Rusty, meanwhile, had stumped over to the gangway. Jussy couldn't help grinning when she saw that the wind-honed little shrimper barely reached Sam's shoulder.

"Heya," Rusty said, offering Sam a gnarled, plaster-encased hand to shake across the narrow gangway. "You Jussy's Yankee, eh?"

"Sam Baker," Sam supplied, gingerly returning the shake.

"Here on business?" Rusty asked in his usual nosy way.

Jussy, feigning disinterest as she wiped the paint from her hands, strained to overhear Sam's response.

"A little." He peered off across the water. "How's the diving around these parts?"

"Divin'?" Rusty sounded as astonished as Jussy was. "Ain' much diving 'round here, bubba. River's too muddy. Ain' nothin' t' see in dem bay, neither. Y'all are better off in Florida."

"I understand there're a few shipwrecks out beyond the bay."

Rusty shrugged. "Maybe."

"Mind if I come aboard?"

The formal request amused Rusty, who grinned widely and made a grand gesture for Sam to step onto the deck. Sam leapt nimbly across the narrow space separating the boat from the dock and came to stand in front of Jussy with his thumbs hooked in the pockets of his jeans.

"Good morning, Jussy."

"Hello. Made it back from Charleston, I see."

"It's one heck of a drive."

"I know."

"There was no one home at your place, so I drove over to Reid's Store. Ella said I'd probably find you here."

"I thought I'd give Rusty a hand with his painting."

"I can see that."

Jussy wondered if their small talk sounded as stilted to Sam as it did to her. But what else were they supposed to talk about with Rusty looking over Sam's shoulder and making no effort to hide his interest?

"The weather's decent for a change," Sam added. "I thought I'd do a little sightseeing."

"Ain' much t' see round here," Rusty responded with a snort.

"Actually, I was wondering if I could charter a boat."

"A boat? For divin', y'all mean?"

Sam smiled. "Not today. My equipment's still in Boston."

Rusty looked up, way up, into Sam Baker's neatly shaved face. The contrast between the small, grizzled shrimper and the handsome Northerner was laughable. "Know your way 'round dem water, bubba?"

"Been handling boats most of my life," Sam said reassuringly.

Rusty jabbed a plaster-encased thumb toward the battered Boston whaler bobbing below them. "That there's mine. I'd be happy to let y'all have her."

"Hey, that'd be great. How much?"

"Oooahh, now. Let me think. Say a hun—"

"Ahem." Jussy glared at Rusty from behind Sam's back.

I'll never paint another brush stroke on this rust bucket again if you take advantage of him, she mouthed.

"Aww, hell," Rusty said, looking wounded. "Forty a day. That's without gas."

From Sam's back pocket emerged the slim leather billfold. "Thanks. Mind if I take her out now?"

Jussy had to hide her grin as Rusty snatched the crisp green bills with amazing speed for a man with both arms in casts. "Y'all go right ahead."

"Want to come along, Jussy?" Sam asked. "I could use a guide. Mr. Simmons doesn't seem capable with those casts of his."

"Oh, hey, that ain' a problem," Rusty said quickly, his eyes on Sam's billfold. "I can always—"

"Why not?" Jussy interrupted. Putting the brush into the turpentine, she gave Rusty a sly smile. "I'll help you tomorrow, Rusty, I promise. See you later."

"Yeah," Rusty said glumly.

Sam and Jussy exchanged amused smiles, and all at once she felt her spirits soaring. She couldn't explain why she was suddenly so happy, although she supposed that it had something to do with the fact that she was eager to be out on the water. She hadn't had a chance to go boating since Caroline and Ashley had moved in with her.

It had absolutely nothing to do with spending the entire morning in Sam's company! Did it?

Sam had obviously been telling Rusty the truth when he claimed to be an experienced boater. In no time at all they had cast off from the dock and were putting downstream.

Sun coins danced on the water and the breeze toyed with Jussy's hair. As the creek widened, Sam increased speed and the whaler responded with a roar of its outboard motor. Sitting next to him, Jussy couldn't help noticing how relaxed he was, how the wind whipped his blond hair and how his white teeth flashed in his deeply tanned face when he turned to grin at her.

"Which way?" he shouted above the roar as the creek opened onto a wide stretch of water surrounded by oyster banks and miles of waving grass.

"What would you like to see?" Jussy called back.

"The bay, the islands, the ocean, anything! You tell me!"

"Okay, head left!"

She would, Jussy decided, take Sam up Cockle Creek, which was a pretty little waterway lined with sandy banks that were ideal for sunning and shelling. Maybe the herons would be nesting and the ibis heading through on their annual migration, and Sam would get to see something of the area's incredibly diverse wildlife.

The tide was still coming in when they reached one of the islands in the middle of the wide, murmurous creek. Jussy tossed out the anchor while Sam skillfully secured the boat and cut the engine. He was over the side before she managed to kick off her sneakers.

Standing in the ankle-deep water, he held out his hands to her.

"Hurry up! It's cold!"

Smiling shyly, Jussy let him pull her over the gunwale. She was unprepared for the heat that sizzled through her the moment his strong hands curved around her hips.

Even though he released her right away, Jussy could feel the warmth of his touch long after he had set her down on the sand.

"Come on," she said, striding away with what she hoped was an uncaring toss of her head. "I want to show you the bird rookery."

They walked in silence, their arms occasionally brushing because the shelving beach was so narrow. Scrub pines, palmettos and tangled cordgrass made up the rest of the island. There was no sound save for the murmur of the tide. Sam paused every now and then to pick up an interesting shell.

"Look up there," Jussy said after a while.

Sam followed her pointing finger to a V of pelicans sailing overhead.

"They've made quite a comeback since I was born," Jussy explained. "Pesticides nearly did them in back in the sixties and seventies, and Hurricane Hugo wasn't too kind, either."

"Charleston was hit pretty hard, wasn't it?" Sam asked. "Any damage to your place?"

"We were lucky. The flooding wasn't too bad because we're on a knoll behind the marsh. The storm surge missed us. Most of the damage came from the wind. We lost a lot of trees, especially magnolias, and a big part of the roof and chimneys."

"That sounds bad enough, if you ask me."

"It really wasn't. As I said, we got off cheap. Most of McClellanville, just south of us, was leveled."

"Were you here during the storm?"

Jussy shook her head. "All of us were evacuated, even my father. At first he didn't want to go, but I made him. I happened to be home from college that weekend. Good thing, too. A few of the locals decided to stay. They've never been found. Neither have their houses or their boats. My father could easily have been one of them."

Sam hated to see the sudden sadness in Jussy's eyes. She'd had more than enough hardship in her life. How could he bring back the laughter they'd shared aboard Rusty's trawler?

"Hey, look at this." Bending, he dug in the sand and came up with a jagged black stone nearly the size of his fist. "It's a shark tooth."

"A good one," Jussy agreed, touching it with her fingertip. The scent of her hair, fresh and sweet, enveloped Sam as she leaned close. "I wonder what kind. Mako? Nurse shark? Or one of those prehistoric things?"

Sam grinned. "Killer whale, judging from the size of it."

"Oh, don't be silly," Jussy protested. "There aren't any—"

Lifting her head, she found Sam's laughing blue eyes only inches from hers. The words died on her lips. She hadn't realized he was teasing. Or that they were standing so close.

"Jussy..."

She hated the betraying shaft of pleasure that speared through her at the way Sam said her name. "What?" she asked breathlessly, not daring to look at him.

"I hope I haven't done anything to offend you or make you angry. Like, um, what happened on the porch last night. I know it can't be easy, finding out that a complete stranger owns the roof over your head."

Jussy stared at him. Was this how people talked to each other up north? Firing both barrels at you when you least expected it?

"It's been something of a jolt," she admitted.

Did she mean his appearance here in South Carolina or the kiss they'd shared last night?

Sam had no idea. He stuck the shark tooth in his pocket. "I've been giving this bed-and-breakfast idea a lot of thought since we talked about it."

Did that mean he'd spent a sleepless night, just like she had? For some reason, the possibility made Jussy's heart beat a little faster.

"Have you made up your mind?" he prodded.

What should she tell him? That she was terrified of the thought of running a real live inn, with paying guests who expected something worthwhile in exchange for their money, like a decent night's sleep, genteel decor, a tasty breakfast? All the things that Jussy just happened to be hopelessly inept at supplying?

"Well?" Sam prodded.

"I—I don't really know what to do," Jussy said lamely. She was mortified to realize that part of her longed to say yes simply because it would mean Sam would be staying a little longer. What on earth was the matter with her?

She became aware that he was frowning at her, no doubt mistaking her silence for pigheadedness. Dismayed, Jussy turned her back on him, her arms hugging her chest.

Although she didn't realize it, the gesture was one of classic noncommunication—a gesture that Sam found oddly, touchingly vulnerable. From out of nowhere came the sudden longing to put his arms around Jussy and hold her close, to assure her that everything was going to turn out all right.

But he didn't dare. He, too, had felt the physical jolt that had flared between them when he'd helped her out of the boat. No matter how tempting, he knew better than to touch her now, because he couldn't be sure the same thing wouldn't happen again.

"Look," he said a little too harshly, "I can't think of any other way to get us out of this mess. Can you?"

Jussy didn't answer. He glanced at her sharply, and a fist seemed to slam into his gut when he saw that she was crying. Not noisily, the way most women he knew cried, but silently, forlornly, with the tears rolling down her cheeks in a way that made him ashamed.

"Jussy, I'm sorry."

She spun away, grinding the palms of her hands into her eyes. "I'm sorry, too," she said with a shaky attempt at laughter. "I have no idea what's wrong with me. I never cry. It's just that I honestly don't know what to do!"

For the first time in his life, Sam Baker knew what it felt like to be a first-class heel. Nobody had to tell him that riding roughshod over this heroic, hardworking woman was a cruel way to handle her, especially after her recent bereavement and the shock of discovering that her own brother had betrayed her.

Putting his hands on her shoulders, he turned her gently toward him. He wanted to tell her how sorry he was. He wanted to assure her that he would never treat her as shabbily as Gerald had.

But the sight of her tear-stained face as it lifted to his drove everything from his mind. His hands were still gripping her shoulders. He tightened them now so that he could pull her close. He didn't stop until Jussy was standing between his legs, with her head tipped all the way back in order to keep her startled eyes on his face.

"Nothing's ever fair, is it?" Sam murmured, feeling the warmth of her slim body all along the length of his. It was a fit of easy pleasure. "Life isn't fair."

Jussy's eyes were fastened on his mouth. That wonderful, sexy mouth that had a way of quirking at the corners like a little boy's when he was feeling sheepishly amused.

Only there wasn't anything little boyish about the way Sam was holding her trapped between his legs. And there was nothing amusing about the way his fingers cruised slowly to the nape of her neck so that he could hold her there, head tilted back, as he lowered his mouth to hers.

Sam kissed her then, a kiss still intended as a wordless apology. His lips were soft, caressing, all lazy pleasure and a bold lack of haste.

Jussy couldn't help it. Her lips parted instantly in response to that wonderful, drugging touch. Sighing, she relaxed into him, into that sensual kiss that was as slow and natural as breathing. Ripples of pleasure spread through her like the lazy waves of a pebble thrown into water.

Sam was cradling the back of her head, his fingers entwined in her silky hair. His other hand was curling around her hip, hitching her closer. In a way that wasn't the least apologetic anymore, his lips moved hard and sure over her own, tasting them, learning them.

Jussy was all softness and warmth, just as he had known she'd be. He felt the wild hammering of her pulse beneath his hand as he curled his fingers around her neck and his thumb came to rest at the hollow of her throat.

"Jussy..." He breathed her name against her parted lips, and she felt the thrill of it spilling through her blood.

Oh, heaven, she'd never been kissed like this before. Her bones seemed to have turned to liquid, a sweet weakening of every limb that left her breathless and dreamy.

She slipped her hands over the width of Sam's chest and clasped them about his neck. Rising up on her toes, she opened her mouth for the bold, mating entry of his tongue.

And all at once Sam realized that he was becoming dangerously aroused. Desire hummed through his body. His pulses hammered. His loins ached as he felt himself growing hard.

Breathing heavily, he seized Jussy's wrists and thrust her away. Bewildered and angry, he watched as her eyes fluttered open. She, too, seemed dazed, unable to comprehend what had happened between them.

Good, Sam thought, chest heaving. Let it stay that way.

Without a word he turned his back on her, fighting for control. It was bad enough that this woman had managed on such short acquaintance to awaken within him a wellspring of feelings he never knew existed: the instinct to protect, to cherish and help. Worse was the knowledge that he now desired her, too. How on earth was he supposed to keep their relationship strictly business when he ached to make love to her?

"I think we'd better go."

Jussy winced at his tone, but Sam's back was turned and so he didn't see. She cleared her throat. "Maybe we'd better. The tide's starting to turn."

In silence they went back to the boat. This time Jussy didn't wait for Sam's help to get in. Rolling up her jeans, she waded through the icy water and climbed over the side by herself.

Scowling, Sam followed. Taking up the anchor, he started the engine and headed for home.

Rusty was waiting for them back at the dock. Stumping over to grab the mooring rope, he asked eagerly what Sam had thought of his boat.

"It's fine," Sam growled, brushing past him. "I hope you don't mind, Mr. Simmons, but I'm in something of a hurry. Where's your car, Jussy?"

"I rode my bike."

"Then I'll give you a lift back to the house."

The wind had picked up during the last few minutes, and once again the sky threatened rain. Even though Jussy didn't really want to, she had no choice but to accept.

Neither of them spoke during the short ride home. Jussy didn't dare look at Sam, and he kept his attention firmly on the road. He didn't cut the engine when he pulled into the drive, but turned around at the front door and left the car idling.

Jussy looked at him.

"I've got a few things to do," he growled, without explaining what they were. "I'll be back later."

"Okay."

Did she sound relieved?

He glared at her. "We need to talk when I get back. Make a decision about your place once and for all."

Jussy stared at the tips of her sneakers. "Ashley gets out of kindergarten at twelve-thirty. We'll be here the rest of the day."

"Okay. See you then."

Jussy stood on the front lawn until Sam's car disappeared around the bend, then went slowly to the aviary. She stayed for nearly an hour visiting with her birds, but for the first time ever their antics and affectionate words didn't lighten her mood.

She couldn't get Sam out of her mind. Despite his button-down shirts and fastidious appearance, he was aggressively masculine, and he had just proved it with the most unsettling kiss Jussy had ever experienced. It had been tender and passionate all at the same time, and she had felt the sizzling heat of it clear to her toes.

Oh, it wasn't fair, having to deal with such an overwhelming man at a time when she was so vulnerable and lonely! Furthermore, she didn't think she'd been this attracted to anyone since she'd gone away to college—if ever! She'd clean forgotten how confused it could make a person feel. And downright awful.

Groaning, Jussy dropped her head into her hands. Why, of all the people on the planet, did her brother have to choose a man like Sam Baker to borrow a fortune from?

Chapter Seven

Ashley was making mud pies out front when Sam returned late that afternoon. Sure enough, the rain had started up again, and the little girl was splashing through the puddles in boots and a bright red slicker. She gave Sam a wide smile as he came up the walk.

"Hi, Mr. Sam. Wanna make mud pies with me?"

Sam considered. "Honestly? No. I'm not exactly dressed for it."

"That's okay. Maybe tomorrow. Did you see the heron out back? He's hunting minnows. I'm not allowed to go there alone, even if I know how to swim. Aunt Jussy says I might fall in the creek." She grinned. "I'd be more wet'er'n I am now, wouldn't I?"

Sam nodded, and wondered if Jussy would ever smile at him as warmly as Ashley did. Probably not. Not as long as they were at such professional odds with each other, and where everything he said and did made her act so cool and wary. "Is your aunt at home?"

"Yup. She's in the kitchen burnin' brownies."

Sam's brows arched. "Burning them?"

Ashley giggled. "She burns ev'rythin', 'cept griddle cakes. But it don't matter. I already got to lick the spoon. That's my favorite part."

"Mine, too," Sam admitted, and he went up to the front door, where the smell of burning brownies greeted him the moment he poked his head inside.

"Jussy?"

"In the kitchen."

She didn't have to tell him where she was. Sam just had to follow his nose. A blackened mess filled the trash can at her feet while she stood at the sink, furiously scrubbing a baking pan. Sam had the urge to laugh, only he didn't, because the look Jussy shot him warned him that personal injury might be forthcoming if he dared.

"Do you see why I'm so dead set against opening a bed-and-breakfast?" she demanded.

"No."

"Oh, come on, Sam! This is what my guests would get every morning!"

"Burned brownies?"

"Burned everything."

Sam refused to believe that. "You're a great cook."

Jussy snorted. For some reason, his spirits rose at the sound. She was in a feisty mood, to say the least, and he was glad of that. It would be easier to deal with her this way, when she seemed intent on sparring with him, than when she opened that sexy mouth of hers in anticipation of his kiss.

"What about the pecan pie I had the other night?"

"That was Ella's."

"Oh. Well, how about the corn bread and muffins?"

"Ella's, too."

"The scrambled eggs," he said triumphantly. "And the pancakes. I actually watched you create them."

Jussy snorted again. "I burned the first batch, in case you didn't notice."

"I guess I didn't," Sam admitted.

Jussy laid the scrubbing pad aside and dried the baking pan. "The point is, I can't cook anything save pancakes and scrambled eggs, and then only if I'm lucky. And housekeeping?" Her nose wrinkled. "You can see how bad I am at that."

Sam knew better than to put his foot into *that* particular trap. He didn't say anything, even though he could have argued that her messy parrots were mostly to blame.

"So hire Ella Reid to cook for you," he said instead. "I bet she'd love to get out of that musty store for a few hours each day. She certainly seems to enjoy doing things for people. I bet she wouldn't charge you much to cook and do a little housekeeping."

It was such a sensible solution that Jussy's irritation vanished. For just a moment she allowed herself the luxury of imagining that she really could succeed at running an inn.

Hope flared, as did a flicker of enthusiasm. For the first time since Caroline had fallen ill, anticipation for the future stirred Jussy's sore heart. Why, it might actually be fun to fix up the house and invite folks to stay.

And Sam clinched it by pulling up a chair and sitting down in Jussy's disorderly kitchen with the air of someone who felt perfectly at home there. "I made some phone calls," he announced, grinning as he sensed that she was relenting. "Cleared my schedule for the next few weeks, so I'm yours if you want me. We could get some remodeling done, buy the things you'll need for your guests and apply for all the necessary permits. What do you say?"

Jussy tried to hide her pleasure, but in the end she couldn't help smiling at him, a bubbling smile of gratitude.

An answering smile curved Sam's lips. He knew without having to be told that she had made up her mind. "We can do this, Jussy," he said gruffly. "And I promise you won't regret it."

We. He had no idea how good that sounded. How weary Jussy had become of doing everything alone, of shouldering all life's burdens by herself.

Strange, she mused, how much stronger a person could feel with someone there to lean on, especially if that someone was as big and broad shouldered as Sam.

And was it really possible that the two of them could turn this old house into a successful inn and make enough money to eventually pay off Gerald's debts? The thought made her feel positively light-headed.

"First thing tomorrow we'll get the permits we need," Sam went on. "And make a stop at the building-supply store. We'd better draw up a list of priorities, too. Oh, and do you suppose I could use one of your spare rooms while I'm here? It's a long commute from Charleston every day."

Jussy's mounting enthusiasm fizzled like a beach ball pricked with a pin. Granted, the house was big enough to accommodate Sam quite comfortably, but in a town like Waccamaw, where everyone knew everybody else's business, strangers didn't simply move in with unmarried women—at least not until the house became a legitimate inn. But how to tell that to Sam, when the mere thought of speaking up on the subject brought a wave of embarrassment crashing over her?

She cleared her throat. "Umm, Sam..."

He looked up, saw the color staining her cheeks and frowned. "What?"

"I'm afraid the house isn't— You just can't—can't..." Jussy stammered inadequately.

"It's too far to drive every day," Sam argued, as understanding dawned.

"I know, but—but people will talk."

"Yeah, I suppose they will." He obligingly averted his gaze from her pretty, blushing face. "But there's got to be someplace where I can stay. I'm not about to commute forty miles each way!"

"I know," Jussy agreed, staring down into her lap, "but I just can't think of any—"

"What about the carriage house, Aunt Jussy?"

They had both forgotten Ashley. Now they turned to find her standing at the back door, dripping wet and grinning toothily.

"The carriage house?" Jussy echoed dumbly.

"Sure." Ashley's haughty expression suggested that both adults were nothing short of dim. "There's plenty of room for Mr. Sam to stay out there, ain't there?"

For once Jussy didn't correct the little girl's grammar. "Well, yes, I suppose there is," she said slowly.

"I could help y'all clean it," Ashley added. "Would you really stay with us, Mr. Sam? Can I have a ride in your car if you do?"

Sam was tempted to give the little girl a great big hug. Just like that she'd managed to solve their conundrum, without really understanding why it had been a problem to begin with. He didn't have much experience with children and wondered if all of them were so darned smart.

"Honey," he said, grinning, "I'll take you clear to Myrtle Beach and back, if you like."

Ashley's eyes popped. "When? When?"

"Now, Ashley—"

But Sam cut smoothly through Jussy's protests. "Why, right this minute, if you like."

The impulsive words surprised him as much as they did Jussy and Ashley. He wondered if maybe he should withdraw the offer, then changed his mind the moment his eyes met those of the wary, half smiling woman drying her hands at the sink. Had Jussy's life been so starved of pleasure that she could welcome such a simple outing with so much enthusiasm?

And what about Ashley? The little girl was clapping her hands and acting as though Sam had just handed her some fabulous present.

Sam had never come across a pair of females who could be satisfied with so little, and he told them as much, laughing, as he shooed them out to his car.

The beachfront, known to locals as the Grand Strand, encompassed miles of powdery sand along the heavily developed main street of Myrtle Beach. Despite the rain, the boardwalk and pavilions were crowded, the arcades and restaurants filled to capacity.

"You'll find a lot of Canadians here this time of year," Jussy explained when Sam commented on the fact, while searching in vain for a parking space. "They vacation early in the spring, before it gets too hot."

"I bet you could lure a lot of them down to Pohicket Creek," Sam said at once. "Give 'em a taste of old-fashioned Southern hospitality at your bed-and-breakfast."

"You've got this all planned out, don't you?" Jussy asked, sounding more amused than angry.

He took his eyes off the road long enough to grin at her. "Sure do."

Despite the rain, the afternoon turned out to be delightful. Sam and Jussy stood side by side, sharing an umbrella, while they watched Ashley compete for prizes in the arcades along the boardwalk. They took turns carrying her stuffed animals while she ate an ice-cream cone, undaunted by the chilly weather. They sat across from each other, listening to Ashley's happy chatter, when Sam took them out to dinner at a Mexican restaurant decorated with straw hats and huge, painted flowers.

Jussy looked more relaxed than Sam had ever seen her. Throughout the afternoon she had laughed with him, traded jokes with him, not once showing any of the wariness that had shadowed their relationship before.

Looking at her across the dimly lit table, Sam suddenly found himself longing to kiss that soft, laughing mouth of hers again, until it kissed him back with all the passion he knew she was capable of feeling.

On the other hand, he knew perfectly well that once he started kissing Jussy Waring, there'd be no turning back—for either of them. Jussy was the sort of woman you couldn't make love to and then simply forget. And that was because she was a woman who believed with all her heart in commitment.

Sam didn't know how he knew that; he just did. And he was not about to be the next man in a long line of others who had ended up hurting her. Because hurt her he would. After all, he was the last man on earth to believe in commitment himself, even though his parents had been happily married for nearly half a century. The fact was, he just wasn't interested in getting married. He liked his bachelor life in Boston, his single-bedroom apartment, and he liked being able to work twelve hours a day and more if he had to. A woman like Jussy would never approve of such unreliable—

Whoa! Sam's thoughts skidded to a panic-stricken halt. What on earth was he thinking? Commitment? Settling down? And arguing with himself as to why Jussy Waring was an unlikely candidate for doing both with?

Get a grip, Sam, he warned himself, and signaled the waiter for another beer.

His discomfort showed after that, despite the fact that he tried hard to hide it. But Jussy noticed immediately when his voice changed and the animation left his face. Sipping the salty margarita Sam had ordered for her, she desperately went over every word she and Ashley had said to him since the meal began. Had they insulted him somehow? Or had he simply grown bored with their company?

The thought was too awful to bear, and Jussy couldn't help becoming terse and ill at ease herself. The trip to Myrtle Beach, which had started out so amiably, ended in self-conscious silence.

She couldn't even bring herself to look at Sam during the long drive home. Every time he turned to say something to her, she felt as though she would jump right out of her skin. This was a hell of a way to start a business partnership, she thought despairingly.

"You gonna stay in the carriage house tonight, Mr. Sam?" Ashley piped the moment the Lincoln halted in the drive. "We can fix it up, can't we, Aunt Jussy?"

Jussy squirmed. She wished Ashley wouldn't be so darned direct. She wished she'd never agreed to a business relationship with Sam. She wished Sam would drop them off at the front door and head straight back to Boston.

"What's it like inside?" Sam asked suspiciously, envisioning the carriage house as a sort of storage garage littered with empty gasoline cans and bags of parrot food.

"C'mon," invited Ashley. "I'll show ya."

Sam turned an inquiring gaze on Jussy.

"Sure," she agreed glumly. What else could she say?

The carriage house had once served as John Owen Waring's art studio. The not-unpleasant smell of linseed oil and acrylic paint hung in the air, but the living area beyond the cluttered front room contained no shred of evidence that it had ever been used for painting or, as Sam had feared, as a feed and storage area.

In fact, the carriage house was in astonishing condition compared to the crumbling old plantation house. Cypress panels graced the freshly painted walls of the living room, whose lovingly restored brick floor was obviously original. White wicker furniture and warm dhurrie rugs softened the cooling effect of the stone, and stuffed chair cushions with boldly colored stripes loaned everything a cheerful air.

"This is incredible," Sam exclaimed, looking around him.

"My father spent a lot of time restoring it," Jussy said.

The way he had his summer studio in Maine, Sam thought, and was racked by a surge of fury toward the charming, easygoing man he remembered. Just like his son, John Owen Waring had obviously been free with his money and his jokes, while never giving anyone the slightest hint that there was another side to him, a dark side that allowed him to live in such cosy luxury while his wife and daughter occupied a house that was literally collapsing from neglect.

"Caroline sometimes stayed here after her treatments," Jussy added softly, so Ashley wouldn't hear. "She preferred being alone whenever she was nauseated. She's the one who fixed everything up so nicely." Her mouth quirked sadly. "Too bad. She's the one who would have made a great innkeeper. Not me."

"I wish you'd stop doubting yourself," Sam said gruffly. "When I see what you did for Caroline and Ashley, I can't help believing that you'll do every bit as well with paying guests."

"But Ashley and Caroline are different! They're family."

"What about your house, then? I know how much you care for it, Jussy. Can't you see that restoring it, and making it work for you, will be a labor of love as well?"

Sam's eyes were holding hers and his voice had grown husky. For some reason, the heat began to rise in Jussy's cheeks. Maybe it was the caressing way the word *love* had rolled off Sam's tongue. She wondered suddenly what it would feel like to love Sam Baker. Or have him love her in return.

"I'm here to help, Jussy," he continued, his voice a rough caress. "But you've got to let me. I'm not going to run out on you."

The way her father had.

"Or pull something behind your back when you least expect it."

The way her brother had.

Jussy's throat ached. Oh, how good it felt to stand here and let Sam's healing words wash over her! To imagine how wonderful it would be to actually accept the help and trust he was offering.

But behind the temptation lay something even more compelling than Sam's involvement in her new business, something she could no longer deny even though she knew it was forbidden.

It had been a long time since Jussy had allowed herself to think and feel like a woman. But Sam Baker was a man who made her very much aware of her feminine side.

Every time she looked at his wide shoulders and wonderfully muscled body, she could feel the pull of his sexuality in a purely physical way. And when he had kissed her out on the creek yesterday, she had wanted nothing more than to shed her clothes and make love with him right there on the sand.

But it was more than that, she realized suddenly. It was the strength of Sam's very maleness that she found herself craving, the haven of safety and comfort she sensed that he alone was capable of providing. An old-fashioned thought, maybe, but at the moment Jussy would have given much to turn her fragile woman's heart into Sam's manly keeping.

"There's a bedroom down the hall," she said, her voice growing cool as she moved quickly to distance herself from such temptation. "You can stay there if you like. Hang on and I'll fetch some sheets and towels from the house."

"That'd be great," he replied, trying hard to hide his frustration. Why did Jussy push him away every time they seemed to be making some kind of breakthrough in their relationship?

"Oh, goody!" declared Ashley, clapping her hands. "I'm so glad you're gonna stay!" And to Sam's surprise, she flew to him and wrapped her arms about his waist.

Going down on one knee, Sam hugged her back. Now wouldn't it be nice if Jussy acted even half as pleased as Ashley to hear that he was staying?

His mouth curved wryly at the thought. Fat chance.

Chapter Eight

Far too early the following morning, Sam was awakened from sound sleep by the most horrifying scream he'd ever heard. Sitting bolt upright in bed, he stared around him for a moment, not knowing where he was. Then he remembered.

The carriage house. He had spent the night in Jussy's carriage house, and the aviary was right behind him.

Groaning, he fell back against the pillows. Those damned parrots! What were they doing, trying to wake the dead? It was a good thing the Waring house was isolated at the very end of the road. No neighbor in his right mind would tolerate that infernal racket day after day!

Sam closed his eyes, but there was no way of going back to sleep. Flipping over on his stomach, he put his pillow over his head, but that didn't help, either. The screaming was still intolerable, even through all that goose down.

At long last the horrible chorus began tapering off. But by the time the birds had settled down to far more pleasing trills and whistles—like the sound effects in a jungle movie—Sam was too wide-awake to consider lying abed any longer.

Groaning, he crossed barefoot to the window and parted the curtains. His room faced south, so he couldn't see much of the sunrise. But the faint brightening of the sky was enough to show him that the clouds had cleared away overnight and that the tide stood high in the waterway. The tips of submerged cordgrass waved in the breeze and a flock of egrets flew by on wings tinged apricot by the dawn.

Beautiful, Sam thought.

Movement on the lawn caught his eye. Sam saw Jussy, clad in jeans, hightop sneakers and a dark green sweatshirt, crossing the dew-spangled grass, carrying a tray loaded with crocks. Balancing the tray on one hip, she fumbled in her pocket for the aviary keys.

Slipping a sweatshirt of his own over a pair of shorts, he hurried outside to help her. "Here, let me do that."

She whirled, startled, and Sam was granted a fine view of wide violet eyes and curling auburn hair before she smiled at him self-consciously and handed him the tray so that she could open the padlock.

"Good morning. Did you sleep well?"

"Yes. Until those feathered monsters of yours started shrieking their heads off."

"They do that every morning. I think it's their way of welcoming the dawn."

"Great," Sam groaned, although he wasn't really all that annoyed. Instead, he found himself thinking how much he enjoyed looking at Jussy's smiling face first thing in the morning and wondering how to coax her into giving him another of those smiles.

Following her inside, he set down the tray. "Need help with this?"

"No, thanks, I can manage."

"Okay. Would you mind if I went for a jog?"

"Of course not. You're welcome to do whatever you like."

Actually, Jussy would be deeply relieved if Sam went away. It was too disconcerting to have him hovering over her this early in the morning with his beefy shoulders clad in a sweatshirt and his running shorts revealing the corded legs of a long-distance athlete. He was standing so close that she could feel the warmth of his body, and it was making her heart do crazy little somersaults.

"I'll be gone about an hour."

"Better take some bug spray," Jussy suggested. Then she added almost shyly, "Do you want breakfast when you get back?"

Sam cocked a devilish eyebrow at her. "What's on the menu?"

Jussy's lips twitched in response. "Burned griddle cakes and overcooked grits."

"Mmm. My favorite." His grin deepened. "Know something, Miss Waring?"

"No, what?"

"You sure are less prickly today than you have been lately."

She cocked an eyebrow right back at him. "Oh? And is that good?"

"Real good," Sam replied, and all at once the teasing note vanished from his voice. Impulsively, he put out his hand and cupped Jussy's chin. With his thumb he caressed her cheek, a gentle gesture that surprised him as much as it did her. What was it about this woman that invited such easy intimacy even though she did her best to keep him at arm's length?

"I'll be back in an hour," he said again, dropping his hand and turning away. Did he sound awkward? He knew he must. He certainly felt that way.

Jussy watched until he disappeared down the drive, side-stepping the puddles left over from last night's rain. While feeding her birds, she tried to remind herself of all the reasons there were to go on distrusting Sam Baker.

But it was hard to summon up negative feelings when all she could think about was the way her heart had knocked against her ribs when he'd reached out to caress her cheek.

She put her fingertips to the spot. Surely it had been nothing more than an impulsive gesture! Then why couldn't she stop thinking about it?

Locking up the aviary, she went quickly to the house. As she crossed the lawn, she was surprised to see the local parcel-delivery truck coming down her drive. A balding man in a familiar uniform waved as he pulled alongside.

"Howdy, Jussy!"

"'Morning, Leonard. What brings you out so early?"

He reached for his clipboard. "Got an overnight delivery that was supposed to be here yesterday. We've been behind real bad on account of the rain. Sorry."

"No problem. What've you got?" For the life of her, Jussy couldn't remember ordering anything by parcel post.

"Bunch of stuff for a fellow named Baker, care of your place. I thought it might be a mistake, but..." He looked at her inquiringly.

"No, that's okay. He's a friend of my brother's," Jussy explained. "C'mon, I'll give you a hand."

"It's heavy."

"I don't mind."

"Aunt Jussy! What's all this stuff?" a sleepy Ashley demanded from the top of the stairs as Jussy and the driver began dragging a strange assortment of crates and boxes into the hall.

"You got me, honey," Jussy answered. She had never seen so many odd-looking things in her life. There was a small black box the size of a portable television set and a crate that contained some kind of generator. There was also a weird-looking machine that resembled the diagnostic computer a service-station mechanic might use to tune a car engine. Two further crates sported labels that might have been hieroglyphics for all the sense Jussy could make of them.

Ashley clumped down the stairs in her nightgown and slippers. Together they examined the boxes, once Leonard had taken his leave.

In the middle of their exploration, the front door opened and Sam stepped inside. He was warm and sweaty from his run, and Jussy, straightening to confront him, was made aware again of his very maleness. She looked away quickly, a blush creeping into her cheeks.

"Hey, this is great!" he exclaimed, his eyes falling on the equipment cluttering the hall floor.

"What is it?" Ashley asked, burning with curiosity.

"Diving gear."

All this was diving gear? What did he plan to do? Jussy wondered. Set up an underwater laboratory?

"This should have been here yesterday," he added, unzipping a duffel bag and inspecting its contents.

Yesterday? That meant that he had sent for his gear on the very day he'd arrived in Waccamaw, the day of Caroline's funeral! Jussy's eyes narrowed. He certainly hadn't wasted any time in making himself at home, had he?

"I'm going to fix breakfast," she announced coolly. "Ashley, time to get dressed for school." Her eyes flicked briefly to Sam. "Do you want to shower before you eat?"

"That'd be great," he began, only to find himself addressing Jussy's retreating back. He stared after her, his hands on his hips. No doubt about it, that was one moody lady!

Jussy was standing on the front porch waving to members of Ashley's car pool when Sam returned from the carriage house. "C'mon," she said in the same unfriendly voice she'd used before. "Breakfast is ready."

"Have I done something to make you mad at me?" Sam asked as he pulled up a chair and sat down at her kitchen table.

Jussy stiffened. Lord, but she'd never get used to his blunt Yankee ways!

But she could be blunt, too, when the subject was as important as the one she'd chosen to tackle the moment he returned. Hopefully it would serve to reerect that much-needed wall between them.

"You left your briefcase here the other night." Her back was turned while she fixed a plate for him. "Some of the papers fell out when I moved it. I couldn't help seeing a report about Pohicket Creek."

"Oh," said Sam, sounding relieved. "I've been wondering where that went."

"Your company does more than design blueprints for marinas," Jussy added accusingly. "It develops them, too, doesn't it?"

"Sometimes. It depends on what our clients want."

"Well?" Jussy prodded, turning toward him. "Want to tell me your plans for Pohicket Creek?"

"There isn't much to tell."

"No?"

Sam smiled at her in a way that made her furious. How dare he look so darned appealing when she was trying so hard to keep on mistrusting him?

"I'm a businessman, Jussy, a thorough one. I don't usually acquire a piece of property without doing some research on it."

"I see."

Did she? She certainly didn't sound any less hostile.

"Just because we run a marketing analysis on a place doesn't mean we intend to develop it."

"Oh no?"

"No." Now Sam sounded curt as well. "No way this area is going to grow along the lines of Charleston or Myrtle Beach, Jussy. No way. It's too remote and much too rural. Besides, development is already going on elsewhere, like Litchfield Beach and even McClellanville, to some extent. A bed-and-breakfast on Pohicket Creek is about as sophisticated as this area is going to get. I swear it."

If only she could believe that!

Crossing to the table, Jussy plunked a plate down in front of him.

"What in hell," Sam said slowly, looking down, "is that?"

Jussy scowled. "What?"

"That gray stuff next to the eggs. It looks like wallpaper paste."

Despite herself, Jussy burst out laughing. "Those are grits."

"Grits?"

"Sure. Haven't you ever had them before?"

"No, thank God."

"Oh, stop being so fussy. Just add some butter and salt and take a big bite."

Sam reluctantly did so while Jussy settled herself across from him, chin in hand, to watch. His expression as he chewed and swallowed made her laugh again.

"Well?" she prodded.

"Are grits always this bad, or is it just because you're such a lousy cook?" he demanded peevishly.

Jussy reached over to pat his arm. "Don't worry," she soothed. "You'll develop a taste for them eventually."

"Not if I can help it," he mumbled as she got up to fetch coffee.

"I heard that."

"Sorry, Miz Waring. I'm only being honest."

She looked at him over her shoulder, and both of them laughed as their glances met. The tension was gone and both were glad.

During breakfast, Sam outlined his plans for fixing up the house. To Jussy they sounded awfully ambitious, and she didn't have the nerve to ask him where he expected to find the money for everything he planned to do. But after a while it dawned on her that maybe money was no problem for Sam, that maybe he had enough of it to treat their remodeling project so casually.

For Jussy, this unheard-of liberty was both forbidden and exciting. Somehow, when Sam talked, she saw all the soaring possibilities that the future could hold. It excited her, and scared her half to death.

"And you expect to do all this in the few weeks you'll be here?" she interrupted at one point.

"Yep. Of course, we'll have to call in a professional when we replace your old furnace with central heat and air, but structurally the house is sound. It really needs nothing more than cosmetics."

"Oh, sure."

"I'm serious, Jussy. Rusty Simmons is going to have to wait. You'll be painting your own house as of now, not the wheelhouse of his trawler."

And hopefully she'd turn out to be better at wielding a paintbrush than she was at grinding coffee beans. Sam wondered if his stomach would stop burning before noon, and if it would be tactless of him to ask Ella Reid to start cooking for them now, before the inn officially opened.

"Bad, huh?" Jussy inquired as he set his mug aside.

He looked up quickly to find a knowing smile playing on her lips. It was impossible to lie to her, especially when she seemed able to read him so well. "Bad, but not fatal."

"Well, that's an improvement, isn't it?"

"Actually," Sam said thoughtfully, "if you could just strain out most of the solids before you pour, you'd be doing just fine."

"I'll start tomorrow, I promise. The Oleander Inn is going to be known far and wide for its coffee."

"The Oleander Inn?"

Jussy colored. "Um, well, yeah. I thought we should have a nice name for the place, one that's fitting. The yard is full of oleanders, and I thought, well, if you think it suits—"

"I like it."

Her jaw dropped. "You—you do?"

"Yes, indeed," Sam said, his eyes on those sweetly parted lips. "In fact, I can already see it, embossed in gold, on letterhead stationery."

"Oh, Sam, really! Spending money we haven't got yet! Letterhead stationery, my foot." But her eyes were shining.

After breakfast, they drove to the building-supply store in Myrtle Beach. Jussy couldn't hide her excitement as they selected paint chips and flooring samples to take home with them and made arrangements for the delivery of new fixtures for the bathrooms and a stove and double oven for the kitchen.

"This doesn't seem real," she marveled as they stopped at a department store to purchase new linens and towels.

And she looked so bewildered and enchanted at the same time that Sam had to kiss her, right there in the domestics department. Her arms were full of towels, so he couldn't hold her the way he wanted to, but he did manage to get his hands on her shoulders and to tilt back her head before his mouth closed over hers.

Jussy gasped and her breath seemed to catch in her throat. But just as quickly the shock fled, replaced by soaring wonder. Sparks danced through her veins, and she sighed and felt the towels bump Sam's chest as her body leaned toward him.

The distant thud as the stack hit the floor went unheard by both of them. Sam's hand was at the nape of her neck, kneading deliciously as his other hand slipped around her waist to draw her even closer.

A moan of pleasure sounded softly in Jussy's throat. Her hands slid through Sam's hair. His tongue slipped between her parted lips, grazing hers. An answering shiver fled through her blood.

"Excuse me." A woman with a shopping cart squeezed past them, sniffing huffily.

Slowly, reluctantly, Sam lifted his head.

Dazed, dazzled, Jussy clung to his eyes with hers.

"Oh, boy," Sam said hoarsely. "Sorry, Juss."

Are you really? I'm not, she wanted to tell him, but he was already scooping up the towels and heading for the cash register. His manner was curt, his eyes smoky with anger.

In silence, they went out to the car. Neither of them spoke as they turned onto the highway and headed for home.

"Look, Juss," Sam said suddenly, "this just isn't working out."

She had been daydreaming, sitting there next to him on the front seat. Now she started and turned quickly to stare at his averted face. "What isn't?"

But of course she knew all too well, and the tone of his voice and the hard set of his mouth made her die a little inside. Rejection loomed, dark and hurtful.

"It might be better if I hired a contractor to do all the work on your house. If I went back to Boston and sent you money as you need it."

No, no, no! she wanted to wail. "Why?" she asked instead. Her voice was hoarse, wobbly.

He ignored that. "All the permits have been applied for, and you won't really need me once the contractor takes over."

"But—but who's going to show me how to run the place?" she demanded, striving to sound uncaring, and failing.

Sam's jaw clenched. "Ella. I can speak to her myself if you like. You know she'll be happy to help out."

"She'll be tickled," Jussy agreed faintly. Her head was spinning. What on earth had she done wrong? Why was he leaving? Surely she couldn't let him go without doing something!

She swallowed hard and plunged on bravely. "I still don't see why you have to go."

Sam shot her a dark look. "Don't you?"

But Jussy could be stubborn, too. For once in her life she was going to stand up to the men who hurt and disappointed her—especially this one. "No."

Sam expelled a deep breath and his hands tightened around the steering wheel. "Look, Jussy, there's no sense in hiding the fact that you and I . . . that we're . . . attracted to each other. If I stay, something might happen. It wouldn't be fair."

To me? Or you? Jussy wondered. *Are you worried because you're starting to feel something for me that you shouldn't? Or just angry because I'm an unwanted complication?*

"I never make a habit of mixing business with pleasure," Sam added harshly.

"Oh," she said. Her heart felt chilled and empty. She'd forgotten about that "strictly business" thing. She'd forgotten that Sam was worldly and sophisticated and that being attracted to an unsophisticated and admittedly bumbling woman was probably annoying to him when it interfered with his work.

Well, she wasn't about to become an *annoyance* to the likes of Sam Baker! He was right; the sooner he hightailed it back to Boston, the better for everyone concerned.

"I'll talk to Ella," she said stiffly. "You just get the workmen hired and the legal stuff done. Ella and I can handle the rest."

"Great," he said, keeping his eyes glued firmly to the road.

Whether by accident or design, they managed to avoid each other for the rest of the day. Jussy pored over the paint chips and flooring samples until Ashley came back from school, then kept herself busy rearranging the kitchen to make room for the new appliances. Sam stayed upstairs, pulling chunks of crumbling plaster from the walls and patching the cracks in preparation for painting.

Around dinnertime he appeared in the kitchen to announce that he intended to run errands.

"I'll grab a bite on the road," he added, when Jussy asked about supper. "Can I get you anything while I'm out?"

"No, thanks. I'm going to the grocery store tomorrow."

"Can I come?" Ashley asked.

Jussy smiled at her, a tender smile that made Sam scowl and fumble for his car keys. "'Course you can, sugar. I'll wait till you're home from school."

"How 'bout you, Mr. Sam?"

Sam cleared his throat. "I'm afraid I'm going to spend tomorrow spackling, Miss Ashley. Want to help?"

"I don't know. What's spackling?"

"It's kind of like smearing Play-Doh on the walls, only you don't get in trouble for it."

"Hey, neat! Can I, Aunt Jussy?"

"How can I possibly refuse you an opportunity like that?"

Ashley's brow furrowed. "Does that mean yes?"

Smiling, Jussy bent down and hugged her. "It sure does." How glad she was of Ashley's company, especially when it kept her from having to be alone with Sam! She felt like she'd been walking on eggs for hours, and that if he didn't leave soon, she'd go plumb crazy.

Fortunately, he did walk out right after that, but an awful loneliness crept over her the moment she heard his car turn down the road. And that only served to make her furious. She wasn't going to start missing Sam Baker on top of everything else!

Grimly she threw herself into her work, cleaning the kitchen with a thoroughness she wouldn't have dreamed possible only a few days earlier. Unfortunately, she ended up using the bathtub bleach on the floor by mistake, and didn't realize her error until she damp mopped the linoleum and the cabbage-rose pattern came off on the sponge.

She had to spend another frantic hour scrubbing and rinsing before the damage was repaired, but even then the floor looked terrible.

And it was still hours until bedtime.

Ashley made things worse by not wanting to play games or be read to that night. After her bath, she played alone with her dolls and then dutifully withdrew to bed. After tucking her in, Jussy went downstairs, where the time seemed to hang even more unbearably on her hands.

Fetching the paint chips from the kitchen, she wandered through the downstairs rooms, envisioning the changes that were to come. Strange, she mused, that Sam had suggested they turn her house into an inn, when it had practically been that during most of Jussy's childhood.

Back in those days, friends of her father's from nearby Pawleys Island or from Charleston had always been dropping in to visit—to sip iced tea on the upper porch, to talk about art and politics and the latest local scandal. A regular flood of "snowbirds" making their annual treck from Maine to Florida were always dropping in without warning, too. Jussy's mother had spent most of her days in the kitchen, frying up endless platters of flounder or shrimp or swordfish and serving them with corn bread and homemade coleslaw at the big farmhouse table on the back porch. Jussy had never been asked to help, because Janet Waring had preferred keeping her kitchen to herself—which probably, Jussy thought now, accounted for her own total lack of expertise in the area of culinary arts.

But those had been exciting days, she thought loyally, even though they had always made her feel that she was something of an afterthought to her busy parents. And then, like an old, worn-out clock, those days had eventually started winding down, before stopping altogether. By the time she was twelve, Jussy's father was spending all but the most-brutal winter months up in Maine. The few short weeks when he was here in Waccamaw were taken up with painting out on the marshes or in his studio. Gerald and Jussy had been forbidden to enter the studio whenever he was there, and Jussy now suspected that her father hadn't just been painting, but had been hiding from his wife—and daydreaming his life away, without thinking once of the needs of his family or caring that their house was falling down around their heads.

Gerald hadn't been much better at taking part in family life. Jussy could remember many times when he had cut school to go crabbing or fishing, or sneaking away in Jasper Oley's pickup truck to shoot dove and quail in the nearby woods and soybean fields. He had always been far more eager to handle a shotgun and a fishing rod than a hammer.

Her lips thinned. She wasn't going to think about Gerald anymore. She would never forgive him for the way he had neglected his wife and daughter and lied to Sam about the money he'd borrowed.

Better to think about the Oleander Inn, and about the bright future that Sam kept insisting lay ahead for her—and *not* about the fact that she was falling in love with him.

"I am not!" Jussy told herself fiercely as the betraying thought came to her without warning.

But of course that was a lie. She'd realized it the moment he'd kissed her in the department store, with her arms full of towels and her head filled with the virtues of no-iron, percale sheets.

The mantel clock in the living room chimed ten melodic beats. Startled, Jussy put aside the paint chips and decided to give up waiting for Sam—which she'd been telling herself all along she had *not* been doing. Still, she couldn't help feeling a nagging sense of worry as she went down to the carriage house to switch on some lights for him.

She knew that she was being silly. Sam Baker was perfectly capable of looking after himself, and there was no reason to believe that some harm had befallen him out on the road.

On the other hand, he had said he was going out to do some shopping, and most of the stores hereabouts closed at nine. Shouldn't he have gotten back by now?

"Don't be stupid, Jussy!"

Just to prove that she still had willpower, she didn't stay in his room any longer than it took to switch on the bedside lamp. She didn't glance at his neatly folded clothes or the shoes standing beside the chair, or venture into the bathroom, where the scent of his cologne left more of a personal mark of male territory than anything else.

See? I'm not the least bit interested in you or your belongings, Sam Baker, Jussy thought, closing the bedroom door firmly behind her. *I'm not in love with you and I don't give a damn where you're keeping yourself!*

Back in her bedroom, she stripped off her jeans and socks, shivering a little in the cool night air. Putting on her nightgown, she brushed her teeth and went down the hall to check on Ashley. The little girl was sleeping soundly, a stuffed bear beneath her arm. Smiling, Jussy closed the door.

Slipping into her own bed, she read for a while, but the paperback mystery held no interest for her. It was nearly midnight when she switched off the light and, sighing, pulled the blanket to her chin.

At the same moment, the headlights of an approaching car splashed across her wall.

"Must've been one hell of a shopping trip," Jussy mumbled to the ceiling.

The car engine died and the lights went off. A moment later Jussy heard the slamming of the carriage-house door. The porch light went out, and then the pump came on in the well house across the yard, as Sam turned on the water in the bathroom.

For some reason, Jussy found the sounds very comforting. It was nice to know that someone else was out here on this lonely piece of property with her and Ashley, someone strong and broad shouldered and very dependable.

Was this why all the married women Jussy knew claimed they enjoyed having a man around?

Jussy had never had a man to depend on before. She found she liked the feeling. A lot.

But that didn't mean she was in love with him.

Soothed nonetheless, she buried her head in her pillow and, closing her eyes, drifted off to sleep.

Chapter Nine

The bell tinkled over the screen door as Jussy stepped into Reid's. Although it was barely ten o'clock in the morning, the ceiling fans were already working hard to disperse the sudden, summerlike heat. Overnight the temperature and humidity had soared, making Ella look all shiny faced and perspiring as she came from behind the counter.

"Lord have mercy," she said.

"Springtime in the low country," Jussy agreed ruefully. "I forgot how it can sneak up on you."

"Sneak up on you?" Ella snorted. "Roars in on a freight train, more like! Whatcha need today, sugar?"

Jussy produced her list, and Ella clucked as she examined it.

"Not plannin' on feedin' that Yankee of yours, are ya? Quickest way to drive a man off, cookin' the way you do."

Jussy laughed. She never took offense at anything Ella said. She loved the motherly old busybody too much for that.

"Actually, now that you mention it, I was kind of wanting to talk to you about my cooking."

"Want me to teach you, eh?" Ella looked triumphant. She'd been making the offer ever since the girl had graduated from high school. Unfortunately, Jussy had always refused. She'd been too busy playing with her parrots and taking her johnboat out on the creeks to learn the things Ella considered most important in attracting and keeping a man.

Well, that was going to change. The best-looking, most-eligible man Ella had seen in years had just arrived in Waccamaw, and she was darned if she'd simply stand by and watch Jussy let him slip off the hook.

"Teach me?" Jussy looked horrified. "Actually, I was sort of hoping that you and I could reach some sort of, um, understanding about *your* cooking."

Ella folded her plump arms across her breast. "I'm not followin' you, hon."

Jussy slid onto the bar stool. "Well, to tell you the truth, it was Sam's idea."

Ella pretended not to notice that Jussy was already addressing the man by his first name. "And just what idea is that?"

Jussy cleared her throat. She didn't really know how Ella was going to take the news that Sam had persuaded her to open an inn, and that he expected Ella to have a hand in running it. A hand? Jussy smiled wryly. Without Ella to run the place, the plan was doomed to failure.

"I didn't tell Sam I was coming here," she confessed, "but he already said that we should ask you—"

The bell tinkled again. Annoyed, Jussy looked up. A skinny fellow in a faded T-shirt and stained jeans came in. He squinted at them, half-blinded by the sunlight outside.

"'Mornin', Ella. 'Mornin', Jussy."

"Hey, Bubba," they chorused.

Bubba Hardin ran the service station out on Highway 17. He had been a boyhood friend of Gerald's and something of a troublemaker before settling down to marry one of the Manigault girls. Fetching a soft drink from the case, Bubba downed half of it before wiping his lips with the back of his hand and heaving a deep sigh. "Man, it's hot. Gonna have us one helluva summer."

"So what else is new?" Ella asked caustically.

"Met that developer friend o' yours last night," Bubba said to Jussy.

She stared at him. "Who?"

"That fella from Boston. Sam Baker."

Jussy scowled. "He isn't a developer."

"Oh, yeah? Said he was interested in turnin' your place into some kind of hotel, and maybe addin' a marina further down the line. Wanted to know what we thought of the idea."

"Who's *we?*"

"All of us over at Skeeter's."

"Skeeter's?" Jussy echoed. For the life of her, she couldn't imagine Sam visiting a place like Skeeter's, the dirtiest, darkest, hole-in-the-wall bar in the county.

"Yeah. Said he was just stoppin' in for a beer on his way back from Georgetown. Nice feller." Bubba belched, finished the rest of his soft drink and plunked his skinny rear down at the counter. "How 'bout some breakfast, Ellie?"

"What did you tell him?" Jussy demanded. "About the marina, I mean?"

Bubba turned up his palms and gave her a boyish grin. "Now, Jussy, darlin', what on earth do I know 'bout marinas? Nuthin', right? Well, that's what I tol' him. Nuthin'. But him an' Davis Wardlaw talked up a storm 'bout it more'n half the night."

"Davis Wardlaw?" Jussy asked faintly. Not attorney Davis Jamison Wardlaw III, who owned a fancy law office on Broad Street in Charleston and reportedly kept his hand in every single new development between here and Kiawah Island? Trust Sam not to waste his time with the little folks!

"What was Davis Wardlaw doin' at Skeeters?" Ella asked skeptically. "I thought they only let trash like you through the door, Bubba."

"Ha ha," Bubba retorted. "Seems to me they had a meetin' all set up. Both of 'em acted like they knowed the other'd be there. Watch them eggs, Ellie. I don't like the middles runny."

Ella responded with a colorful oath although Jussy paid no attention. Zombielike, she collected her few groceries from the shelves. So Sam had told everyone at Skeeter's—half the town of Waccamaw, most likely!—that he was interested in building a marina behind her house, while never once saying a single word about it to her. And meeting with a prominent real-estate attorney like Davis Wardlaw after telling her he was going grocery shopping? How come? Why was he lying to her?

I don't care, Jussy thought tightly. *I'm not hurt. I'm not!*

"Jussy?"

"Hmm?" She looked around to find that she had placed her groceries on the counter and that Ella had already bagged them and totaled her bill.

"I said thirty dollars and twenty-eight cents."

"Oh. Sorry." Jussy fumbled in her back pocket for the money.

"Where is he today?" Ella asked while making change.

"I don't know. When I got up to fix breakfast this morning, he was gone."

Ella waited until Bubba had crossed to the cooler for orange juice before leaning over the counter. "You mean he's *stayin'* at your place?"

"No, he ain't—*isn't*. He's living in the carriage house. Ella, we gotta talk. Can you call me tonight?"

Ella clearly wanted to know more right then, but Bubba was on his way back, so she nodded reluctantly and went to flip the eggs.

Jussy drove home slowly, her arm dangling out of the car window, the hot breeze fanning her cheeks. When she rounded the curve in front of Jasper Oley's ramshackle bungalow, she couldn't help slamming on the brakes. What on earth was Sam's Lincoln doing in the driveway?

She stared at the car as she went past. There was no sign of anyone on the front porch, and the house windows were dark. Jasper's ancient Chevy was gone, which meant that the two men must have driven off somewhere.

Deeply suspicious, Jussy drove home. Unlocking the aviary, she took out two of her parrots for company while she unloaded and put away the groceries. All of them wanted attention, but she chose Mr. Binks, who could be something of a feather plucker if left on his own too long, and Mango, her Moluccan cockatoo, who immediately climbed to Jussy's shoulder and rubbed his downy cheek affectionately against hers.

Soothed, Jussy talked softly to them while she brewed herself a cup of coffee. She had gotten up at six to hand feed some newly hatched chicks down in the aviary before readying Ashley for kindergarten, and now she was tired. Sam hadn't shown up for breakfast, and Ashley had come downstairs after brushing her teeth and collecting her book bag to announce that she'd just seen him driving away in his car.

Jussy had had no idea where he was off to so early, but now, of course, she knew that he was spending time with Jasper Oley. No doubt because somebody—Davis Wardlaw, most likely—had told Sam that Jasper owned a lot more land along Pohicket Creek than the Warings did. Surely Sam wasn't thinking of building a marina right next door, was he?

He better not, Jussy thought furiously.

But how in the world was she going to stop him if that's what he really intended? And why hadn't he told her right away?

It hurt to find out that he could be just as bad as her father and brother when it came to confiding in her. Only she wasn't going to admit as much to herself.

Sipping her coffee, jaw stubbornly clenched, Jussy was startled by a sudden shriek from Mr. Binks. She whirled to see what had alarmed him.

"Good morning." Sam was standing in the doorway, looking far too handsome in worn chinos and a faded blue T-shirt that hugged his muscular arms and wide chest.

"Good morning," Jussy answered, striving to sound cool and detached.

If he noticed, he gave no sign. "Mind if I fix myself some breakfast?"

"Go right ahead." She'd be darned if she'd offer to do it for him.

"Mama," a clear voice said into the silence, "who's that?"

Sam, mixing up pancake batter next to the sink, stared in disbelief at the small gray parrot on the kitchen table.

"Mama?" Mr. Binks persisted.

"That's Sam," Jussy answered calmly.

"Sam," the parrot echoed, repeating the name several times, as though trying to figure out where he'd heard it before.

"Hello," the big, salmon-colored bird chirped, though the word was nowhere near as distinct as the African grey's had been.

"That's Mango," Jussy added, in response to Sam's questioning gaze.

"He's beautiful. What kind is he?"

"A Moluccan. They're the largest of the cockatoos."

"I've never seen one before."

Jussy's expression softened as she stroked the cockatoo's head. "That's because they're endangered in the wild. As a matter of fact, their natural habitat—"

Her voice was drowned out by Mr. Binks, who had been pacing the checkered tablecloth with increasing agitation and now shouted loud enough to wake the dead, "Sam go!"

Sam was visibly startled. "I beg your pardon?"

"Sam go! Sam go now! Mama, say Sam go!"

"He can't mean that," Sam protested in disbelief.

Jussy looked embarrassed. "I'm afraid he can. He's very particular about who—"

"No, I don't mean the way he feels about me. The way he knows how to tell you what he wants. He can't possibly understand what he's saying, can he?"

"Sam go! Bad Sam! Go now, please!"

Jussy fixed the bird with a threatening stare. "Hush," she said sternly.

Amazingly, he obeyed, although he continued to glare at Sam malevolently.

"A lot of people believe parrots merely mimic the words and phrases they hear," Jussy said. "To some extent they're right. But Mr. Binks is nearly thirty years old. He's been around longer than I have, and you can't convince me that he doesn't know exactly what he's saying whenever he talks. When he's in the mood for certain kinds of food, he tells me. When he wants me to kiss him, he asks. When the telephone rings, he'll warn me to keep it short. Of course, he's exceptional even for a grey, and I've already told you how well African parrots can socialize. But my Amazons are the same when it comes to their vocabulary, and so is my scarlet macaw. They've been around people long enough to know exactly how to communicate with their human flocks."

"They've got to be incredibly intelligent then," Sam said doubtfully.

"Oh, believe me, they are."

"Sam go now," Mr. Binks declared again. "Mama kiss Inks. Mama kiss Inks now."

"Oh, that's right," Sam reflected, grinning. "Ashley told me he can't say his name because parrots don't have lips."

"I do so," Mr. Binks retorted, glaring.

Sam threw back his head and laughed, throaty, masculine laughter that warmed Jussy clear to her toes. It was hard not to laugh along with him, even when she knew that she had no business feeling the least bit charitable toward him. He had deceived her and he had lied. He was plotting things behind her back, which made him just the sort of slick Yankee developer nobody in his right mind should trust.

But, hang it all, whenever Sam laughed like that, she found it impossible to keep her wits about her. She forced herself to glare at him, if only to let him know that she hadn't lost them yet.

Sam's laughter faded the moment he intercepted that look, and he glared right back. So she wanted to indulge in another of those temperamental mood swings of hers, did she? Laugh with him like a delightful child one moment and be the haughty ice queen the next?

No woman he'd ever known had made Sam want to laugh as much as Jussy did. Or leave him jangling with frustration a moment later. Of course, he was honest enough to admit that a lot of that frustration was sexual in nature, because he didn't think he'd ever wanted a woman as much as he was finding himself wanting Jussy Waring.

That's why the warning bells were going off in his brain once again as he met those flashing violet eyes of hers. Finding himself attracted to a woman while on a business trip was both distracting and demoralizing, and definitely *not* his style.

And neither was Jussy Waring! Okay, so she had a cute nose and gorgeous eyes and a very appealing figure when she didn't go around hiding it in the shapeless men's wear that passed for her clothes. And she was intelligent, warm and caring, too. But those attributes, however appealing, were certainly not sufficient to make him throw all caution to the wind, which was something Sam Baker never, ever did. That kiss yesterday had been a mistake, and so had the one before *and* the one before that! The sooner he put them—and her—out of his thoughts, the better.

Not that he'd been dwelling on them!

Annoyed with himself, he went over to the T-stand to admire the Moluccan cockatoo. At the moment, even a bird was a welcome distraction from his feelings for the woman sitting at the table behind him.

Mr. Binks, perched nearby destroying a paper-towel roll Jussy had given him, pretended Sam didn't exist. But the Moluccan extended his wings and gazed up at Sam with bright, expectant eyes the moment he approached.

"He wants you to pick him up," Jussy explained, watching.

Gingerly Sam extended his arm as he had seen Jussy do. The cockatoo stepped trustingly onto his wrist and then walked boldly to his shoulder, where he nuzzled Sam's ear.

"He's heavy," Jussy agreed, seeing Sam wince.

"It isn't that. I'm worried about my ear. He isn't going to eat it, is he?"

Jussy snickered. "No. There's nothing more gentle than a Moluccan. And he likes you already."

"He does?" For some reason Sam felt flattered. He wasn't much of an animal lover. Dogs were too messy for his liking and cats too aloof to win his approval. But this big pink fellow was surprisingly engaging. "There's another thing I'm worried about."

"What's that?"

"My shirt. He won't, um, soil it, will he?"

"Of course not. He'll tell you when he needs to go."

Sam stared at her. "You mean . . . in words?"

"Mmm-hmm. He'll say 'potty' and wait to do his business until you put him back in his cage."

"Get out of here!"

"I'm serious."

"Are you trying to tell me that he—that parrots—can be housebroken?"

"Not all of them. And it takes a long time before they get the idea. Now, Mr. Binks knows perfectly he's supposed to do his business in his cage, but he refuses."

"That doesn't surprise me."

Chuckling, Jussy crossed to his side. "Here, I'll take him from you."

"Thanks."

"And here you go," she added, setting a stack of pancakes in front of him. Sam had forgotten all about them, and this time it had been Jussy who had rescued them from burning.

"Hey, thanks."

"Need anything else?"

"Not at the moment, no."

Jussy watched as he poured the syrup, feeling an ache inside her. How come it felt so darned good to have him chatting with her here in her kitchen, which was the last place he belonged? Especially after he'd made his feelings all too clear by glowering at her with such smoldering animosity?

Angrily, she went to the sink and began washing the dishes. "By the way," she said casually, "I saw your car over at Jasper Oley's place earlier."

"Yeah, he flagged me down when I got back from Charleston. Said he'd been wanting to meet me."

"Did the two of you have an interesting chat?"

"Sure did," Sam said around a mouthful of pancake. "He's quite a character. Took me on a tour of the town in that old jalopy of his. I think he remembers everything that's ever happened here."

"He ought to. Not counting his tour in the army, he's never left the place."

"He told me things were pretty wild in Waccamaw when your father was alive."

"My father had a lot of friends," Jussy explained coolly. Her father was the last one she wanted to talk about at the moment. She took a deep breath and gestured toward the marsh, which lay calm and lovely beyond the kitchen window. "Sam, are you going to build a marina out there?"

His head came up. "What makes you ask that?"

"I was told you were discussing it in Skeeter's Bar last night. You and Davis Wardlaw. And now you're going to buy land from Jasper, aren't you? And develop it just the way you Yankees did Myrtle Beach, right? Or should I say *ruin* it?"

Sam's hands sank into his lap. He said slowly, "Is that what you think?"

Jussy merely turned her back on him, her eyes stinging with sudden tears.

"Jussy." His chair scraped and then his hand was on her arm, his voice so low and raw that it made the tears run faster. Was it possible she had hurt him?

Angrily, she shook free of his grip. Who cared about his feelings? What about hers? Not once had he come out and admitted those damned marina plans to her! Instead he had lied, assured her he had only her best interests at heart, and that Pohicket Creek would always remain the same sleepy place it had been for centuries.

Men! she thought furiously. How come you can never trust them?

Whirling, she headed for the back door, wrestling with the knob because tears were suddenly so close. She couldn't bear the humiliation of breaking down and crying in front of Sam.

But he was right behind her, again taking her arm in a hard grip. "Jussy, we have to talk about this."

"There's nothing to say!" she cried, rounding on him furiously. "Now, will you please let me go?"

But he wouldn't. He just stood there looking at her with his fingers wrapped around her upper arm, while she hiccupped and gulped and the tears began to run down her face.

Wordlessly, he reached to brush them away.

"Let me go," she quavered. "And don't touch me!"

But again he refused to oblige. Instead, the hand that had brushed away her tears slid through her hair to cup the back of her head. His other arm went around her waist and he drew her slowly, deliberately, toward him.

"I'm not going to build a marina on Pohicket Creek, Jussy," he murmured in a voice that throbbed with urgency and sent an answering shiver through her blood. "Not now or ever."

"But Bubba Hardin said—"

"I don't care what Bubba Hardin said. I don't even know who Bubba Hardin is. Those guys at Skeeter's got the story all wrong."

"But Davis Wardlaw met you there."

Jussy was finding it awfully hard to concentrate on what she was saying. Her thoughts were skittering out of control, and all she really seemed aware of was the way her body fit so deliciously against Sam's. "He's one of the top real-estate attorneys in the state."

"So? That isn't why I asked him to join me."

"Then why did you?"

"It's called networking, Juss. I met him once or twice in Maine, at your father's place. I thought it might be a boost for the Oleander Inn to let him know about it."

Jussy wished Sam wasn't holding her so close. Her breasts were crushed against his chest and his capable fingers were kneading the nape of her neck. Oh, it felt too heavenly for words! "You didn't tell me you were planning to meet him."

"That's because I didn't know it myself. We ran into each other by accident in Georgetown."

"Did you really?" she asked, wanting so much to believe it.

"Yes, we did," Sam said roughly. "Believe me, Jussy. Believe *in* me. That's all I ask."

Oh, if only he knew how much she yearned to, how she craved to let him in, but how frightened she was of doing so! She opened her mouth to frame words of refusal, but found that she simply couldn't bring herself to speak.

But somehow it didn't matter any longer. A look of tender understanding had softened Sam's face, and for the first time in her life Jussy knew the thrill of a shared moment between a man and a woman that needed no words.

"It's okay, Jussy," he whispered, his voice sending shivers down her spine. "Trust me. Just trust..."

The words faded away as he lowered his head and his mouth found hers. She was salty with the taste of tears.

Once again he truly meant for the kiss to be a simple gesture of comfort, like the last one had been. But the innocence ended the moment he touched his mouth to hers.

Passion exploded between them. There was none of the slowly seeping delight of before. This was hot and fierce, a mating of lips and tongues and hands, a desperate need that had been simmering between them for much too long.

Instantly Sam felt himself growing hard, a betraying reaction to that pure, sexual heat. Jussy felt it, too, and it was the most erotic thing she had ever known. She couldn't bite back a moan of pleasure as Sam took her by the hips and settled her intimately against him.

"Oh, God," he whispered. "Jussy..."

Her fingers threaded through his hair. Desire had done away with all restraint, all sense of reason. She wanted Sam, *needed* him.

Her flattened palms slid over his chest, feeling the steel beneath his shirt. His heart thundered, and Jussy gasped with the stunning knowledge that she was the cause of that pounding pulse. She made a desperate, needy sound deep in her throat.

With parted lips she nuzzled Sam's jaw and the hollow of his throat, feeling his quick jerk of response. Then he was lifting her chin with cupped hands and kissing her, kissing her so slowly and deeply and passionately that Jussy felt as if she were drowning. She never wanted the moment to end.

But it had to, and she was the one who ended it. Even while her heart betrayed her, while her body bloomed with readiness, her hands were letting go of Sam's glorious shoulders and sliding down his chest to push him away.

"Jussy—"

"No," she said with a sob. "I can't."

Because she wasn't brave enough to let Sam ride rough-shod over her heart. Because she couldn't be sure that she could trust him to keep it safe after they made love.

Business partners. That's what they were, and Sam was a man to whom Jussy owed a veritable fortune. Fate would never favor them to be anything more.

"I'm going down to the aviary," she said in a choked voice.

This time Sam let her go, knowing better than to try and stop her. He was beginning to know better about a lot of things where Jussy Waring was concerned.

But it was hard. Harder than anything he'd ever done before.

The door slammed behind her. Sam cursed savagely as he spun away.

"Damn, damn, damn!" echoed the forgotten Mr. Binks.

"Hush your mouth, bad bird!"

Chapter Ten

"Wow!" said Ashley, covering her ears as she stepped into the hall.

Jussy, coming through the front door behind her, did the same. She hadn't known what to expect when she confronted Sam again after they'd nearly undressed each other in the kitchen earlier, but it certainly hadn't been the roar of a power tool.

"All the neat stuff happens when I'm at school!" Ashley yelled, as a dense cloud of dust blew down on them from the staircase above.

"Believe me," Jussy shouted back, "I wasn't expecting this!"

Abruptly the hall fell silent and Sam appeared on the landing above. His blond hair was disheveled, his shirt covered with chalky powder. He grinned as he caught sight of Ashley. "Hi, squirt. Back from school?"

"Aunt Jussy fetched me. Whatcha doin'?"

"Cutting plaster. This wall here has got to go. Hope you don't mind the mess," he added, turning his gaze on Jussy.

"You could've given me some advance warning," Jussy chided, trying to sound aloof, although she was mainly trying to cover the fact that she found him enormously sexy with a tool belt riding low on his hips and his muscular arms covered with plaster dust.

Following Ashley up the stairs, she saw that the hall was covered with drop cloths. Chunks of plaster lay everywhere. The wall behind the radiator was stripped to bare lathing.

"Look at this," Sam said enthusiastically. "Your forefathers used a mesh of horsehair and creek mud to frame their walls. I've never seen anything like it."

"It ain't creek mud," Ashley protested. "It's called pluff mud."

"Pluff mud?" Sam had to laugh. "You folks sure have a strange way of talking."

"Uh-uh. Y'all are the ones who're weird."

"You mean us Yankees? Just how many Yankees do you know?"

Ashley thought a moment, then held up her forefinger.

"One? Only one? Then how do you know all Yankees are weird? Am I weird?" As he spoke, Sam scooped the little girl into his arms and turned her upside down.

Ashley shrieked with laughter.

"It's 'you guys,'" he insisted, holding her over his head. "Not 'y'all.'"

"Put me down!"

"Not until I hear you say it—*you guys* are weird. Got it?"

Although breathless with laughter, Ashley obeyed.

Watching them, Jussy felt a heaviness around her heart, a funny mix of sadness and envy and longing. Why couldn't she and Sam get along so easily? Why did everything have to be so complicated between them?

Because you desire this man, Jussy thought. *And you're falling in love with him.*

And that made everything so very complex.

"Can I help you spackle now?" Ashley asked eagerly.

"I've got something else for you to do," Sam announced. He gestured toward one of the unused bedrooms down the hall. "A job of your own, if you want one."

"What?" she demanded, following him.

In the doorway, he hunkered down so his eyes were level with hers. "Well, I've been thinking that some of the guests who'll be staying here might have little girls of their own. Maybe they'd enjoy sleeping in a room near yours, where you could invite them over to play with your dolls before bedtime—but only if you wanted them to."

Ashley considered a moment, then nodded vigorously.

"Well, how about fixing up this room for them?"

"How?"

"You can start by picking the colors for the walls and trim. Trim means the doors and window frames. You have to choose something you think another girl your age might like. Then your aunt Jussy can have the room painted just the way you want it."

Ashley's eyes were bright with excitement. "Me? I can pick out the colors?"

"Why not?"

"Can we buy new furniture, too?"

"We'll start with a new bed, then we'll see."

"How 'bout a bedspread?" Ashley asked excitedly. "And curtains?" Her face fell. "Oh. But who's gonna sew them, Aunt Jussy? Momma was the only one who knew how."

Jussy felt her throat tighten.

An awkward silence fell.

"Curtains?" boomed a cheerful voice from the landing. "Did I hear y'all mention curtains?"

"Miss Ella!" Ashley cried.

Ella swept into view, arms spread wide to welcome Ashley's hug. "Howdy, darlin'! Howdy, Mr. Baker. Oh, hey, Juss, you're here too, hmm? Well, here I am, reportin' for duty as requested."

Sam got to his feet, smiling as he towered over her and held out his hand. Ella pumped it enthusiastically.

"Glad you could make it," he said cordially.

Jussy looked blankly from one to the other.

"He called me this mornin'," Ella explained, grinning. "Said you'd be needin' a heap o' help gettin' the Oleander underway. Shoulda told me sooner, Juss, 'stead of keepin' it a secret."

"I didn't do it on purpose."

"I know, but the sooner we get started, the better, don't ya think?"

We?

"Then—then you're going to help?" asked Jussy, overwhelmed.

Ella let out her trademark snort. "Didn't expect to run a place like this on your own, did ya, Juss? Run people off would be more like it!"

Jussy's heart skipped a beat. "Then—then you think it's a good idea?"

"Best this town's ever seen!"

"Do you mean that?"

"Can't think why nobody's hit on it before."

"All it took was a superior set of Yankee brains," Sam explained, tapping his forehead.

Ella snorted again. "Go ahead and believe that if you want to. The rest of us know better. Oh, your brother thinks it'll go over big, too."

It took Jussy a moment to realize that Ella was talking to her. She stared at Ella, bewildered. "*My* brother? You mean Gerald?"

"Who else?"

"But how does he know?"

"Bubba Hardin called him last night and told him all about it. Said Gerald sounded sorry he didn't come up with the idea on his own."

"That figures."

"Oh, the hell with him," Ella said dismissively. Drawing Sam over to the window, she produced a sheaf of papers from her purse. "I made up a list 'fore I came out. Kitchen's as primitive as they come, ain't it?"

"I'll say."

Ella looked over at Jussy, grinning. "No offense, Juss, but if we're gonna run a decent inn, we gotta have us a decent place to cook."

"I know," Jussy said, hoping she sounded suitably cheerful. To tell the truth, she was feeling far from cheerful all of a sudden, even though she should have been thrilled that Ella had agreed to help out. Every time Gerald's name cropped up, her mood soured immediately.

But she was honest enough with herself to know that there was more to it than that.

Standing in the doorway, watching Sam with Ella, Jussy could feel her throat tighten with hurt. She knew why Sam had wasted no time in getting Ella involved—because he wanted to get out of Waccamaw as fast as possible, before that *something* he had warned her about could happen between them.

Jussy supposed she should be grateful to him for being so conscientious. From the very first he had assured her that she could trust him. Apparently he'd meant in every aspect of their relationship, not just the business part.

Yes, Jussy certainly had every reason to be grateful. Then how come she felt so darned miserable?

Down in the kitchen, Ella clucked approvingly over the recent cleaning Jussy had given it. "And this floor! Why, it looks brand-new. How'd ya do it, hon?"

Jussy laughed. If Ella only knew she'd bleached the color clean off it by mistake! "Trade secret," she said with a wink.

"Land sakes. Didn't think you had it in ya! Come here, Ashley, and show Miss Ella where the new 'frigerator's gonna go."

"I have to admit I'm worried about you, Jussy," said a soft voice in Jussy's ear.

She whirled to find Sam towering over her, hands on his hips, where the tool belt hung. There was a look in his eyes that made her knees grow all wobbly.

Oh, his eyes! They were as blue and piercing as a crisp autumn sky. If he left tomorrow and she never saw him again, Jussy would always remember the way he was looking at her now with that burning blue gaze, as though his eyes were telling her what he dared not: that she had indeed come to matter to him.

She swallowed hard, knowing it was a lie. "Worried about me?"

"You know, because of the inn. I realize this is a big step for you, Jussy, and you're not sure that you can pull it off. I'm wondering if you're not having second thoughts today. Earlier, I thought maybe you'd started to believe you could do it."

That's because I thought you were going to be here with me, Jussy ached to tell him. *You make me feel like I can do anything.*

"I hope you're not getting cold feet again."

I am. Because you're leaving. You said so yourself.

Sam's voice dropped to an urgent whisper so that Ella and Ashley wouldn't hear. "Believe in yourself, Jussy, please. Successful innkeeping has nothing to do with being able to cook or make beds or brew the perfect cup of coffee. Ella can do all that. What's in here," he said, tapping his heart, "is all that really matters. The ability to do for others, and you wrote the book on that. You took in a dying woman and her only child, and cared for them both to the point of exhaustion. Providing a comfortable bed for tired travelers should be a cinch after that. That's where your strength lies, sweetheart. In giving."

He sounded so tender and sincere that Jussy's heart swelled with a wondrous warmth. No one had ever told her before that her foibles and failures were unimportant. No one had ever suggested that she draw on the strengths she did have, the ones inside that people didn't automatically see.

But Sam had seen them.

And he believed in her.

Or was this just his way of telling her goodbye?

Ella came up behind them. "Sam? I been meanin' to ask about the dinin' room. How many guests you think we'll be feeding on average?"

Sam's eyes expressed intense regret at the interruption, but he turned without comment and followed Ella from the room.

Jussy's heart went after him, and she would have stood there, mesmerized for who knows how long, if Ashley hadn't danced up to her with the paint chips she had left on the counter last night.

"Can we pick out the colors now?"

Jussy started as though waking from a dream. Her chin came up as she saw the happy expectancy on Ashley's face. "You bet, sugar. And we're going to choose carefully, okay?

We want to make sure our guests have the best of everything, right down to the paint on the walls."

"Oh, that reminds me," Ella called from the other room. "There's an oyster roast at the VFW tonight. Y'all care to come?"

"Now how does paint remind you of an oyster roast?" Jussy asked in bewilderment.

"They just finished paintin' the VFW hall. Myron Manigault come into the store this' mornin' for the last gallon of paint. That's when he told me about it."

"What's an oyster roast?" Sam asked.

Ella grinned. "Honey, if you don't already know, you'd better come find out."

Sam turned to Jussy, brows raised.

"It's a cookout, sort of," Ashley explained before Jussy could. "The oysters get steamed till they open, and then you shuck 'em with a knife."

"I've never eaten steamed oysters," Sam said doubtfully.

"They're not for everyone," Jussy warned.

"'Specially Yankees," Ella taunted.

"Oh yeah? What time does it start?"

"Around seven." Ella looked smug. "The first batch'll probably come off the fire 'round eight." She looked at Jussy. "You're comin', too, right?"

But Jussy shied away from the thought of socializing with Sam. It was hard enough to hide her feelings from him while they were busy discussing the inn.

"I haven't got a sitter for Ashley."

"I can stay at Susannah Middleton's house." Ashley piped up immediately. "Could I spend the night? Please?"

Jussy knew there was little sense in arguing at this point. Ella had that she-warrior look on her face, and Ashley hadn't been to a sleep-over in ages. Neither of them appeared ready to give in. Besides, she didn't have the will-power, after all, to turn down an evening with Sam.

"Okay. I'll call Susannah's mom and ask."

Ella and Ashley looked delighted. So did Sam. If Jussy needed further proof that she'd fallen in love with him, she had it in the way her heart started singing the moment she realized he was glad she was coming along.

That, and the way her throat tightened when Sam showed up at the house later that evening, after showering and changing his clothes. Jussy had warned him to put on something old, but she should have known that "old" to Sam merely meant clothes that were nicely worn in and very, very masculine.

Tonight he was wearing soft moleskin pants the color of sage, with cuffs that gathered neatly at the top of a pair of well-worn hiking boots. The collar of a dark green flannel shirt was folded casually over the neck of a cable-knit sweater of gunmetal gray. It was an outfit straight from a glossy Ralph Lauren spread, with Sam's rugged good looks merely enhancing the image.

Jussy, of course, had taken "old" quite literally. Her jeans were faded a powdery blue and worn through at both knees. She had slipped an oversize army green barn jacket over her bulky navy sweatshirt. She looked shapeless and bedraggled, and was suddenly very much aware of it as Sam's eyes raked her up and down when they met in the hall.

"No, no, no," he said at once, "that'll never do."

"For an oyster roast?" Jussy countered, scowling. "You have no idea how messy you'll get."

"Maybe so, but as the proprietor of the Oleander Inn, you've an image to maintain from now on."

Jussy tossed her head. "Who says so, Mr. Baker?"

A slow grin crossed his face. "Feisty tonight, aren't we?"

No, just happy, Jussy wanted to shout. But she wasn't about to tell him how much she was looking forward to an evening with him.

"I'll change," she offered, striving to sound haughtily generous, even though she would gladly have done anything for him at the moment. Hurrying back upstairs, she had to consciously refrain from whistling.

There followed a lengthy period of agonized indecision as Jussy rummaged through the incredibly messy contents of her closet.

She had an image to maintain, Sam had said. What sort of image? Businesslike? Pleasingly domestic?

Actually, she was glad for the chance to put on something different, after having gotten an eyeful of Sam dressed in his male-model best.

On the other hand, she didn't want to wear anything that would make Sam think she was trying to spark his interest. Did she?

But there was a wicked part of Jussy that wouldn't be denied tonight. She told herself there was no sense in fighting it, so she didn't even try. Ten minutes later she appeared downstairs in a pair of black leggings that clung to her long, shapely legs and a lavender sweater whose subtle color brought out the deep woodland violet of her eyes. She had put on a touch of eyeliner and lipstick and twisted her hair in a lovely French braid that emphasized the delicate beauty of her face.

Sam, who had been pacing the hall with typical male impatience, drew up short at the sight of her. Not a flicker of emotion crossed his face, but Jussy had to hide a smile of joyous triumph as she halted on the bottom step, her eyes level with his.

She knew. Oh, she knew, as a woman somehow always knows these things, that Sam found her beautiful, and her heart exulted. Tonight, just for tonight, she was going to indulge in the forbidden pleasure of imagining he was hers, and that they were going out together, just the two of them.

"Ready?" she asked, smiling innocently into his eyes.

He nodded. He had to clear his throat before he could speak. "We'll take my car."

Both of them were silent as they rolled away from the house. No doubt about it, Jussy had really rattled him.

After a moment, sounding more awkward than Jussy had ever heard him, he asked, "Will your parrots be okay?"

She had to hide another jubilant smile. Here she was, almost thirty years old, and she'd just learned the first lesson in snaring a man! Tomorrow she was going to throw every last one of her father's old shirts and sweaters—the bulk of her wardrobe—into the wood stove!

"They'll be fine," she said seriously. "Anybody would be crazy to steal them. They're extremely talented at gouging out eyes and snapping off fingers."

"Temperamental lot, your birds," Sam agreed, grinning. He hunted around for something else to say. Had she put on perfume? No, that was the clean, fresh smell of soap clinging to her skin. And what on earth had she done with her hair? She hadn't been upstairs more than ten minutes, and still it looked as though she'd spent hours braiding it into that soft, sexy style.

He found he had to clear his throat again. "I noticed a lot of avian-science books in the library the other day. Textbooks?"

Jussy nodded. She wanted to preen every time she felt his gaze on her.

"So what's it like?" Sam asked. "Working toward a Ph.D. in parrots?"

Actually, she was glad for something to talk about, too. She was feeling decidedly foolish tonight, and there was danger in letting one's heart get ahead of one's head. So she obligingly described her childhood wish to be a veterinarian, and how her undergraduate studies at Clemson University had steered her toward the avian sciences. She talked about her growing commitment to saving endangered parrots and their fast-disappearing habitats. She described her graduate work, which involved the breeding and rearing of the very rare Lear's macaw, of which less than twenty were known to survive in the wild. It was a species faced with certain extinction unless breeders like herself could successfully reintroduce bonded pairs back into the Brazilian scrub.

"I only have a single breeding pair," she concluded, "but I've managed to get them to nest twice. Unfortunately, one clutch was infertile, and we lost the second before hatching. I think the incubator humidity was to blame. When I get back, I'm hoping to try again."

"You didn't bring them here?"

"No. I was afraid of disrupting their routine. And the risk of injury and disease always increases when you remove them from the aviary."

"I'd like to see them sometime."

Jussy couldn't hide her pleasure. Normally people got a glazed-over look in their eyes right about now, and she had learned to curb her enthusiasm and keep her parrot lectures short so as not to bore anyone to death.

But Sam was different. He seemed genuinely interested in her studies. His questions revealed a lot of enthusiasm, and he had shown himself to be a darned good listener. Was there anything about this man that wasn't perfectly wonderful?

A low, cinder-block building appeared through the trees ahead. Jussy directed Sam into the parking lot, where he slipped between two pickup trucks and cut the engine.

"Are you warm enough?" Jussy asked. The temperature had dropped sharply with the coming of darkness.

Sam grinned at her. "Yes, ma'am."

She grinned back. "Sorry. I'm used to being with Ashley."

"No harm done. But I will admit that I'm starving."

"C'mon, then, and I'll show you how to shuck oysters."

"Lead the way. I'm able and willing."

"Oh, and Sam . . ."

He paused, his hand on the door latch. "Hmm?"

"Be prepared. This isn't the Boston Debutante Cotillion."

His white teeth flashed in the darkness. "Don't y'all fret none, young lady," he said in a surprisingly passable Southern drawl. "I already done got a hint of that last night at Skeeter's."

Chapter Eleven

Ella Reid had been on the lookout for them, and she pounced like a cat the moment Sam and Jussy reached the building. She was wearing a Citadel Bulldogs sweatshirt and had clipped her dark hair away from her face with a silver barrette. She was carrying a cup full of beer, and a cigarette dangled from her shiny red lips. This was Ella's way of dressing up for the night.

"Howdy!" she yelled. "Glad y'all made it! How ya doin', Sam?"

"Glad to be here, Ella."

"How 'bout a beer?"

"Maybe later," Sam replied, but Ella slipped her arm through his and hauled him off to the back patio anyway.

Here, a boom box wailed a mournful Waylon Jennings song. Oysters were being steamed, a bushel at a time, on a wide piece of sheet metal covered with wet towels. Underneath them, a wood fire smoldered. The air was heavy with the smell of smoke and simmering salt water.

Following more slowly, Jussy reached the back patio just as Jasper Oley came out the screen door.

"Howdy, Jussy! Met that young houseguest o' yours," he boomed in his best staff sergeant's voice. "Nice feller! Tells me he's turnin' your place to an inn."

"Yes, sir."

"Whatcha think about that?"

"Well, I'm sort of hoping we—"

"Don't know if your daddy would've liked it much."

"No, sir."

Jussy's father had hated any kind of change.

"How 'bout you?"

"Well, I—"

"Now looka there!" the old man exclaimed, peering over her shoulder. "Earl Horry's done brought along a date! Hey, Earl! Earl, over here!"

Jasper waved frantically, but the other man disappeared into the darkness. "Always was half-deaf," Jasper complained. "Looks like I gotta chase 'im down. Nice talkin' with you, Juss."

"You, too, sir," Jussy answered, hiding a smile. Conversations with Jasper always went this way.

A lot of other people came up to Jussy after that to ask curious questions about Sam. Everyone seemed to think he was a developer, and they were all astonished when Jussy explained that he was merely planning to turn her house into an inn.

Every one of them had firm opinions about that—both good and bad—and didn't hesitate to let Jussy hear them. She did her best to sound upbeat, but she had to admit that some of their concerns scared her a little.

When Sam appeared, the probing questions stopped immediately. People drifted away, pretending they couldn't care less about having such an intriguing stranger in their midst.

He was frowning as he joined her, which made Jussy feel a whole lot better. She couldn't resist teasing him. "What did you do—lock Ella in the ladies' room?"

Sam groaned aloud. "Doesn't she ever take no for an answer? Where's her husband, anyway?"

"Alabama, I think. He ran out on her a couple of years ago."

"Oh." Sam looked apologetic. "I didn't know."

"Not to worry. She got to keep the store, and Curtis got stuck with a bimbo. At least that's the way Ella tells it."

Sam grinned at her.

"What?" Jussy asked, meeting his gaze.

"You never worry about speaking your mind, do you, Jussy Waring?"

Not true, Jussy thought. *I don't have the nerve to tell you that I'm in love with you.*

"It's okay," he added, misinterpreting her blush as one of embarrassment. "I find it very refreshing."

Refreshing? Jussy had been called a lot of things in her life, but never "refreshing." After thinking about it, she decided she liked it. One approving word from this man, in fact, and she was ready to walk on air.

"'Sters!" someone yelled.

"Hungry?" Jussy asked, drifting back down to reality.

"I'm not sure. They're raw, you say?"

"Yeah. Nice and slimy."

Sam countered her wicked grin with one of his own. "Okay. Show me how to shuck 'em."

"You sure?"

"I thought I told you before. We Bakers aren't afraid of anything."

They found an empty place at the long wooden table where the oysters, hot and dripping, had been heaped in a mound. Slipping a heavy gardening glove on to her left hand, Jussy scooped up a fat cluster and pried open the shells with a blunt-handled oyster knife. Then she showed Sam how to dip the succulent oyster into spicy sauce and wash it down with beer.

"Think you kin handle that?" demanded Bubba Hardin, nudging Sam with his elbow from the other side.

"I don't know," Sam responded with a wry grin. "We'll see."

"You gotta suck 'em down quick."

"Er, thanks. I'll try to remember that."

Jussy watched with interest as Sam pried open a nice fat shell and scraped out the half-transparent, dripping oyster. Dragging it through the sauce, he swallowed without chewing, then looked at Jussy with an expression of surprise.

"Good?" she pressed.

"Hard to believe, but yes."

"Man ain't right 'less he likes oysters," Bubba pronounced, pleased.

Jussy felted warmed inside, though she couldn't explain why. Maybe because an oyster roast was such a distinctively low country sort of tradition, and it was important to her that Sam approve.

"Heard you was gonna build a resort out on Pohicket Creek," the elderly Myron Manigault said to Sam in his gravelly voice.

"Not a resort," Sam corrected. "A bed-and-breakfast."

"Oh? I thought it was gonna be a resort." The old man sounded suspiciously pleased.

"What's a bed-and-breakfast?" somebody else asked.

Sam explained.

"That don't sound so awful," someone else put in. "How come you tol' me he was out to ruin the place, Myron?"

"I didn't say no such thing," the elderly man protested huffily, although everyone knew that he had.

"You kin have my property if you decide on a marina," Bubba told Sam. "You can build anythin', long as the price is right."

"Who'd wanna build a fancy dock in your corner of the swamp?" demanded Tod Slater, who owned one of the Victorian houses in town. "Ain't no call for marinas in the middle of a dump, Bubba."

"How 'bout build one smack on top of the *Mary C?*" inquired someone else. "That trawler of Rusty's is the biggest eyesore in Waccamaw."

"No, she ain't. Your ex-wife is," Rusty retorted.

Everyone laughed, including Sam.

Jussy looked from one animated face to another in the bright glow of the overhead lights. Waccamaw boasted a small but diverse population, and most of them were here tonight. Shrimpers, farmers, a few young couples with children, and the requisite polyester-clad retirees crowded around the ever-increasing mountain of oyster shells. Sometimes the townsfolk could be clannish, and Jussy had worried that they would resent a Bostonian in their midst. But her heart rejoiced when she saw that no one seemed to mind Sam's presence.

As a matter of fact, she noticed that a lot of the women, especially the unmarried ones, seemed more than a little pleased to have Sam here. The more she looked, the more she noticed the dreamy glances being turned his way.

Not that she could blame them. And, oh, wouldn't it be wonderful if she could let them know in no uncertain terms that Sam belonged to her?

"Next batch!" announced Jasper.

Room was made for the wheelbarrow bringing the oysters from the fire. The talk changed to more general topics: the weather, the fishing, the basketball play-offs. People were too busy shucking oysters and downing beer to single out Sam any longer.

Sam left the table a few minutes later to replenish his own beer, and fetch another for Jussy. When he returned, he found her standing between the rake-thin Bubba Hardin and that bandy little shrimper whose boat Sam had rented. Jussy was shucking oysters with astonishing speed and laughing at something Bubba had just said. The chilly March wind had whipped color into her cheeks, and Sam paused in the shadows to look at this Jussy he scarcely recognized.

What was different about her tonight?

She's happy, he thought. Not brooding or sad, the way she sometimes seems at home.

He was deeply glad that she had had this chance to get away from her troubles for a while. He wished he had the means to wipe away her worries for good.

But how was that possible, when he was leaving in just a few days? And doing so because that, too, was for Jussy's own good?

Looking at her, Sam knew suddenly that he had made the right decision in turning his responsibilities over to Ella Reid. Because just by looking at Jussy, he found himself yearning to kiss that laughing mouth of hers, to mold the lovely curves of her body with his hands and to make love to her with all the explosive passion they'd shared in her kitchen. Oh, those legs of hers in those clinging black leggings! Didn't they ever quit? What would it feel like to have them wrapped naked around him?

Sensing his eyes upon her, Jussy looked up at that moment, and their glances locked. She felt her heart lurch as she saw the smoky gleam in Sam's eyes. She knew right away what caused it, and an answering shiver slithered through her blood. Desire.

Here, in front of all these people, surrounded by a noisy web of talk and laughter, Sam desired her.

Through the silky material of her bra, Jussy could feel her nipples growing taut. Heat sizzled through her. If Sam could make her react to him so physically just by looking at her, what would it feel like if he ever put his hands on her? Undressed her? Made love to her?

She popped the lid of the unopened beer can Rusty had just set down at his elbow and all but guzzled the contents. She wasn't much of a beer drinker, but at least it gave her something to do. A way to hide from Sam's all-knowing eyes.

"Plannin' on partyin' tonight, Juss?" Bubba Hardin asked approvingly. He and Gerald had spent most of their school years trying to get her drunk, and failing disastrously.

"No," Jussy said curtly, but she accepted the next beer he handed her.

"You was always too much of a goody-two-shoes," he reflected.

"I still am," she assured him. But the alcohol was starting to shore her up a little. She found that she could forget about Sam's burning look and concentrate on the oysters.

Luckily, Sam didn't return to the table. Jussy caught glimpses of him now and then talking with Jasper or Rusty or Myron Manigault, and once or twice laughing with some unattached female who cornered him in a shadowy area of the yard. Jussy harrumphed everytime she saw this and wielded her knife more viciously. The beer helped, and Ella, Bubba and several others made sure her cup was never empty.

At midnight, the beeper on Jussy's watch went off. Quickly she peeled off her glove, put down the knife and washed her hands.

"You leavin'?" Ella asked.

"Yup."

Ella leaned forward to whisper in her ear, "Wouldn't care to leave Sam behind, would you?"

Jussy grinned. "That isn't up to me, Ella. Besides, I need him to drive me home."

"Rats."

"But I can always suggest that he comes back."

"Oh, would you?"

"Would she what?" asked Sam, coming up behind them.

Jussy had been doing all right as long as Sam stayed away from her, but now that he was there at her shoulder, she could feel the goose bumps rising along her arms. There was no denying that something was happening between them tonight. Electricity seemed to crackle whenever he was near. Now that he had made it clear that he was leaving Waccamaw sooner than expected, there was an urgency between them that had never existed before.

"Jussy wants you to take her home," Ella said glumly.

Sam frowned. "Why? What's wrong?"

"Nothing. It's midnight. I've got to go home and feed my macaws."

"Oh." He'd forgotten about Jussy's birds. "We'd better go, then. Come on."

Jussy turned to follow him, but she had misjudged the distance around the table. She whacked her hip hard against the corner and would have stumbled if Sam hadn't caught her elbow and steadied her.

"You okay?" he asked roughly.

Jussy smiled at him dreamily. "Okay. Just had a couple of beers, that's all."

Sam's lips twitched. "A couple?"

Jussy grinned and traced the toe of her sneaker through the sand. She looked like a guilty, adorable child. "Okay, maybe more than that. How about you? Can you can drive?"

"I can manage."

"Oh, yeah? See that guy over there?"

Sam leaned down to follow her pointing finger. "The one wearing the Atlanta Braves jacket?"

"Right. That's Joey Ritter, Waccamaw's spanking-new police chief. Actually, he's the only policeman we've got, but he's a stickler for the law. I sure would hate to see you charged with DWI."

"Trust me, it won't happen." But Sam wasn't really paying his words any mind. While bending to talk to Jussy, he had caught the fresh, clean scent of her, and right away it started playing havoc with his senses. Since when had the combination of lavender soap and woodsmoke and the tang of the ocean become such an intoxicating fragrance?

"Let's go," he said gruffly.

Jussy's brow furrowed. "You know, I'm not sure I can walk."

"Just how many beers did you have?" he demanded, trying to hide his amusement.

"Um, I don't know. I think maybe..."

She wobbled a little as she spoke and Sam, laughing openly now, scooped her up against him and carried her off to the car. His gallantry was rewarded with applause and hoots of laughter as people saw what he was doing.

Jussy, embarrassed, tried to struggle from his grasp, but Sam merely tucked her against one hip and freed his right hand to open the car door.

"Allow me." Rusty was there to do the honors, bowing and grinning as Sam hustled Jussy into the passenger seat. The catcalls and laughter kept up as he got behind the wheel.

Rolling down the window, he waved and bid everyone good-night. Moments later the Lincoln was bumping down the road to a chorus of farewells.

"What a night! You can sit up now, Jussy. Nobody can see you."

She scowled at him. "You better have a good explanation for manhandling me like that!"

"Certainly. I didn't think you could get to the car on your own."

"Don't be ridiculous! I'm not drunk!"

"No?"

"No! I just—I'm a little tipsy, that's all."

Tipsy. What a quaint word. Sam felt his heart fill with fondness as he looked into Jussy's sweetly angry face. "You don't do this often, do you?"

Jussy bristled. "You pick me up like that again, Sam Baker, and I'll poke your eyes out!"

"Oh, really?" But he was already thinking about doing just that. Of lifting Jussy against the length of him and holding her close, and all of a sudden he realized that it wasn't fondness that stirred within him whenever he looked at her. It was something else, something far more elemental and hard to ignore: a raging thirst in the blood that could only be slaked by giving in to his desire.

"I'm very good at poking out eyes," Jussy added, because Sam wasn't saying anything, only looking at her in a way that was making it hard for her to breathe.

"Bloodthirsty little savage, aren't you?"

He meant to sound teasing, but his voice was rough with everything that was going on inside him. The result was just as unexpected as a slap in the face.

Instantly Jussy turned away from him and hunched against the car door.

"Jussy, I'm sorry."

But it was too late. The playful mood between them had vanished.

They drove on in silence for some time.

"I have to admit, tonight was a first for me," Sam said, in a vain attempt to clear the air between them.

"I guess they don't have oyster roasts up in Boston," Jussy agreed, hoping to accomplish the same. The silence was so charged with tension that she wanted to scream.

"No, they don't. The only thing that remotely comes close is a clambake on Martha's Vineyard, I guess."

"What are those like?"

Sam hesitated. How could he possibly explain? The clambakes usually took place at somebody's historic colonial beachfront home, not in a rundown, cinder-block building. There would be cutlery and table linens, not a rough wooden table and a roll of paper towels for wiping off your fingers. Beverages included a choice of vintage wines, not watered-down beer from a keg. Accents were moneyed, old guard, and talk usually centered around the Newport Regatta rather than the latest football scores of the Southern Big Ten.

"It's hard to say when you've never been to Martha's Vineyard," Sam said lamely.

Oh, how that hurt! Jussy realized immediately that he was telling her she was simply too unsophisticated, too *country,* to comprehend such a fancy Northern tradition.

Her eyes smarted with self-pitying tears. Oh, why had she brought him along tonight? She'd scared him off for good with a taste of the primitive socializing Waccamaw had to offer!

Or was it her? Had she disgusted him completely with her silly, drunken behavior?

"Turn left here," Jussy instructed dismally.

Sam obliged. Up ahead, the lights from Jasper Oley's bungalow glimmered through the trees.

"How many birds do you have to feed?"

"Only two for now. Most of my breeders will be going to nest now that spring's come. If the hatches are as good as last year, I'll have my hands full."

"I'd like to watch them hatching sometime," Sam said.

"You won't be here," Jussy reminded him sadly.

For that matter, she doubted he would last till the end of the week. He probably couldn't wait to get back to Boston.

Jussy had always wanted to ask him about that other world, but now more than ever she was afraid to. She had a feeling Sam moved in circles that made her existence here on Pohicket Creek seem even more embarrassingly rustic than it already did.

Once again a feeling of inadequacy reared up inside her. What on earth had led her to believe that Sam Baker desired her? She must have taken complete leave of her senses!

Swallowing hard, she willed herself not to cry.

Back at the house, Sam parked the car beneath the big oak tree and cut the engine. For a while he sat there, saying nothing. Jussy sat beside him, staring down at her hands.

"I guess I better feed my birds," she said at last.

"Need any help?"

"No, thanks."

"You sure?"

No, she wasn't sure. Despite her agony over Sam's rejection, she was perfectly content to go on sitting there beside him. The night air was chilly, and Sam's big body was a haven of warmth. More than anything, she wanted to lay her weary head against his shoulder.

Unwisely, she turned to look at him and found that his big, comforting shoulder was barely inches away. She lifted her eyes higher and found that his gorgeous cleft chin and sexy mouth weren't much farther.

Jussy Waring was struck suddenly by a thoroughly outrageous thought. Supposing she were to twine her fingers through Sam's thick blond hair and bring his mouth down to hers? More than anything else in the world she wanted to kiss him right now.

"Jussy?"

She looked at him guiltily. Her heart started knocking crazily as her wide eyes met his burning blue ones. He knew. He *knew* what she was thinking!

"Wh-what?" she breathed.

"You understand why I have to go, don't you?"

Her eyes slid away from his. She nodded.

"You'd be sorry if you got tangled up with me."

Would she? How did he know? Or was he just trying to convince himself of that?

"I'm old enough to know my own mind," she said stubbornly.

"So am I. And I know it would be a mistake for us to— If we—" He broke off, rubbing a hand across his eyes.

"If we made love?" Jussy sat up, glaring at him. "Why are you so scared to say it, Sam?"

"Jussy—"

"Are you scared of what might happen if we do? It's hard for me to believe you're the type to fret about casual sex! Could it be you're worried that this thing between us isn't so casual?"

She didn't know who was more surprised by her outburst, she or Sam. Was this really her talking? Sounding so bold and fearless, willing for once in her life to stand up for what she wanted?

"I am not scared." Sam's eyes were chips of ice. "Damn it, Jussy—"

"Then prove it. Kiss me. Kiss me just once, and tell me you're not running back to Boston because you're scared of this thing between us."

With a low growl, Sam took her by the shoulders and jerked her hard against him. Jussy came without resistance. She fitted perfectly into the circle of his arms, but he didn't give her time to savor the fact. Roughly he lifted her chin with his cupped palm, then closed his mouth over hers with all the agonized arousal he could no longer deny.

Uttering a choked cry, Jussy flung her arms around his neck.

Passion exploded, rocking them both.

Groaning, Sam leaned her back against the car seat. Jussy clung tightly as he moved over her, pressing his body against hers. They meshed perfectly, heatedly. His hands were beneath her heavy sweater, finding and caressing her naked skin.

Jussy arched at his touch. She breathed his name against his throat as he drew off the sweater and unhooked her bra.

"Oh, Juss!" It was all he said before lowering his head to find her rising nipples with seeking hands and tongue.

The effect was pure magic. Jussy moaned, and her head fell back against the seat. Her hips settled against his, where she could feel the growing heat of him through her clothes, enflaming her with the force of his arousal.

"I thought you were scared," she whispered.

"Oh, God, never," he answered raggedly. "Not of this."

Stripping away her leggings, he revered her with lips and hands, leaving her trembling, every limb aching with want of him. Leaning over her, he captured her mouth in a searing kiss, while his hands slid to her panties and drew them slowly, tantalizingly, from her hips.

Jussy felt her thoughts skittering away. She could feel the taut control Sam was trying to exert over himself all but snap as he lowered his lips to her passion-flushed skin.

"Ah, Juss—"

From somewhere in the house, the telephone rang.

Jussy froze.

Sam's body went limp above hers. His breathing sounded ragged in her ears. He swore harshly.

The ringing continued. The house windows were open, and the sound came to them clearly on the still night air.

"Let it go," Sam whispered.

"I—I can't. What if it's Ashley?"

She heard him swallow hard. Then he reared back and released her. She prayed the phone would stop before she got out of the car, but it kept ringing, insistently. Pulling her sweater over her head, Jussy went running up the walk. Out of breath and anxious, she reached the front hall.

"Warings'."

"Jussy! Glad you're there! Is Sam on his way back?"

For the first time in her life, Jussy felt a surge of hot anger toward Ella Reid. She stood there grappling with the urge to scream into the phone. She also wanted to cry, because she realized in the same moment that she had no right to be mad. She should be thankful that Ella had stopped her and Sam from doing what they'd been doing.

I can't make love with him, Jussy thought, agonized. *I can't! Because I was wrong. He's not the one who's scared. I am. I don't want to find out what he means to me. I don't want to know what it'll be like, saying goodbye to him, loving him the way I do. If I even love him at all. Which I don't! I don't!*

"Jussy?"

"What?" Her voice came out in a croak.

Ella was immediately contrite. "Oh, honey, you were sleeping! I'm sorry. I didn't mean to wake you up."

"It's all right," she said wearily.

"What about Sam? Is he on his way back here?"

Jussy cleared her throat. Through the hall window, she saw a light go on in the carriage house. For a second Sam was framed in the doorway, then the front door slammed and the blinds were drawn.

Over. It was over. She'd played her bravest hand, and fate had turned the cards against her.

"Well?" Ella prodded.

"I don't think he's coming back, Ella."

"Oh, shoot, it figures. Say, you okay, hon? You sound strange."

"I'm just tired."

Thankfully, Ella's maternal instincts kicked in at that. "Why, I'll just bet you are! Look at all the work you been doin' lately! Go on back to bed, honey. Sorry I bothered ya, and we'll talk tomorrow, okay?"

"Okay."

Jussy put down the receiver. For a moment she leaned her head on the banister and closed her eyes.

The phone rang again.

"Oh, for crying out—hello!"

"Howdy, Juss."

Wearily she closed her eyes. Her throat ached. "Hello, Gerald."

"What kind of lame greeting is that for your only brother?"

Anger flowed through her again, worse than before. "More than you deserve, Gerald Waring! Who in hell do you think you are to—"

"Whoa! Whoa, kid! I didn't call for an earful of this! What're you so mad about? I hear y'all are gonna make a killin' on the old place—turn it into a fancy inn, Bubba Hardin said. If you ask me, you ought to be turnin' cartwheels.''

He sounded like he always did—carefree, charming, totally unconcerned about any trouble or heartache he might have caused her.

Jussy couldn't deal with it. Not tonight. ''It's late, Gerald. I'm tired.''

''I know. But about this inn. It's why I'm callin'. Any chance I can come down and—''

''And what?'' Jussy interrupted scathingly. ''Help us out? Sand and paint and remodel bathrooms?''

''Umm, no. That wasn't exactly what I had in mind.''

Of course not. It never was. What he wanted was a share of the profits. Never mind that those would be modest, if there were any at all, and that all of them would be owed to Sam.

Sam.

Oh Lord, she didn't want to think about him, either. She wanted to go up to her room and have a good cry.

Gerald was still talking. He sounded a little less sure of himself now. Jussy's silence had probably worried him.

Sure enough, she could hear the old, familiar wheedling in his tone and could just picture the endearing smile on his handsome face, the one she'd always had trouble resisting. The one Caroline had found so hard to say no to as well—at least in the beginning.

''Drop dead,'' Jussy snapped suddenly, and she slammed down the receiver.

She stood there in the dark for a long time, breathing deeply, until the anger faded and she stopped shaking.

Slowly, tiredly, she crossed the hall. Cool night air caressed her bare legs and she realized that she'd forgotten to close the front door. She remembered, too, that she had left her underwear and leggings out in Sam's car. Well, she wasn't about to fetch them now.

Wearily, she started up the stairs. Moonlight splashed across the landing, eliminating the need to switch on a light. Barefoot, Jussy made her way down the hall.

She had forgotten about the construction work Sam had started earlier. Piles of debris were scattered across the floor. Jussy screamed as she stepped on a piece of unseen lathing and felt a nail pierce her bare heel.

Groaning, she collapsed on the floor. Oh, God, it was the last straw. Putting her head in her hands, she burst into tears.

Chapter Twelve

"Jussy? Are you all right?"

She wiped away the tears and bit back a moan of pain.

"Jussy, where are you?"

Sam was looming over her in the shadowy hallway.

"I—I'm all right."

Swearing softly, he lifted her up and carried her into her bedroom. Switching on the light, he laid her gently on the bed. Leaning over her, he smoothed back her hair.

"What happened?"

"It was dark. I stepped on a nail."

Wincing, Sam lifted her foot to examine the heel. Seeing that it was bleeding, he fetched a soapy washcloth and disinfectant from the bathroom.

"When's the last time you had a tetanus shot?"

Jussy thought a moment. "After the hurricane. They recommended everybody have one."

"How long ago was that?"

"Almost six years."

"That should be okay. But I want you to call your doctor in the morning, just to make sure."

Sam sat down beside her as he spoke. Propping her foot on his lap, he washed and treated the wound, then applied the ointment and a bandage. "It'll be sore for a few days."

Jussy grimaced. "I know. I can tell."

"At least it isn't fatal," he teased.

Jussy felt her heart turn over at the way he was looking at her. Her leg was still resting in his lap, and his strong, capable hand was caressing her ankle. To tell the truth, she had forgotten all about the pain and her tears the moment he'd sat down beside her.

"Better?" he asked.

Jussy smiled and nodded. And sighed deeply, aware that she should thank him and tell him good-night. She should be embarrassed, too, considering that she was sitting here with her foot on Sam's lap while her sweater was riding immodestly over her thighs and her panties were out in his car.

She knew she should tug the sweater back down, but it was too late. Sam's gaze had followed hers to her long, sunbrowned legs, and now his eyes swept up to her pinkening cheeks.

They stared at each other.

"What were you doing in the house just now?" Jussy asked a little breathlessly.

"Coming to talk to you."

"Oh," she said in a small voice. "What about?"

His voice grew husky. "You know."

Oh, yes, she did. And a shiver slithered down her spine.

Sam turned away from her and ran his hand through his hair. "Actually, I should be apologizing to you for what happened out in the car." He sounded as though he was trying to convince himself as much as her that he was sorry, but still the shiver in Jussy's blood died away. Disappointment seeped in.

"Oh, Sam—"

But he didn't let her finish. Boldly, his hand moved up her ankle, then along her knee to her thigh. And all at once the shiver was back, dancing down Jussy's spine.

"Do you know what?" Sam asked roughly. "I truly don't feel like apologizing."

"Y-you don't?"

He leaned closer, so that their faces were nearly touching. "No. As a matter of fact, I don't think either one of us has any reason to be sorry. Do you?"

Jussy swallowed and shook her head.

"Good. There's nothing more to be said, then. Where was it we left off?"

Jussy stared at him, bewildered.

"Was it here?"

Slowly he took her face in his hands and kissed her, warmly and deliciously, the way he had out in the car.

"Or was it here?" His hand slid along her bare thigh, caressing her.

"I—I'm not sure," Jussy breathed.

"I know we didn't stop here," he insisted, his voice rough as his hand curved slowly, erotically over her naked buttocks. "You left your panties in my car."

"We must have gone further," Jussy agreed. Her breath hitched as Sam lowered his head to her breasts. "I don't remember this," she whispered with a sigh.

"Neither do I." Sam's mouth closed over a firm, silken swell, bringing an answering moan to Jussy's throat. "Should I stop here, or keep on going?"

Actually, he couldn't have stopped now even if she asked him to. The taut control he had kept on himself since he'd found her crying at the top of the stairs had unraveled completely. He could no sooner deny his desire for this woman than he could the need to breathe.

But he could not forget the hurts Jussy had suffered at the hands of other men. He would not be so callous as to use her for his own ends. He couldn't. Unbearable tenderness poured through him as he worshiped her slim, lovely body. Even as the blood pounded and he ached for release, he held himself back, loving her gently, slowly.

Jussy moaned her assent as his hand found its way between her silky thighs. His fingers stroked and caressed, tantalized and teased, while his kisses continued to work their magic on her. Their tongues mated and their breath mingled while the world slipped away and only Jussy and Sam remained.

The pleasure was intense, hovering on that thin line at the edge of pain. Jussy quivered and lifted herself to Sam's wondrous touch. Never before, never, had she felt like this. Sliding her hands beneath his sweatshirt, she skimmed her palms across his wide chest. Her mouth plucked at his lower lip, making him groan with agonized bliss. Maddened, he unbuttoned his jeans, wanting to feel her, all of her, closing around him.

Eagerly, Jussy stroked her hands down the wall of Sam's chest to his rock-hard belly. She could feel the force of his arousal straining there, and she touched him boldly, wonderingly.

Sam sucked in his breath and reared back, away from her.

Undaunted, Jussy came up on her knees to face him. Slowly, she drew the tails of his flannel shirt from his jeans. Easing it from his shoulders, she kissed him where his skin was exposed to the moonlight, then traveled lower, her lips tracing the contours of his chest.

Sam shuddered and caught her hard against him. Freeing her hair from its braid, he let the silky strands slip through his fingers.

"So good," he murmured. "I never dreamed it could feel so good to have you undress me...." He took her face in his hands and kissed her, still kneeling before her on the bed.

Jussy murmured in pleasure, while her hands continued their work until his jeans fell away with a whisper of rough fabric. He straightened then and lifted his mouth from hers.

Dazed, Jussy opened her eyes to find Sam above her. Her fascinated gaze traveled over his hard chest and flat belly to the length of his manhood, displayed in full arousal before her. A fiery blush stole into her cheeks, but it was not a blush of embarrassment or shame.

"You're so beautiful," Sam said hoarsely, echoing her own thoughts about him. Once again his hands were trailing through her hair. "If you only knew how long I've wanted to touch you, to look at you like this, to love you...."

Jussy closed her eyes in bliss as his mouth trailed from her throat to her breasts. His tongue kissed her nipples as his hands skimmed down her rib cage and then to her hips. Cupping her buttocks, he lifted her against him, then dropped back with her into the sheets while his kisses trailed lower, across her stomach and farther still.

Jussy couldn't stop the moan of pleasure that rose in her throat. Making love with Sam was unlike anything she had ever imagined. It was far more intense than any longing, more passionate than dreams, more consuming than fire. A desperate need for him pulsed through her blood, drowning her in sweetness, demanding release.

Murmuring his name, she arched her hips invitingly beneath him. She could wait no longer.

"Jussy..."

Sam's voice seemed to come from very far away.

Jussy's eyes fluttered dreamily. "Hmm?"

"Wait."

But she didn't want to wait. Her arms reached for him as she murmured passionate pleas that Sam struggled to ignore. Rearing back from her, he leaned over and scooped his jeans from the floor.

"What is it?" she asked.

"I'm sorry," he said hoarsely. "It can't wait."

Jussy knelt behind him, rubbing her cheek against his shoulder as he fumbled with his wallet. In the moonlight she saw him remove a packet of condoms.

"Oh." She turned her face away. "Do you always keep those in there?"

Now it was Sam's turn to look embarrassed. "Not usually. I, um, I got them the other day in Myrtle Beach."

Jussy sank back on her heels. So he had been hoping—planning—all along to make love to her!

Sam turned toward her, uncertain now, but Jussy's smile was joyous. Eyes shining, she opened her arms to him, and he came to her when he was ready, smiling in that slow, wondrous way she had come to love so much.

Drawing her into his arms, he took her back down with him onto the bed.

"Oh, Juss..." Her name was a ragged murmur against her lips. His voice was raw with hunger.

The knowledge that he desired her so much made Jussy quake inside. Her fingers slid in a tantalizing path along his shuddering body. Almost wonderingly, she took hold of his engorged member.

Sam gave a groan of stunned delight. Then he was rolling her across the bed; his kisses ravished her, making her dizzy with want. She continued to caress him, glorying in the erotic pleasure of arousing him the way he had aroused her.

When she sensed a change in him, her hand fell away.

They were silent, looking at each other.

"Oh, God, Juss," Sam murmured. "I want you under me. I've got to feel you now."

"Yes," she breathed.

Her fingers twined through his hair, while at the same time, Sam took her hips and gently guided her body around so that she was lying beneath him. With his arms propped on either side of her head, he came down fully on top of her. The tip of his manhood nestled against the heated juncture of her thighs.

Once again he breathed her name, and it was both a ragged question and a glorious affirmation.

Starry-eyed, Jussy responded by opening herself to him. Up swirled her hips in wordless invitation, and Sam gave in with a moan of surrender. Desire lured him down as surely as the silken legs that wrapped themselves around him, and he thrust, hard and aching, into her.

It was a moment of shattering pain for Jussy.

Unprepared, unsuspecting, she cried out.

Instantly Sam reared back on his elbows. In the moonlight, she saw the shock on his face.

"My God!"

She swallowed hard, trying to sound unconcerned. "It doesn't matter."

He was still burrowed inside her, throbbing, lost in tormented pleasure, but the look on his face was hard with accusation.

"You—you're a virgin! Why didn't you tell me?"

"I said it didn't matter."

But to Sam, apparently, it did. Jussy could see the emotions warring on his face. She could feel his inner struggle between the need to withdraw and the urgent pull of their bodies, still tightly sheathed together.

Her eyes stung with scalding tears. She had made up her mind that she wanted this man, and even though the unexpected pain of his possession clouded her desire, she would not give him up.

"Sam, please." Her hands trailed down his back, while her lips curved imploringly along the arch of his throat.

"Jussy, no."

"Yes," she breathed, her arms tightening around him as he tried to ease away from her. Up swirled her hips to capture him again, the erotic invitation impossible to ignore.

Sam gave a moan of anguish. He could no longer still the pounding command of his own desire. Closing his eyes, he came back to the woman beneath him.

The world rocked as he slipped deeply inside her.

Trustingly, gladly, she lifted her hips to his.

Slowly, carefully, Sam filled her. Though he could scarcely control his own driving need, he took his time to be gentle. When he was completely wrapped inside her again, he paused, even though his body and his senses pounded with the force of approaching release.

"Are you all right?" he asked softly.

"Yes," Jussy said with a sigh. "Oh, yes."

Slowly, slowly, he began to move inside her. His lips trailed heated kisses over her closed eyes.

The sensation was pure magic. Already the pain was receding, giving way to feelings that were heat and light and liquid pleasure.

The intimacy was unbearable. Groaning, Sam began to move more forcibly inside her. Jussy felt the wonder of it lifting her up and out of herself.

The pain was forgotten as every savage thrust carried her higher and higher. Feelings soared, and she cried out his name as a wave of sheer ecstasy swept her away. Shimmering, shuddering, she clung to him, while Sam groaned aloud with the intensity of the explosion. Endless moments passed while he poured all of his tormented fury into her.

It took a long time for the tilting, swaying world to right itself again.

But then Sam shifted away from her. Rising up on his elbows, he took Jussy's face between his hands. Even in the dim moonlight she could see the intensity of his gaze.

"For God's sake, Jussy, why did you do that?"

She had anticipated the question, of course, but now she couldn't think of a suitable answer. For heaven's sake, how was she supposed to think, with Sam's gloriously male body still an intimate part of hers?

Sam's voice was harsh with recrimination. "If only I'd known! I wouldn't have— We shouldn't—"

Jussy touched a finger to his lips. "I told you before, it doesn't matter."

"But it does." Now he sounded angry. "You're twenty-eight years old, Jussy! Something like this, something you've been saving for so long, should have been given to somebody special!"

You are somebody special, Jussy ached to say, but she was afraid to.

Besides, Sam didn't give her the chance. Easing himself away from her, he got up and went into the bathroom. She heard the water come on. Swallowing hard, she laid her arm across her eyes to hold back the threatening tears.

This should have been a special moment for her. She was still soft and dewy from lovemaking, and her heart was filled with the wonder of what Sam had meant to her in that most intimate of moments. It wasn't fair!

He came back, carrying a towel dampened with warm water. "Here," he said, sitting beside her. "I thought you might need this."

He watched, aching, as Jussy pushed back the sheets and wiped the blood from her thighs. Her head was bowed and her lips were trembling. But Sam saw only the way the moonlight sparkled in her glorious red hair. He felt the turmoil inside him seeping away as he looked at her. He wasn't angry with Jussy, only with himself.

His heart tightened with guilt as he realized the enormity of what he had done to her. He should have stopped this thing between them the moment he'd discovered her inexperience. He had taken something that rightfully belonged to another man, a precious gift that Jussy had had no right to give him.

No, that wasn't exactly true. Jussy had every right to bestow that gift upon whomever she chose. Sam only wished she'd chosen someone more worthy.

Because he clearly wasn't. And he could never be. If she expected anything from him in return, she would only end up being hurt. And hurting her was the last thing he wanted.

"Oh, Juss . . ."

He gave a despairing sigh.

Jussy laid the towel aside and turned toward him. To Sam's surprise, there were no tears in her beautiful eyes. Instead she was smiling, that tender, pansy-eyed Jussy smile that he was coming to crave far too much. Her arms curved around his neck and she brought her lips to his ear.

"It's late," she whispered. "Let's go to sleep."

And then she was drawing him down with her into the softness of her bed, as though she'd been doing so every night of her life. Laying her head against her heart, she twined her legs around him and breathed a long, contented sigh. Her eyes fluttered shut. Her breathing quieted.

Sam could feel the rigid set of his own muscles seeping away into lassitude. Damn, but she felt good to cuddle with. Much too good.

He shifted slightly so that her head came to rest in the curve of his shoulder. With his free hand he stroked down the length of her rib cage to her hip and kept his hand there, holding her intimately.

Jussy murmured her approval. Her soft hair tickled his throat. Her breath warmed his skin. With a contented sigh of his own, Sam closed his eyes and gave himself over to sleep.

Chapter Thirteen

Morning came with the raucous burst of parrot song. Groaning, Sam burrowed deeper under the blankets.

Gentle laughter forced him awake. He looked up. Jussy's lovely violet eyes were dancing right above his own.

"Mmm," he murmured, curling a bare arm around her waist and dragging her down beside him. "You're a hell of a sight first thing in the morning, lady."

She wrapped herself around him, still smiling. "Bad or good?"

Sam nuzzled her silky hair. "Better than good. Fantastic."

As was the fact that he found her so playful. She had twined around him like a cat, and those long, gorgeous legs of hers were riding intimately against him. Sam had expected a shy, withdrawn Jussy when they woke up in the same bed together. This mellow, smiling creature was a delight.

They held each other, savoring the moment of rare warmth and companionship. Save for the screaming of the parrots, the room was still. A reddish dawn beat against the shades.

"Shouldn't you go down and feed them?" Sam murmured at last.

"Eventually."

He lay there with his eyes closed, enjoying the heaviness of her head against his heart and not really caring about the noise.

"What about the ones in the incubator?" he asked after a while.

"I got up to feed them last night."

Sam's eyes opened. His hand, which had been stroking her hair, stilled. "You did?"

"Mmm-hmm. Around two o'clock."

"I didn't notice."

"Of course not. You were dead to the world."

Sam gave her a devilish grin. "Can you blame me?"

She considered. "No. But shouldn't a sexy man like you have more fortitude than that?"

Sam came up on one elbow. "Sexy, am I?"

She nodded, blushing prettily.

"And you say I have no fortitude? Because I slept like a log after making love to you only once?"

The blush deepened. Her lips curved in an impish smile. "Well, to be fair, I'll admit that once was plenty."

"Oh." For some reason, Sam felt disappointed.

"But that was last night," Jussy added, nuzzling his neck. "This is now."

Sam's quirky smile all but melted her heart. And the feral look that crept into his heavy-lidded eyes made Jussy's breath hitch and her heart beat faster. She was sure he could feel it as he reached under the sheet to curve his hand around her breast.

"Is that a request, Miss Waring?"

"Is that an answer, Mr. Baker?"

Sam moved closer so that she could feel the heat of his arousal against her thigh. "No, ma'am. This is."

Laughing, Jussy slipped her arms around his neck. Sam's mouth stilled her laughter, and she gave a dreamy sigh as the kiss deepened and his tongue found its way between her lips. She felt him against her, throbbing, insistent.

"I don't want to hurt you again, Jussy," he whispered, drawing back a little.

"You won't," she breathed.

"Are you sure?"

Yes, she was sure. And she let him know it with her kiss, and the way her body softened and her legs parted as he moved above her.

There was really no need for him to doubt her. Dewy and receptive, she received him with ease, and this time there was none of the pain that had stunned her last night.

"Oh," she breathed as Sam became a part of her.

"You feel good," he whispered against her willing mouth.

Just in case, he held himself still, worried that he was rushing things, wanting her to get to know the feel of him.

But he needn't have worried. Jussy rose gladly to meet his gentling strokes, and a moment later they were moving together in a wonderful, timeless rhythm.

Jussy held him cradled in her arms while he whispered encouragement in her ear, inflaming her, making her heart glory in his giving.

She met every impassioned movement of his body with a mounting passion of her own, taking him deeper, loving him, until the world was swept away again and reality turned itself inside out and was gone.

* * *

Later, Jussy left Sam to shower while she went outside to feed her birds. The morning was humid, but Jussy didn't notice. Every muscle in her body—even some she'd never dreamed she had—seemed to ache, but she'd never felt so good before. One brief night in her life had ended and the dawn had come as it always did, and yet she had never known such happiness. Never in her life had she felt so sure and confident, not only of herself, but of Sam's love.

Jussy's heart did a little dance as she remembered how angry he had been last night when he'd found out that he was the first man she had ever had. Why would he have reacted that way unless he cared? That thought alone was what had made her brave enough to initiate their lovemaking this morning. She never would have dared if she hadn't been so certain that Sam had finally fallen in love with her.

She hummed aloud as she fed her birds, joyously anticipating the day ahead. A day spent with Sam, tearing down plaster walls and nailing and taping drywall, seemed like the most wonderful treat in the world. Jussy couldn't think of anything she'd rather do.

When she went back to the house, she brought Alfredo, her scarlet macaw, along with her. Alfredo had originally belonged to a language-arts teacher at the College of Charleston, and had been left behind when the woman returned to her native Barcelona. He spoke only Spanish, and was bad-tempered and aggressive.

Since the weather was warm, Jussy left him on the back porch. She wasn't sure Sam would appreciate being nipped by a macaw any more than he enjoyed Mr. Binks's harping about his unwanted presence in her kitchen.

Coming through the back door, Jussy found Sam at the stove, frying bacon and eggs. His hair was still damp from the shower, and his jeans hung low on his hips, emphasizing his sexy waist.

For a moment Jussy stood in the doorway watching him. Her heart ached with love. Then he turned from the stove to transfer the eggs onto plates and saw her. He straightened and his hands stilled.

"Glad to see you're the one cooking," Jussy teased. "This way breakfast will be edible."

He didn't return her smile or respond to her teasing. Instead he just kept looking at her, his blue eyes unreadable.

Jussy smiled brightly and crossed to the refrigerator. "Want some orange juice?"

"Thanks." He sounded tense.

Jussy gave up pretending. "What's the matter?"

"Nothing."

But there was, and both of them knew it.

Jussy put her hands on her hips. All her life she had retreated into self-conscious silence at the first hint of male displeasure. But that had been before last night, and before Sam had taught her how to approach any problem with head-on Yankee stubbornness.

"Shouldn't the woman be the one wallowing in a morning-after snit?"

Her direct attack worked. Sam put the frying pan into the sink and turned to face her. Propping his hip against the counter, he crossed his arms in front of his chest. "I'm sorry, Juss. It just wasn't a good idea."

"What? Being civil with each other?"

"That's not what I meant."

He looked so grim, so unsmiling, that all of Jussy's budding self-confidence vanished like a puff of smoke. She tried to still her rising panic. "Then what do you mean?"

Sam gestured helplessly. "This. Us. I've been thinking about it all morning. What we did last night was wrong."

"Wrong?" Jussy tried to hide her hurt and anger. "When two consenting adults are in—"

"Consenting adults?" Sam interrupted harshly.

"Oh, forgive me," Jussy said stiffly. "One consenting adult and a virgin."

Wincing, Sam turned away from her. Sometimes he didn't know what to do with this woman. One minute she could be an adorable innocent, the next a shrewd, experienced lover with a tongue that cut much too deeply. Part of his fascination with her was due exactly to this exhilarating paradox, but at the moment her insight was much too difficult to bear.

It hurt, damn it! More than he had thought it would!

"I wasn't belittling your lack of experience," he said harshly. As a matter of fact, the truth about her loomed before them larger than life, a wordless accusation. After all, Jussy had obviously remained a virgin for so long simply because she'd never fallen in love—until now. And now, of course, she was waiting—expecting—him to say that he loved her back.

Only he couldn't.

"Damn it!" Sam spun away from her, running an agitated hand through his hair. He did care for Jussy. He cared about her happiness, about her vulnerable heart, about the fact that the Oleander Inn was the single best hope she had of making a decent life for herself and Ashley. Furthermore, he cared plenty that her brother and her father had been so unfair and hurtful to her throughout her life, and that she had been burdened with so much hardship of late.

But love?

Sam swore softly, his back still to her. He couldn't afford to fall in love with Jussy. Love meant commitment, sharing, always being there for one another. He had a return ticket to Boston on Wednesday, for Pete's sake!

"Look, Jussy—"

"Sam, don't worry about it."

He whipped around, startled by the calm reason in her tone.

She came up behind him, her deep violet eyes soft with understanding. "I said don't worry about it. My brother, Gerald, let you in for much more than you bargained for. I'm not going to make matters worse by involving you in— in an affair. Just help me get this inn started, okay? Then you can go back to Boston and not worry anymore."

There wasn't a hint of bitterness in her voice. She sounded so sincere that Sam didn't know what to say. Frowning, he searched her face for a sign that she was burying her own misery and bravely letting him off the hook.

Her eyes were like soft, purple pansies, her dark, curling lashes framing them like a poem. And there was nothing in them to tell Sam she was lying.

"Okay," he said, striving to sound lighthearted himself. "You've got yourself a deal."

"Good." She smiled at him and turned away. "Oh, do you feel like reheating those eggs? Nothing worse than cold eggs for breakfast. I'd be happy to set the table for you in the meantime."

"Aren't you going to eat with me?"

"Nope," she said cheerfully. "I've got to go back down to the aviary. I'll grab a bite later."

Sam turned to look at her, a hard, piercing look. But she had learned over the years to keep an unwavering smile on her face no matter how difficult it might be. So she pinned it there now and kept it up while Sam's blue eyes nailed hers.

Not until he turned away did she let the uncaring facade drop. Exhausted and aching, she wiped the single tear from the corner of her eye, but only when she was sure Sam wasn't looking.

* * *

Tearing out plaster walls, Jussy discovered, was impossible work. Dust and plaster got everywhere—on her clothes, in her hair, in her eyes. Moreover, every inch of debris had to be hauled outside to the trash pile by hand. Eventually she got so fed up with doing this that she simply started tossing giant chunks of plaster and wood lathing out of the upper-story window, not caring where it landed.

Ashley found this extremely fascinating when she returned from her sleep-over.

"Can I do that, Aunt Jussy?"

"Be my guest. Just watch out for nails. I stepped on one last night."

"I will." Grinning wickedly, Ashley sent a huge piece of plaster sailing across the yard like a Frisbee. "Where's Mr. Sam?"

Jussy shook the dust out of her hair. "I don't know. I've been working up here all morning."

"I'm in the library." Sam's voice came from below. "Is that you, Ashley?" He appeared at the foot of the stairs, looking up at the little girl as she hung over the railing. "How was your sleep-over?"

"Fun!" Ashley called back.

They grinned at each other, and Jussy felt a pang of longing to share the easy comradery of their relationship.

"Whatcha been doin' in the library?" Ashley asked curiously.

"Goofing off. I thought I'd take a break from demolition."

"Demo—what?"

"Wrecking things. I've been checking out my diving gear."

"Are you goin' diving?" Ashley asked eagerly.

Sam cleared his throat self-consciously. "I don't think I'll have time, squirt. I'm going back to Boston in a few days."

"Aww, shucks. How come you gotta?"

"Time for lunch, Ashley," Jussy interrupted briskly.

"But I ain't hungry!"

"I am not hungry," Jussy corrected automatically. "And why not? Did Susannah's mother fix you breakfast?"

"Her daddy did. Heaps. So can we skip lunch and go divin' with Mr. Sam?"

"Of course not."

"Of course you can," Sam said at the same moment.

They looked at each other, Jussy scowling down at him from the landing, Sam grinning up at her from below. No one could have guessed that only a few hours ago he had said such hurtful things to her.

Because he doesn't care, Jussy thought. And she had no right to blame him for that. He'd warned her from the outset, hadn't he?

"Well, why not?" Sam prodded, while Ashley began jumping up and down. "The weather's great. We could both use a break."

Jussy compressed her lips. She hated it when Sam acted impulsive. He was so much harder to refuse when he put that endearing smile on his face and acted as though nothing of import had ever happened between them. Ashley only made it worse by tugging on her arm and demanding to know why they couldn't go.

The reason was simple, but Jussy couldn't tell it to Ashley. Sam had hurt her deeply, no matter how hard she tried to pretend he hadn't, and his cheerfulness only made the pain all the harder to bear.

On the other hand, she was sick to death of breathing plaster dust and pulling nails. And in a few days Sam would be gone. Where was the harm in being together, just the three of them, for a few hours on a gorgeous spring day like this? After all, it would probably be for the last time....

She couldn't fight that thought any more than she could Ashley's imploring gaze. "Okay," she said, already certain that she was going to regret it.

"I'll get my swimsuit!" Ashley crowed, racing for her room.

Jussy looked down at Sam. His mouth softened.

"That was nice of you."

Jussy made herself smile back. She wasn't about to let on that she was hurting so much inside. "You, too."

"Oh, come on. She's a good kid."

He seemed to mean it, and Jussy had to struggle against threatening tears. No matter what had happened between her and Sam, she had to admit that in the space of a few days' time, he had done more for Ashley than Ashley's own father ever had. Some men were just naturally good with children. Sam was one of them. Jussy couldn't remember Ashley ever having warmed so quickly to a stranger.

"I'd better pack a lunch," she said, laying aside her hammer.

"I'll do it," he volunteered quickly.

"I can handle peanut-butter sandwiches," Jussy informed him coolly.

"Oh yeah?" Sam pointed to Ashley, who had returned unnoticed from her room. The little girl was hanging over the railing, making choking noises, while her tongue protruded and her hands were wrapped around her throat.

Jussy scowled. "Oh, cut that out! They're not that bad! Are they?"

Ashley grinned toothily. "Just kiddin'."

Oh, why was it so hard to stay mad at either one of them? Jussy wanted to go on feeling sour and hurt at everybody, but it just wasn't possible. Her heart was already brimming with anticipation as she slipped into a bathing suit and shorts, braided her hair and grabbed a pair of boat shoes from her closet.

Downstairs, she found Sam and Ashley packing the car. The tall man was leaning over the trunk, stowing something inside, while laughing at whatever it was Ashley had just said to him. He was giving her his full attention as she danced around him, hands clasped behind her back, the ribbons on her little swimsuit fluttering.

Something long dormant stirred in Jussy's heart as she looked at them, something that suddenly made her hurt and her sense of betrayal seem unimportant. The yearning for a family of her own, and the sense of belonging and acceptance a family could give, flowed through her being.

Once, she had dreamed of having a family just like this, back in the days when she had still been too young to let reality sour her dreams. Back in those days she had still believed in love and commitment. But people were fickle, she had learned. Married couples were often highly incompatible, and there was no guarantee of receiving a parent's unconditional love.

Maybe that's why she had started raising parrots. From the first little cockatiel someone had given her for her tenth birthday, she had learned the sweet satisfaction of having a devoted and loving friend. Once you earned a parrot's trust, you never lost it. None of Jussy's parrots, however wild or temperamental, had ever given her any reason to doubt their affection.

While the people around her...

Sam looked up just then and saw Jussy standing on the walkway watching them. He waved at her and smiled, a smile that was not at all like the one he'd just given Ashley. This one made Jussy's breath hitch and her heart skip a beat. In that one moment she knew she'd done an unforgivably stupid thing to let herself fall in love with this man.

Stupid because in a few days he'd be gone.

Stupid because she'd end up being hurt even more when he left.

But Jussy's was a heart made for love, and she could no sooner deny Sam Baker when he smiled at her than she could the need to breathe. Resolutely she put tomorrow from her thoughts and made herself forget that only this morning Sam had all but thrown her love for him back in her face. At the moment he seemed willing to accept her friendship, and while that would never be enough for Jussy, she knew that at the moment it was all she had.

Whatever time Sam gave her, and however short, she would accept it and be damned grateful.

Chapter Fourteen

The afternoon was warm and very still. With Sam at the helm, the whaler seemed to fly over the glassy water. The weather was beautiful, the scenery more so. Billowing clouds dotted the sky, and the sun turned the water a bright, translucent green. The barrier islands were deserted save for the gulls, and gentle waves broke along the sandy shores.

Ashley could scarcely sit still. Because of her mother's illness, she had rarely been out in a boat, and Jussy could understand her excitement. She herself loved nothing better than being out on the waterway.

A half mile out, Sam cut the engine. Jussy tied the boat fast to a channel marker.

"Here, squirt." Sam handed Ashley a small blue-and-white flag and showed her where to display it. "This will signal anyone who comes close that we're a cover boat with a diver below."

"What are you going to look at down there?" Ashley asked, peering into the water.

"A British freighter called the *Portcullis*. The guidebook says it went down in a hurricane right after World War II."

Ashley's eyes widened. "Do you think they had treasure on board?"

Sam laughed. "Doubtful. And if they did, someone picked it up a long time ago."

"Have you ever found any treasure?"

Sam was busy slipping into his wet suit. "Some. Nothing spectacular, I'm afraid."

"Like what?"

"Oh, a few gold coins, old bottles, the hilt of a sword—stuff like that."

Ashley threw Jussy a fascinated look.

"Do you think there's any treasure out here?" she breathed. "Not on that British ship, but somewhere else?"

"Oh, plenty." Sam winked at Jussy over the little girl's blond head. The gesture gladdened Jussy's heart, even though she didn't want it to. "Edward Teach, better known as Blackbeard, supposedly buried a treasure chest filled with gold somewhere between here and Cape Hatteras. It's never been found."

"What about Stede Bonnet?" Jussy added. "Do you remember the book we read about him, Ash?"

Ashley's brow furrowed. "The gentleman pirate from Charleston?"

"That's the one. He supposedly buried his booty out on Sullivans Island somewhere."

"Where's that?" Sam asked.

"At the mouth of Charleston Harbor."

"Why don't you hunt for it while you're here, Mr. Sam?" Ashley urged.

Sam had to laugh at her eager expression. The thought of buried treasure never failed to fire anyone's imagination, and Jussy's niece was no exception. Neither, apparently, was Jussy. Sam found he had to look away from the glowing depths of her violet eyes and from her sweet, smiling mouth.

Where on earth, he had been wondering all along, had Jussy come by those clinging shorts and that sexy bikini top, anyway? From what he had already seen of her wardrobe, he would have been less surprised to see Jussy in a baggy T-shirt with ripped armholes and a pair of her brother's cut-off jeans.

More predictable, yes, and certainly much less distracting. But he had made himself a promise not to look at Jussy anymore. At least not in that way. Lord knows pretending to be so cheerful, to act as if nothing had ever happened between them, was bad enough. Wanting her all over again was an agony of its own.

"You could spend the rest of your life looking for treasure and never find a single thing," he explained to Ashley gruffly. "Besides, those stories could well be old wives' tales. There may not be anything out here at all."

"That's not true!" Ashley protested. "Not long after Momma and I moved down here, all this gold treasure was found in Florida. We saw it on the news."

"Yeah, I heard about that. A Spanish plate galleon, wasn't it? But don't forget that those treasure salvors had already spent countless years and millions of dollars searching before they struck it rich."

"I suppose so," Ashley conceded gloomily.

"But that doesn't mean nobody ever gets lucky," Sam added slyly. "Why don't you learn to dive and look for treasure yourself?"

"Me?" The little girl looked startled.

"You'll have to wait until you're a little older," Sam admitted, "but your aunt Jussy could start right away."

"What?" Jussy demanded.

"Oh, please, Aunt Jussy! Do it!"

"It wouldn't take long to get certified," Sam added, smiling into Jussy's astonished eyes. "Just find a reliable dive shop in Charleston. I could even give you lessons myself."

"You're leaving in a few days," Jussy reminded him quietly.

A muscle in Sam's jaw tensed. He didn't say anything. Retreating to the stern of the boat, he shrugged into his wet suit.

"Can you give me a hand?" he asked after a moment.

Jussy was furious to find herself blushing as she helped him with his zipper. The black wet suit hugged his muscular body like a second skin. In it, every masculine curve was displayed to perfection. Jussy couldn't help remembering the feel of that magnificent body, naked, pleasuring hers.

"Now the BC," Sam instructed.

Jussy's blush had deepened to scarlet. She kept her face averted, hoping he wouldn't notice. "The what?"

"That vest over there. Careful, it's heavy."

He was right. The air tank was attached, and Jussy struggled to hold it upright while Sam slipped his arms inside. Ashley did her best to help, even though she only succeeded in getting in the way.

"What a luxury," Sam told both of them with a grin. "I'm not used to having help."

Ashley looked pleased. Jussy tried not to.

"What did you call that thing you're wearing?" Ashley asked curiously.

"This? It's a buoyancy compensator. A BC. By inflating or deflating it as needed, I can adjust my buoyancy underwater."

"Very clever," said Jussy, who had never heard of such a thing but was more than glad to think about it now.

"Would you hand me my mask, please?"

She did so, and watched as he worked the strap over his tousled blond hair. Only this morning those same strong hands had roved her body with hungry familiarity. She had belonged to Sam this morning, as he had to her. Now she was afraid to even look at him, let alone touch him, because he didn't belong to her anymore. He'd made that perfectly clear. But it maddened her to know that she could desire him still, even here on the open water, in a boat with her niece.

Thank heaven for Ashley, whose stream of excited chatter hadn't slowed for a minute and was actually helping to distract Jussy from her painful thoughts.

"What's that for?" Ashley asked now, watching Sam clip on a heavy belt and an odd-looking meter.

"This is a weight belt. It helps me stay submerged. And this is a depth gauge. It tells me how deep underwater I am."

"And that?"

"A compass."

"What about this?"

Patiently, Sam answered all of her questions and even persuaded her to draw a few breaths from the mouthpiece of his regulator. Then he guided her through a predive check, smiling at her serious expression as the little girl did her best to help.

Jussy leaned against the console, arms crossed before her as she watched them. Not until Sam had pulled down his mask and adjusted his watch did he look back at her.

"I won't be long. Will you be all right?"

"Of course we will."

Ashley's lower lip thrust out stubbornly. "Yeah! We're not the ones risking our lives in some rusty old wreck!"

"I'm not risking my life," Sam assured her.

"Are you certain?" Jussy asked, suddenly wondering if maybe he wasn't. "I thought you weren't supposed to go diving alone."

"Actually, you're not."

"Sam—"

Jussy took a step toward him, but he merely plunged backward from the side of the boat into the water. Flashing her a thumbs-up signal, he disappeared below the waves.

Ashley ran over to the side, watching the bubbles that marked his descent. "He'll be okay, won't he?"

"Of course he will," Jussy said firmly, but the thought of Sam swimming far below her, weaving in and out of dark, dangerous places, preyed on her mind. She was sure that he was a careful diver, but suppose he ran into unexpected trouble? How on earth would she know?

Before she headed into full-fledged panic, she took a few deep breaths. This was crazy. She wasn't about to sit there and fret about him. Not when it was so peaceful out in the channel with the boat bobbing gently on the tide and the sun dancing across the water. She was going to make a point of relaxing with Ashley until Sam returned.

"Come here, hon. Let's put more sunscreen on your nose. Then go find the binoculars. Maybe we'll get lucky and see some porpoises."

In the shallow water a number of feet below, Sam was carefully adjusting his BC as he made his descent. The water was surprisingly clear, and already the shadowy bulk of the British freighter was visible below. Though badly rusted and covered with sand, its hull was intact and promised intriguing exploration.

Unfortunately, the image of Jussy's dark, hurting eyes kept interfering with Sam's concentration. So did the memory of those long, tanned legs in those skimpy shorts of hers.

No matter how hard he tried, Sam couldn't convince himself that he didn't want her again. If Ashley hadn't been on board with them, he would have returned to the surface immediately, stripping off his wet suit as he went, and would have made love to Jussy right there on the deck. The thought of pressing his cold, wet body against Jussy's sun warmed one was acutely arousing.

No doubt about it. His desire for Jussy was a physical thing, pulling him relentlessly no matter what he kept telling himself. Worse was the knowledge that Jussy wanted him, too. Sam had seen as much the moment he had looked into her smoky eyes after she'd helped him on with his wet suit.

Thank God he was leaving Wednesday for Boston.

The minutes ticked by. Up in the boat, Ashley sang to herself as she scanned the nearby islands with her binoculars. Jussy forced herself to study an article on do-it-yourself plaster repair in the *Old House Journal*. But every few minutes she found herself checking her watch.

Hadn't Sam told her he'd be gone only twenty minutes? How long had it been, anyway? It felt like an hour, maybe more. What if something was wrong?

"Aunt Jussy?"

"Hmm?"

"Think I'll see any pterodactyls out here?"

Ashley was scanning the horizon with her binoculars.

"Oh, dozens, I'm sure."

"How 'bout whales?"

"More probable than dinosaurs."

"Shouldn't Mr. Sam be back by now?"

Jussy laid aside her magazine. "Don't worry so much, Ash. He'll be fine."

"I'm getting hungry."

"We'll eat lunch when Sam gets back."

"Yeah, if he does."

"Ashley. He's a conscientious diver. That means he's careful. Yesterday he told me he's been diving for nearly twenty years and has never had an accident."

"You sure?"

Not really. That was why Jussy couldn't help scanning the water herself, and leaning over the side with bated breath the minute the timer on her wristwatch started beeping.

Seconds later, Sam's head broke the water. He grinned at her as he pushed back his mask and flashed her a thumbs-up.

"Don't tell me you were worried," he taunted.

"Of course not." Meeting him at the ladder, Jussy helped him off with the BC as though she had been doing so all her life.

But she was lying, and both of them knew it.

"Well? What did you see?" Ashley demanded.

Dropping his gaze from Jussy's, Sam began toweling his hair. "Not much. A lot of rusting metal. The sand and the current have done a lot of damage."

"Find any buried treasure?"

"I looked real hard, squirt, but nothing turned up."

"Shucks."

"There is one treasure I would like to find," Sam admitted, peeling back his wet-suit sleeves. "Not a treasure, exactly. A mystery. Have either of you ever heard of Theodosia Burr?''

To his surprise, both of them nodded.

''She was Aaron Burr's daughter,'' Ashley explained, proud of her knowledge. ''And she married Joseph Alston, a Charleston rice planter, didn't she, Aunt Jussy?''

''Mmm-hmm. And in the middle of the War of 1812 she sailed north from Georgetown to visit her father. Her ship never arrived in New York. No one knows what happened to it—a hurricane, an attack by a British man-of-war, a maritime disaster. The wreckage was never found.''

''How do you know all this?'' Sam demanded, astonished.

''The Warings and the Alstons were once related,'' Jussy explained. ''But that was hundreds of years ago.''

''Yeah, and we got a book about it,'' Ashley added. ''My momma read it to me before she got sick. Do you wanna find Theodosia's ship, Mr. Sam? Was there any gold on it?''

''Probably not. Besides, I'd rather find out what happened to Theodosia herself. That would really be one for the history books.''

''So stay here and look for her ship,'' Ashley suggested, with a child's inescapable logic. ''You don't really have to go home just yet, do you?''

Jussy pretended to be busy with a wayward curl that had worked itself loose from her braid. Sam started rinsing off his wet suit with the water jugs he'd brought from home. His mouth was a thin, grim line.

''Well?'' Ashley prodded.

''I'm afraid I do, squirt.''

''But why? Why can't you stay here with me and Aunt Jussy? How come—''

"How about lunch?" Jussy interrupted. "Didn't you tell me you were hungry, Ashley?"

The little girl nodded, instantly diverted. "Can we picnic on one of those islands over there?"

Sam obligingly started the engine. "Just tell me which one."

Jussy unfolded beach towels while Sam carried the cooler from the boat. The tide was low, and a strip of powdery sand led down to the water. Ashley hunted for minnows while pretending she was Theodosia Burr stranded on a deserted island.

Jussy, who had forgotten all about Theodosia Burr, was trying hard to ignore Sam as he stripped off his T-shirt. But she couldn't help watching the play of corded muscle under tanned skin as he unpacked the cooler.

It galled her, this fascination with Sam's body, and the fact that it was especially hard to ignore now that she knew the pleasure it was capable of giving.

And the pain. Was this what love was all about? Pleasure and pain? Happiness and hurting?

She had promised herself that she wasn't going to hurt anymore. She was going to savor these last few days with Sam as though they were an unexpected present. They would be all that were left her once he was gone.

With a tired sigh, Sam settled down next to her, elbows propped on his knees. "Ready to eat?"

She wasn't really hungry, but she nodded.

"I'm sorry, Jussy," he said softly, watching her, understanding her.

She blinked. "I'm sorry, too."

"I can't stay."

"I know."

"I never meant—"

She put a finger on his lips. "Shh."

He caught her wrist and turned it so that he could press a kiss into her palm. They stared at each other without speaking, their faces nearly touching, their hearts beating very fast in the narrow space between them.

Desire and regret burned in Sam's dark gaze. "I've never seen you in a bathing suit," he said, dropping her hand to run his finger boldly down the thin strap of her bikini.

"I've never seen you in one, either." Jussy willed her eyes to stay right were they were: level with Sam's, not dropping down to his gym shorts, which were all he had worn underneath his wet suit.

"You're one sexy lady, did you know that?" His voice was a husky whisper.

Ever since last night, yes, Jussy yearned to say. *Because you showed me how to feel that way. . . .*

"Hey! Are y'all gonna kiss?"

They broke apart guiltily.

"Well? Are you?" Ashley demanded.

"Don't be silly." Jussy's voice wobbled. "We were just unpacking lunch."

Ashley hunkered down between them. "Whatcha bring?"

"You'd better ask Sam. He fixed the sandwiches."

Sam made a great show of unwrapping the tinfoil to cover his own embarrassment. "I brought a veritable cornucopia of delights. Watercress-and-cucumber sandwiches on toast points for the lady, and peanut butter on whole wheat with banana slices and raisins for Princess Ashley."

Jussy blinked. "Excuse me?"

Ashley was giggling, liking the idea of being a princess. Her opinion about lunch was a little different, though. *"Yecch,"* she exclaimed.

Sam quirked his brow at her. "Does that mean you object to peanut butter with banana and raisins? I bet you've never had it before."

Ashley shook her head. "Sounds gross."

"Try it before you condemn it. You, too, Jussy."

"I'm not condemning anything. I want to know where you found watercress within a hundred miles of Pohicket Creek."

Sam winked at her. "That's my secret."

Another secret he'd been keeping from her was the fact that he could cook so darned well. Jussy's eyes widened as he withdrew numerous homemade salads and side dishes from the cooler. Everything was accompanied by rich sauces or extravagant garnishes.

"When did you do all this? I never dreamed—"

"I made them all the other night as a surprise for you and Ashley. You should be forewarned that I'm full of surprises."

He was. And Jussy, knocked off-balance, said a foolish thing. "Then maybe *you* should stay and cook for the Oleander's guests. You're better qualified than Ella for the job."

She regretted that the moment she said it. In effect, she was asking him to stay, to become a part of her new business, her life.

"Jussy..." Sam sounded pained.

Even though she had always known how he felt, she hadn't been able to stop harboring just the faintest hope that maybe he'd end up changing his mind.

Despite her misery, she couldn't remember when she'd ever been happier than she was right now, eating a picnic lunch with Sam and Ashley, listening to his teasing and her happy chatter. Jussy's heartache was bearable because she knew she could turn her head at any time and find Sam right there beside her, within easy reach of her caressing hand.

But of course it was too much to ask for. Way too much.

"I'm sorry," she said a little breathlessly. "I was only kidding."

His expression had closed like a book. "I know."

Jussy scooted to her feet. Any second now she was going to embarrass herself by bursting into tears. "I'm going for a walk."

"Jussy..."

She ignored him. Putting on her sunglasses, she stalked away down the beach without a backward glance.

Chapter Fifteen

Ashley was exhausted after their outing, so Jussy put her to bed early that night. After a bath and a bedtime story, the little girl fell asleep without a murmur of protest.

Tired herself, Jussy toyed with the thought of skipping her nightly check on the parrots, but knew that she couldn't.

Quietly she went outside. Lights blazed in the carriage house below. Sam's rental car stood by its front door.

Jussy hurried past, glad for the concealing darkness. She and Sam had scarcely exchanged another word for the rest of the day. On the boat ride home, they'd avoided so much as looking at each other. In the car, Ashley had done all the talking. At home, Sam had taken his diving gear down to the carriage house and had not come out again.

Jussy knew he was avoiding her deliberately. Or, better, avoiding the issue that had sprung up like a thunderstorm out there on the beach. The issue about their relationship, and where it was headed.

No woman on earth would be stupid enough to believe that Sam Baker was ready to settle down, especially Jussy Waring. Sam had made that clear to her time and again, and she'd been silly to hope that she could somehow get him to change his mind. Obviously, what had happened between them was not of significance to him.

The trouble was, Jussy had come to the painful realization that things had become pretty serious for her. Maybe her conservative upbringing had something to do with that. Love wasn't a casual thing for folks around here, and love, the physical kind, was never offered to another without a loyal heart standing behind it.

Well, Jussy had offered her loyal heart to Sam Baker. And he had flat out rejected it. He'd come to Waccamaw to sell Gerald Waring's house and had ended up having an affair with the man's sister. Big deal. In just a few days he'd be back in Boston and the whole thing would be forgotten.

Jussy's eyes burned as she fumbled with the keys to the door of the aviary. Dashing away the tears, she walked quietly past the cages, inspecting the breeding pairs that had settled down to roost.

Only Mr. Binks was still awake. When Jussy passed his cage, he tucked his head beneath his wing and refused to look at her.

Stepping nearer, Jussy noticed a few downy feathers in the sand below his perch.

"Plucking again, are you?" she asked sympathetically. "Can't say that I blame you. I've been feeling like pulling out my own hair lately."

At the sound of her voice, the gray parrot looked up. "Mama kiss Inks?"

His hopeful tone made Jussy laugh. "Need some company, do you?"

"Mama stay. Mama stay, please."

How could she possibly refuse a request like that?

"Okay. But I'm not spending the night out here with you. You can come inside with me."

Actually, she was glad for the company.

Mr. Binks seemed equally pleased. He sat obediently on the back of Jussy's chair as she ate a quick snack in the kitchen. He perched quietly on the towel rack while she took a shower, then cuddled with her as they watched television together in the parlor.

Ten o'clock came and went. Mr. Binks sat nodding in Jussy's lap.

"Come on," Jussy said. "We're going to bed."

She set up a cage in her bedroom and covered it with a towel after putting him inside so that he could fall asleep in the dark.

He talked to her softly while she readied herself for bed. After she had slipped beneath the covers and switched off the light, he made soft kissing sounds that soothed her aching heart.

"Good night, Mr. Binks," she murmured.

"'Night, Mama."

The room grew still.

Jussy drifted off to sleep. She was too exhausted to dream.

Down below, the clock chimed the passage of another hour.

"Jussy?"

She lifted her head, groggy and confused. A light was shining out in the hall. Sam's broad-shouldered shadow fell across her pillow.

"Jussy? Are you awake?"

"I think so," she said hoarsely. "What is it?"

"May I come in?"

She sat up, brushing the hair out of her eyes. "Now?"

He chuckled softly. "I know it's late. But I couldn't go to bed without appeasing my conscience."

Had it been bothering him? Jussy tried to be perversely pleased by the thought, but instead felt a giddy hope stealing through her.

"Oh?"

Sam stepped into the room and closed the door behind him. Jussy couldn't remember having invited him in. But she couldn't really convince herself that she minded.

Moonlight fell on the rugged planes of Sam's face as he neared the bed. His expression was troubled. "We have to talk, Jussy."

There was no sense in pretending that she didn't know what about. "Yes, we do."

He paused next to the bed, hands in his pockets, looking more uncertain than Jussy had ever seen him. "You know that I've got to go home, Jussy. I can't stay away from my job much longer. I've got commitments in Boston, and people who depend on me."

What about the people who depended on him here? What about all the time and the help he had promised to give her?

"I know," she said bravely. She wasn't going to make it hard on him.

But the thought of his leaving was not only painful, it was downright scary. Running a bed-and-breakfast and making a success of it when you couldn't even cook or clean house—and when a little girl's future hung in the balance—was a frightening prospect.

In the short time Sam had been a part of her life, Jussy had come to realize just how strong-willed, capable and efficient he was, the sort of man you could depend on for anything. He could cook and wield a hammer, charm the locals, win the heart of a five-year-old girl and make the conversion of a two-hundred-year-old dump into a successful inn sound easy. That strong shoulder of his was just right for leaning on, and Jussy wished with all her heart that it would always be there for her.

Furthermore, all those reasons for wanting him to stay didn't even take into account the fact that she loved him. Somehow, in just a few short days, Sam had managed to do away with all the awful loneliness and uncertainty Jussy had suffered for most of her life. In the process, he'd become as necessary to her as breathing. How did you let go of a man like that?

"What's the matter, Juss?"

Sam's voice was so tender that tears sprang to her eyes. She wanted so badly to be angry with him, but found she couldn't. It wasn't in her to be vindictive or mean.

"Nothing." *But don't call me Juss,* she thought. *It's too intimate, too sweetly familiar.*

Silence fell. Sam took his hands from his pockets and ran them through his hair. "You really want me to stay, don't you?"

Jussy made no answer. What could she possibly say?

"Are you in love with me, Jussy?"

Before she could even think of a response to that, he was shaking his head. "I'm sorry. I had no right to ask."

"Why not?" she demanded bitterly. "Would it make a difference if I was?"

"There can't be anything more between us than business, Jussy," he said harshly, desperate to make her understand. "It just wouldn't work. *We* wouldn't work."

"Why not?" she demanded again, her chin raised defiantly.

He struggled to explain. Everything had seemed so simple when he'd gone over this conversation in the carriage house. But it was hard to think straight now, with Jussy glaring up at him, all disheveled and sleepy, from the middle of her bed.

"Oh, sweetheart. We're like oil and water. Two different worlds. You'd never be happy in Boston."

"But you could be happy here."

She hit him with that, fast and hard, then pressed on with the next attack. "I've seen the way you've changed since you've been here, Sam. You're much more relaxed, and you smile a whole lot more. Hell, you even *dress* differently."

"That isn't true," he protested, although he didn't sound as convincing as he would have liked. Was she right?

"Oil and water. They don't mix too well, Sam, but we do. *We do.* So how can you say we won't work?"

"Oh, Juss—"

But she didn't give him a chance to say more. Instead she took his hand and pulled him down onto the bed. When he was sitting, jumpy as a cat, beside her, she leaned against him, showing him how much she, too, had changed. This bold, passionate Jussy was willing to fight for what she wanted.

Sam couldn't know how scared she was. She had let go of his hand, so he couldn't feel the pulse slamming double time in her delicate wrist. He couldn't know how much she felt like crying even as she trailed a feathery kiss across his averted cheek and steeled herself for the moment when he would push her away and storm out of the room.

But he didn't. He just sat there, letting her go on touching him, caressing him with her teasing, parted lips.

Then slowly, almost unwillingly, his hands came up to frame her face.

Jussy held herself very still as Sam tipped up her chin. Her heart thundered. Or was that his? There was no telling anymore where she ended and he began.

For a moment that felt like a hushed eternity he peered at her through the darkness. Then, just as slowly and deliberately, he lowered his head until his lips fastened themselves upon her waiting mouth.

A choked sob tore from Jussy's throat. All her love, all her loneliness and need were there in the way she kissed him back.

Desire ignited like a spark off flint, hot and urgent. They came together almost desperately.

Sam groaned as his hands slipped under Jussy's loose nightshirt and found her naked underneath. His mouth trailed along her throat, while his thumbs brushed the straining tips of her breasts.

Jussy shivered at the intimate touch and her nipples rose taut against his palms.

"Oh, you feel good," Sam breathed. Too good. How could he resist her?

Tossing her nightshirt aside, he lowered his head so that his tongue could finish what his hands had begun.

Jussy groaned as he worshiped her full, straining breasts. Liquid fire seemed to pour through her at his touch. The rough material of Sam's shirt scraped her bare skin. His head was heavy against her heart.

Then Sam shifted on the bed so that they knelt facing each other. Jussy took pleasure in unbuttoning his shirt and feeling the muscles of his chest grow taut as her seeking lips caressed his naked flesh. Her unbound hair spilled across him as she lowered her head and unzipped his jeans, savoring the shudder that shook him as she eased off his boxers and the heat of him sprang free into her hands.

Sam whispered her name as he pulled her against him. Jussy wrapped her arms around his neck and they kissed, their tongues mating. Naked skin seared where it met and meshed.

Then Sam took her by the waist and lifted her into his lap. Jussy's thighs rode across his hips and the heat of him throbbed against her womanhood.

The moment was electric, stunning them both. For a breathless eternity they clung together, arms locked, mouths joined, silky woman's skin pressed against hair-roughened man.

Then Sam laid her back on the bed. Poised above her, he scorched her with his eyes.

"You're wrong, Jussy," he whispered raggedly. "We don't just mix. We burn."

And to prove as much, he took her, impaling her in a joining that made Jussy gasp aloud with the sheer magnificence of it.

Perfectly gloved, they moved together. Desire pulsed with every heartbeat while Jussy moaned Sam's name. Her head fell back and he pressed his lips to the hollow of her throat, whispering to her, encouraging her. They clung together, their breathing harsh, their hearts clubbing wildly.

Release came like an explosion. For Jussy, it was a moment of soaring perfection, made poignant by the desperate awareness that it could also be the last time. She shuddered and clung to Sam convulsively while he poured himself into her, holding her tightly as he moaned her name.

Afterward they lay silent, shaken by the power of their joining. Long moments passed before their breathing quieted and the slamming of their pulses faded away into the steady rhythm of human hearts at rest.

Lying on his back, Sam held Jussy wrapped in his arms while she sprawled intimately across the length of him. Laying her head against his chest, she breathed deeply of his now-familiar scent. She knew that she had to commit this moment to memory forever. It would be all that remained of Sam once he left.

The thought was unbearable. Turning her face into his shoulder, she clung to him. She made no sound, but Sam could feel the shudder that wracked her slim body.

Closing his eyes, he swallowed hard. His hands caressed her naked back. "Jussy?"

"Mmm."

"I still have to go."

She didn't say anything.

"It might even be better if I left tomorrow."

"Oh?" Her voice was muffled against his chest. "Why is that?"

"Do I really need to tell you?"

Slowly, Jussy lifted her head.

A chill ran through Sam's blood. Her violet eyes were the coldest he had ever seen.

"I really wish you would."

Sam's hands halted their slow, hypnotic stroking. "I don't think I should."

"Why?" Jussy came up on one elbow, glaring. "What are you scared of, Sam? Of admitting that maybe you've fallen in love with me?"

"Jussy, don't."

"Why not?" she persisted. "Why does it make you so uncomfortable to admit that something special happens whenever we make love? *Are* you scared?"

Sam folded his arms behind his head in a deliberate attempt to appear unflustered. "Don't be ridiculous."

"There, you *are* scared!"

"Of what?" he demanded, glaring right back at her.

"Of the same things I'm scared of," Jussy insisted. "That there's more to the two of us than just great sex. That it feels too darn *right* whenever we're together. You came here to sell my brother's house. I only wanted to buy it back from you. But now there's a whole lot more between us, isn't there?"

"Come on, Jussy!"

"Do you know what I think, Sam?" She went on as though he hadn't spoken. "I think you really have fallen in love with me, even though you didn't mean to. And that's what scares you the most, isn't it?"

"Aw, damn it, Jussy!"

Sam escaped to the edge of the bed and sat there with his head in his hands.

"What's wrong with falling in love, Sam?" Jussy demanded, following him. "What's wrong with realizing that maybe you've found someone who's right for you? I'll admit it might not be true, but shouldn't you stay long enough to find out? Don't you owe us that much?"

Sam didn't know how to answer her. His mind seemed to have stopped functioning. Was this the same Jussy Waring he had met in Ella Reid's store, the one who had been so fragile and grieving? Was this the same Jussy who had been so wary of men that at first she'd scarcely dared make eye contact with him?

There was no time to think it over, not when her ridiculous accusations were making him hopping mad. Rolling out of bed, Sam began throwing on his clothes with a haste that told Jussy he couldn't get away from her fast enough.

"I'm sorry you think that," he said, "because it isn't true. I'm not in love, Jussy." He raised his voice, as though by speaking loudly he could further enhance his credibility. "Did you hear me? I am not in love! Sorry to be so blunt, but I don't want you believing something that just isn't true!"

Jussy sat on the bed with her legs tucked beneath her, her throat so tight that she couldn't speak. She had no idea what to say anyway. Even though she was convinced that Sam was flat out lying—to himself, not to her—she didn't know how to convince him otherwise. She had bravely gambled everything, and it seemed she had lost.

"I'm not in love, Jussy," Sam repeated harshly. "I want to make absolutely sure—"

From under the cover of the bird cage came a sudden scream. It startled even Jussy, who had at least known that Mr. Binks was there in the room with them.

"Sam, bad! Sam, go! Sam go now!"

There was electrified silence.

Then Sam swore softly. "I think that about says it all, don't you?"

And without a backward glance, he pulled open the door and stalked from the room.

Chapter Sixteen

When Jussy returned from driving Ashley to school, she found the Lincoln parked in front of the carriage house with the trunk standing open. Most of Sam's diving gear was already stowed inside.

Slowly, Jussy cut the engine and got out.

Sam emerged from the carriage house with his suitcase. He set it down when he saw her. Jussy looked at it, then peered into his face.

"Were you going to leave without saying goodbye?"

He avoided her eyes. "I've got to be at the airport before ten."

"What about the inn? You told me you'd help me get it started."

"I made some phone calls this morning. Myron Manigault recommended a general contractor. I've put him in charge of the remodeling. Ella's going to handle the management end."

"I see."

"It won't be as hard as you think, Juss. In a few months you should be ready for your first guests."

She didn't say anything.

Sam stowed the suitcase in the trunk and slammed the lid. From the breast pocket of his sport coat he withdrew a checkbook. "I've told Ella to open a business account in the Oleander's name. There'll always be enough in it to cover expenses. Meanwhile, I want to make sure you and Ashley won't have to worry—"

"Don't," Jussy said fiercely.

He looked at her, frowning.

"You don't owe us anything, Sam."

"Jussy—"

Hitching her purse over her shoulder, she started for the house.

"Hello, pretty! Ha! Ha! Ha!"

"Oh my Lord!" Jussy froze and stared in disbelief at the small gray parrot that came waddling around the corner of the aviary. "It's—it's Mr. Binks!"

Mr. Binks was clearly in a fine fettle. His wings were spread aggressively, his feathers were ruffled, his tiny eyes were beady with excitement. Over the grass he marched, right to the sidewalk where the two of them stood.

"Bad Sam!" he shrieked. "Bad, bad, bad!"

Sam stepped quickly out of reach of that menacing beak. "Where in hell did he come from?"

"That's what I'd like to know! I locked him up in the aviary before I left with Ashley."

"Then how do you suppose he got out?"

"Somebody must have unlocked his cage."

"On purpose?" Sam demanded incredulously.

"Don't touch him!" Jussy said in a fierce whisper as Sam bent toward the bird. Even though his wings were clipped, he could still become airborne and escape. "He doesn't like you."

Sam stood still as Jussy approached the agitated parrot, talking soothingly all the while. Bending down, she put out her hand. Fortunately, Mr. Binks stepped willingly onto her wrist.

The moment she had him, Jussy clapped her other hand over his back. Mr. Binks shrieked like a banshee, but Jussy ignored him and held on.

"Here," she said, thrusting the struggling bird at Sam. "Lock him up somewhere. I'm going to check the others."

"Jussy, wait!"

But she was gone, leaving Sam holding the screaming, squirming and now biting bird. Cursing, he set it down on the front seat of the car and opened the windows a crack. He'd be darned if he'd carried that feathered monster all the way up to the house!

Mr. Binks screamed and lunged at him.

Cursing, Sam shut the door and raced after Jussy. She had to be out of her mind to think someone had broken into her aviary! More likely than not, she'd just neglected to close Mr. Binks's cage tightly—or maybe the little brat had ingeniously opened it himself.

Calling her name, Sam raced around the corner of the aviary. Jussy was standing as if frozen in the open door, and Sam nearly knocked her down as he burst inside.

"What's going on?" he demanded, catching her by the arms and shaking her.

"Oh, God," she said in a choked voice.

Looking around him, Sam went still. His hand dropped away from her. The workroom they were standing in was in total disarray. Bins and crates had been overturned or smashed, feed sacks had been spilled and tools were scattered on the floor. Worst of all, in the aviary beyond, the cage doors all stood open. The flights were empty. Only a few parrots remained, some of them perched in the rafters near the ceiling, others in their nest boxes, where they cowered together as though too scared to come out. The rest had disappeared.

"What in hell is going on here?" Sam railed. "Do you have any idea who did this?"

Jussy didn't answer. She was still standing in the doorway, her arms hanging at her sides. Her eyes were wide, unseeing, and her face was drained of color.

"Jussy," Sam said urgently, shaking her once again.

She came alive the moment he touched her, jerking away from him like a scalded cat. Her eyes swept up to lock with his, and he wasn't prepared for what he saw in them.

"Oh, Sam, how could you?"

"What?" He stared at her, stunned. "Now, wait just a damned minute! You don't think I—"

But Jussy was pushing past him as though he didn't exist. "Where's Rico? And my sulphur-crests and tritons? Angel? Caesar?" she called. Her voice caught on a sob. "Oh, God, even Mango's gone! I've got to catch them! They can't have gone far!"

She was crying now and wringing her hands as she hurried through the empty aviary.

There was no time to find out why in hell she blamed him for this, Sam realized. She was obviously in shock, and it was time for him to take control.

"How do you catch an escaped parrot?" he demanded, hurrying up behind her.

Jussy didn't answer.

"Jussy!" He grabbed her arm and spun her around.

She looked at him furiously. "What?"

"We've got to move fast. Your birds are scared and confused. They've got to be captured now, before they have a chance to fly farther. My guess is that all of them except for Mr. Binks escaped to the marsh side of the house. Tell me what we need to do, what equipment we've got to get together, okay?''

His voice was rough with anger, but it served to calm Jussy's skittering panic.

''We'll need cages for catching them,'' she said tremulously.

''Good. What else?''

She drew a shaky breath. ''Feed. In a metal can so they'll hear it rattle.''

''Fine. I'll get it. You hunt down those cages, okay?''

She nodded.

Fortunately, Sam had been right: most of the birds had headed for the water when they'd been released from their flights. In fact, nearly a dozen brightly feathered birds festooned the branches of the oak trees near the creek, looking like colorful streamers. Those whose wings were clipped were foraging in the grass below. Mango and another cockatoo, Angel, were among them, and Jussy burst into grateful tears as she caught them up on her wrists.

Unfortunately, the parrots with unclipped wings were much harder to catch. The untamed breeder birds had been badly spooked by their sudden release, but even the domestically hatched ones were wary of everything, including Jussy.

A few of them came willingly when the feed can was rattled, but others remained where they were, or flew even higher into the branches. There they sat, ruffled and nervous, giving Sam the impression that any sudden movement would send them bolting for the horizon.

''I don't see my scarlet macaw,'' Jussy said anxiously, making a head count. ''And one of the corellas is missing.''

"How about the others?"

"They're all up there, I think."

"Good. Do you think they'll come down when they're hungry enough?"

"I—I hope so."

Sam could tolerate anything but the hopeless despair in her eyes. Never had he met a woman whose face could mirror her emotions the way Jussy's did. Or was it merely that he could read her so much better than any other woman he knew?

Either way, the sight of her pain was more than he could bear. At the moment he was willing to do anything to stop her from hurting. Hurrying back into the aviary, he hunted around until he emerged with a trio of small wire cages.

"Are your birds familiar with these things?" he called. Parrots, he remembered Jussy telling him, were extremely suspicious of anything new.

Jussy nodded. "They've all been in them at one time or another, on their way to the vet or whatever. And they're used to seeing them hanging on the back wall. What are you going to do?"

"I want you to prop the doors open and fill the bottoms with their favorite treats. Seeds, peanuts, whatever. They've got good eyesight, right?"

Jussy nodded.

"So they should come down when they're hungry enough, right?"

"I—I hope so."

"Oh, come on, Juss! Don't you think a hungry parrot would gladly give up its freedom for a peanut?"

Jussy didn't answer. She was trying hard not to start crying again.

Sam had hoped that the birds would come swooping down the moment Jussy returned with their treats, but they didn't. Instead they stayed put and watched as she rattled the cages and made a big fuss about putting the treats inside. At least they didn't fly off to a more-distant tree. "Let's wait over here," Sam suggested, pulling her toward a bench in the camellia garden. From there they could watch the birds without being too noticeable themselves.

And wait they did. None of the birds seemed in a hurry to come down. They sat contentedly preening themselves or shredding the bark from the branches. A few of them even seemed to be napping.

It didn't take long for Sam to grow extremely frustrated. He had never been able to tolerate not being in control of a situation, and this one was particularly nerve-racking. Beside him, Jussy couldn't sit still, either. She shifted constantly, toyed with her hair and dug holes in the dirt with her heels.

Watching her, Sam was plagued by the desire to put his arms around her and hold her tight. But she was as jumpy as a cat and he knew better than to touch her. Besides, that accusing way she'd looked at him when Mr. Binks had first appeared still rankled.

"Sam!"

Jussy's nervous whisper was accompanied by slim fingers digging into his arm. Sam's hand moved quickly to cover her own. A bright green blur came swooping from the top of the tree to land near the cage.

"My Amazon male," Jussy breathed. "He's the bravest of the bunch. If he goes in, the others may follow."

They watched with bated breath as the Amazon hopped closer.

"Steady now," Sam whispered as Jussy began to shiver beside him. "Steady."

The rest of the capture was surprisingly anticlimactic. In less than a minute the Amazon had decided that the cage posed no danger, and with a happy squawk, hopped inside and lunged for a peanut.

"Wait," Sam cautioned as Jussy made a move to rise. "See if the others follow."

They did. The morning sun had grown brighter and the birds were becoming more active. Hunger and the need to forage was driving them out of the trees. One by one they fluttered in a flashy procession down to the lawn. Their lust for adventure had given way to older, more driving instincts, and Jussy and Sam, moving slowly and quietly, were able to gather most of them up.

Only three birds resisted capture. Jussy's wild-caught umbrella cockatoo refused to come down from the tree even after his mate had been shut into her flight and given a liberal, and noisy, feeding. Another Amazon, a female, did the same, as did a nervous little Senegal parrot. The missing corella and Alfredo, the scarlet macaw, hadn't shown up at all.

"Maybe they'll come back later," Sam said encouragingly. "They might even be roosting somewhere close by. As for those guys up there, leave their flights open. They may decide to return on their own."

Jussy's shoulders slumped. "I wish I could believe that."

Sam looked at her standing forlornly in her vandalized aviary, and his heart hurt for her. Coming up behind her, he slipped his arms around her waist. "You're exhausted. Come up to the house. I'll fix you something to eat."

Oh, how wonderful it felt to lean back against Sam's muscular chest, into the spot where her head seemed to fit so perfectly beneath his chin and his strength surrounded her like a benediction and he made her feel safe and protected and cherished.

But then she remembered what shock and the lengthy capture of her birds had driven from her mind. With a cry, she struggled from his grasp.

"You!" she said furiously, round on him. "You aren't going to fix breakfast for anyone, least of all me! Get out of here, Sam! Right now!"

She was halfway across the yard before he caught up with her. Grabbing her arm, he spun her around so hard that she crashed against him. "Are you still blaming me for what happened to your birds?" His eyes blazed.

Jussy's blazed right back. "You bet I am! Of all the vindictive, awful things—"

"Damn! You don't really think I'd resort to that just to get back at you? Come on, Jussy! I haven't been in the aviary all morning!"

"You were here alone when I took Ashley to school!"

"I took a shower! Somebody must have driven up while the water was running!"

"Do you honestly expect me to believe that? How dumb do you think I am?"

Sam let her go long enough to run shaking hands through his hair. He'd never seen Jussy like this, a wounded wildcat spewing fire and venom. "Jussy, I swear to you—"

"Oh, stuff it, Sam. Get out of my life."

He watched her run back to the house and knew an empty despair like nothing he had ever felt before. She wouldn't believe anything he said to her now, and he didn't even know if he could find the right words. She had stripped him down to nothing with the force of her fury and her pain.

Chapter Seventeen

Jussy spent hours cleaning up the aviary and repairing the damage done to the cages and storage bins. She had arranged for Ella to pick Ashley up from school and keep her overnight. Ella had agreed that the little girl shouldn't be made aware of what had happened.

Ella had been aghast herself. And unfortunately, she had gone and done the one thing Jussy had forgotten to ask her not to do: spread the news around town. As a result, a steady stream of visitors had been invading the place all morning.

Actually, their curiosity and concern turned out to be a blessing, because everyone promised to keep watch for the missing corella and scarlet macaw. And as folks showed up to look over the damage and offer their sympathy, they also pitched in with helping hands.

It was the first visit to the aviary for many of them, and Jussy found herself obliged to answer a lot of questions about her parrots. To her surprise, everyone seemed genuinely interested, and she received a number of inquiries about acquiring birds for pets.

Strange, Jussy thought. The worst thing that had ever happened to her aviary was turning out to be the best thing in terms of educating people about her parrots.

The irony of the situation would have amused her at any other time, but not today. She had been upstairs in her room when Sam's Lincoln had rolled away from the house and out of her life. She hadn't really believed until that moment that he would actually leave.

Now there was nothing left to do but pick up the pieces—in the aviary and in her heart.

Ashley came home very tired and subdued the next morning. She had heard from Ella that Alfredo and another bird had escaped.

"Will we get them back, Aunt Jussy?"

"We'll have to wait and see."

They were sitting on the back porch, watching the rain come down. The air was humid. Clouds hung low over the marsh.

"I wish you wouldn't be so sad, Aunt Jussy. They'll come back."

"I know, hon."

"Then why are you crying?"

"I'm not."

The phone rang. Ashley slipped from her chair. "I'll get it."

She was gone a long time.

Probably one of her friends from kindergarten, Jussy thought dully. Even at the tender age of five, Ashley already spent a lot of time talking and giggling on the phone.

Thunder rumbled in the distance. Jussy stared out across the creek. Tomorrow the contractor Sam had hired was arriving with a crew to begin major renovations. Jussy had spent most of yesterday evening showing him around. Soon the old house in which Jussy had been born, in which she had fallen in love, would be forever changed.

I should feel sad, Jussy thought. *But I don't. I'm too empty to feel a thing.*

"Aunt Jussy?"

Ashley was peering around the kitchen door, grinning.

"Who on earth have you been talking to?" Jussy asked, mustering a smile for her. "You've been gone for ages."

"Guess."

"Susannah?"

"Nope."

"Caitlin?"

"Nope."

Jussy ran through the names of every playmate she could think of. "I give up."

"My daddy."

Jussy looked blank.

"Daddy," Ashley repeated, "and he's still on the phone. He wants to talk to you."

Understanding dawned. Jussy hurried into the kitchen.

"Gerald?"

"Hey, Juss."

"Where are you?"

"At home."

For some reason, she felt relieved. "What's up?"

"You tell me. I talked to Bubba Hardin last night. He told me what happened out at the place."

"I had no idea you were still such good friends with Bubba."

"Well, I am. Any idea who's responsible?"

"No."

"You don't sound too good, kid."

Trust Gerald not to understand what a shock yesterday had been.

"Gerald, I've lived here all my life. I know everybody in this part of the county. Who on earth would deliberately vandalize my aviary?"

"Hey, calm down! I get the picture. Any suspects?"

Jussy thought of Sam. Her heart squeezed every time she remembered how unfairly she had accused him. "None. Joey Ritter came out to poke around. I didn't want him to, but Ella—"

"Joey Ritter?"

"Oh, yeah. You wouldn't know. We've got a police chief now."

"You called in the police?" Gerald sounded stunned.

"It's embarrassing, I know. But I told you, Ella called him. She was furious."

"Can't say I blame her. So..." Gerald shifted, uncaring, to the next topic. "How're you and Sam getting along?"

Jussy's hand tightened around the receiver. "He went back to Boston yesterday."

"What? But I thought—" Gerald fell silent.

"What? What did you think?"

"No need to get mad, Juss! I was just wondering... Well, umm, Bubba thought maybe the two of you kind of had a thing for each other."

"Well, Bubba was wrong. And I don't appreciate your talking behind my back like that! Bubba should mind his own damned business, and so should you!"

"This *is* my business."

Oh, really?

"So is the house. Did Sam give you enough money to fix it up right?"

Jussy had never considered herself as having a temper before. Now she had to fight down a surge of hot anger. "That's none of your business, either, Gerald Waring! Not after you lied to Sam in the first place! You had no right, *no right,* to use Caroline as an excuse to—"

"Cut it out, Juss! It cost a hell of a lot more to open a restaurant out here than I thought! Sam would never have given me the money if he knew what I really needed it for."

"So you lied about Caroline."

"It wasn't really a lie."

Jussy closed her eyes. What was the use in trying to talk to him?

Gerald took her silence to mean that the subject was settled. "About this inn. I've got plenty of experience now, even if my restaurant went under." His voice brimmed with enthusiasm, his mind obviously racing over all the possibilities. "First thing we should do is think of a better name. The Oleander sounds so dumb. And you know as well as I do that the winters are gonna be slow. I was thinking about booking hunting clubs for that time of year. Sam could buy us a coupla boats and we could shoot ducks out on the marsh. You'll have to ask hi—"

Slowly, deliberately, Jussy hung up.

A few minutes later Ashley appeared in the kitchen.

"How come you're crying again, Aunt Jussy?"

"Oh, honey, I'm not."

"Did Daddy make you mad? He always made Momma real mad."

Jussy hugged her close. "You're too sharp, kid, you know that?"

"Is he gonna come here?"

"Why? Would you like to see him?" Jussy asked carefully.

Ashley considered. "Not really. Aunt Jussy?"

"Hmm?"

"How come Mr. Sam had to go?"

Yesterday morning Jussy would have had a whole different answer than she did now. Yesterday morning she would have firmly believed that Sam was going back to Boston because he had fallen in love with her. He was not impulsive, like Jussy. He went into things headfirst, not heart first, the way she did. And when he found himself confronted by something he hadn't planned on, something that didn't fit his nice, orderly sense of the world and his place in it, naturally he'd hightail it for home.

Or so Jussy would have said, before her aviary had been vandalized. Now she realized her belief in Sam's love had been mere wishful thinking. Because if you really loved someone, you didn't leave them when they needed you most. You didn't walk out when you still had no idea who had broken into the aviary and done so much damage—to the birds and to Jussy's sense of security, and to her faith in the people she'd known since childhood.

On the other hand, she'd hurt Sam back by accusing him of being responsible. Never mind that she'd realized right away that he would never stoop to anything so petty; the damage had been done.

Was that why he'd left so abruptly?

"Sam had to go home to Boston, honey. That's where he belongs."

Unlike me, Jussy thought, pulling Ashley onto her lap and pressing her cheek against the little girl's downy hair. *I belong wherever Sam is. I know that now. And it hurts. I hurt. Worse than I ever thought I could.*

Sighing, Ashley snuggled into Jussy's arms. "I wish Mr. Sam would come back. He was funny. He made me laugh. He made *you* laugh, Aunt Jussy."

"Sometimes."

"Daddy doesn't make you laugh. He never made Momma laugh, neither. But he was funny on the phone. And you know what?"

"What?"

"He said he might come out'n see us."

"Oh?" Jussy tried hard to hide her dismay. "Would you like that, Ash?"

As always, Ashley gave the matter careful consideration. Then she said honestly, "Not if he makes you mad. And only if he brings me a present. But I still wish Mr. Sam'd come back."

So do I, thought Jussy.

"You know what? I like the chintz better. It's more formal, but not in a put-offish way. What d'ya think, Jussy?"

"Hmm? Oh, it's fine, Ella. I've always liked blue."

"Sure." Frowning, Ella laid down the bolt of curtain material. Behind her, Jussy was staring out of the parlor window. She looked pale and tired, as though she hadn't been getting enough sleep.

"Maybe we should talk curtains later," Ella suggested. "Why don't you take a walk? Get some fresh air or somethin'. It's much too pretty outside."

"Okay."

Barefoot, Jussy strolled across the lawn to the small floating dock that the construction workers had installed yesterday. Here, the Oleander's guests would be able to watch the sunset or make use of the johnboat that was tied up below. Sitting down, Jussy let her legs dangle as she looked out across the creek.

The construction crew had begun work last week as promised. They had started immediately ripping out plaster walls, installing duct work and refinishing the old heartpine floors. Faced with all that noise and the fumes from the floor sealant, Jussy had packed up the car and taken Ashley to Georgia.

They had spent three days in Athens, where Jussy had met with her professors and formally withdrawn from the university. She had donated her pair of Lear's macaws to their avian-research department and had promised to let them know when the Oleander opened for business. Everyone had been supportive and kind, and had promised to spend a long weekend with her once the inn was up and running.

Then she and Ashley had driven home, her bridges burned behind her.

The next few days had been spent selecting paint and material and poring over the blueprints for the new kitchen. Ella never went anywhere without a big leather satchel crammed with notes and measurements. She carried a business checkbook, too, and paid for everything with its beautifully embossed checks.

Jussy figured that Sam must have put in plenty of money, given the size of the work crew swarming like ants all over her house. And Ella never thought twice when it came to overstepping the budget. But Jussy never asked. Sam's name didn't come up at all.

From the dock, she had only to turn her head to see her house clearly through the branches festooned with hanging moss. So many changes had already taken place. The plumbing had been updated. A central furnace and air-conditioning had been installed. Next week the painting crew was due to arrive and new, energy-efficient windows would be put in place.

To escape the noise and the dust, Jussy and Ashley had moved into the carriage house. Jussy had been toying with the idea of staying there permanently, so that all of the bedrooms in the main house could be made available to paying guests. Word about the inn had already gotten around, thanks to Davis Wardlaw in Charleston, and Jussy had already fielded a number of inquiries.

The more she thought about it, the more Jussy liked the idea of staying in the carriage house and maintaining a feeling of privacy for herself and Ashley. That way she would be able to keep an eye on her birds, too, which she'd been doing much more closely ever since the break-in last week. Any guests curious about her parrots would have to visit with the few Jussy intended to keep in the front hall, but they would not be able to venture down to the aviary itself.

At least none of the birds had suffered ill effects from their dramatic escape. And on the day Jussy and Ashley returned from Georgia, Alfredo, the scarlet macaw, had been captured and returned by a kindly farmer near McClellanville. The corella was still missing, but Jussy hadn't given up hope that it, too, would come back.

Sighing, she flipped a pebble into the slow-moving water. It wasn't really the corella's return that she was counting on. But more than a week had passed since Sam had left, and Jussy knew it was foolish to go on dreaming.

Still, she couldn't prevent her heart from doing a crazy little dance when she suddenly saw an unfamiliar car come zooming down the drive from the direction of the main road. She knew all of the construction workers' vehicles by now, and this was a brand-new rental car.

Jussy got up and forced herself to walk calmly toward the driveway. The car stopped under the huge oak tree where Sam had always parked. Someone was getting out—a tall man with sandy, windblown hair.

Jussy's heartbeat accelerated. So did her footsteps. She was almost running by the time she crossed the lawn.

"Well, howdy, Juss! Good to find you home!"

The features were unmistakable, because they looked so much like Ashley's. But the grin was trademark Waring.

"Gerald." Jussy's voice was numb with disbelief.

"Surprised to see me, huh?"

She didn't answer. Her throat had closed up. Her mind had simply ceased to function.

Gerald opened the trunk and hefted out a pair of suitcases. "Looks like you've got quite a crew inside. Where should I put these?"

"Back in the car."

Gerald's smile faded when he saw that she was serious. "Not welcome, am I? Whoo boy. I thought that might happen. It's still my house, Juss."

"No, it's not. It belongs to Sam Baker."

"Then what're you still doing here?"

Jussy's chin came up. She wasn't going to let him intimidate her. "I'm running the inn for him, with Ella's help."

Gerald chuckled. He wasn't taking her request to leave seriously at all. "Ahh. I've been wonderin' how you were gonna feed decent food to payin' folk."

"You can't stay, Gerald."

"Why not?"

"You know why."

He looked at her, suitcases still in hand, smiling his father's charming smile. "You can't stop me."

"I can try."

"Whooee! Is this my little sister talkin'? What put starch in your backbone after all these years, I wonder?"

Nursing your wife through terminal cancer, Jussy wanted to say. *And falling in love with a man who showed me there's nothing scary about standing up to you men.*

But she wasn't going to start explaining that to him, either.

"Why are you here?" she asked again, wearily.

"I told you. It's my house. And I got a right to help run it."

So that was it. Somebody had given him a hint that the Oleander Inn just might prove successful. And now he wanted his share. More than his share.

On the other hand, he was still her brother. And he owed Sam a lot of money. Was there really any harm in letting him help pay it back?

Gerald was watching her warily. He wasn't taking any chances that Jussy would refuse to welcome him. Nobody had to tell him that she had changed. He only had to look at her to see that. She was softer, and much prettier than he remembered—a real woman, not a kid sister anymore. But there was something tough about her, too. Starch in her backbone, a little hardness around the heart that had never been there before. He could see it in the tilt of her chin and the way those big eyes of hers met his without flinching.

"I got a right to all this," he insisted, gesturing toward the house. "And a right to stay. I'm Ashley's father, don't forget."

It was the wrong tack to take.

Jussy expression became cool, watchful. "Oh?"

"I wouldn't want to take her away from all this."

"Is that a threat?"

Gerald gave her his trademark grin. "Now, I didn't say that, did I?"

But he had implied it. Jussy looked down at the ground. "You'd really do that, Gerald? Use your own daughter to get your way?"

The grin faded. "I don't want things to get ugly, Juss."

They already had. "You're not taking Ashley."

"Says who? I'm still her father. I got more right to her than you do."

"Is that so?"

"Yeah, that's so. Any court of law would rule that she belongs with her biological father no matter what that judge decided when Caroline was still alive."

A little trickle of panic seeped into Jussy's heart, but she'd be damned if she let Gerald see it. "You'd subject her to a custody battle. Your own daughter." She couldn't believe it. "Just to be sure I let you help out with the inn."

"Partners, not help. We'd split everything fifty-fifty." Gerald sounded as though she ought to appreciate his generosity.

Jussy's heart was beating double time. She wasn't sure if she was going to burst into tears or bash Gerald's head in with the golf clubs she could see in the back seat of his car. "What about the money you owe Sam? I'd planned on paying him back first, before I took a penny of the profits."

"That figures. You always had a lousy head for business, Juss."

"Get out of here, Gerald."

"What?"

"Get off the property. Now."

He set the suitcases down. The charming smile was gone. "You can't make me leave."

"Yes, I can. If you don't go, I'll call the police."

"That Ritter fellow?" Gerald snorted. "Tod Slater told me all about him. Said he was a pansy, nothin' to be scared of."

"Tod Slater's only mad at him because he got busted for walking around town with an open beer can."

That had been on the day Sam arrived in town, Jussy remembered. The day of Caroline's funeral.

"I wouldn't take anything Tod Slater says seriously," she added through clenched teeth. "He stays drunk all the time and sits on his front porch hooting at girls. If he says Captain Ritter's nothing to be scared of, then stay here and find out. Because I'm going in right now to call him."

"Sure you are," Gerald scoffed.

"Try me."

"If I leave, I'm takin' Ashley with me."

That stopped Jussy in midstride. She tried to keep her voice from trembling. "You wouldn't dare."

Gerald reached into his pocket, drew out what looked like a ticket folder and waved it under her nose. "I already figured I might have to, especially after Tod's idea failed to put you off. I got two return flights to L.A., Jussy, not one."

"What idea?" Jussy prodded, stalling for time. In her mind, she was going over a number of desperate plans to keep Ashley safe. If she could keep Gerald talking, maybe Ella would see them from the house, guess what was going on and drive away with the girl. But how long could they keep her hidden?

"Your aviary." Gerald was smiling again, but in a way that wasn't charming at all.

Jussy stared at him.

"I asked him to give you a little warnin'," Gerald explained. "Just to let you know I was serious about wantin' in. I was gonna mention it on the phone the other night, but you hung up on me. Remember, Jussy? You hung up on me, your own brother."

"But—but why hurt my birds?" Jussy asked faintly. "What were you trying to prove?"

"Answer the lady, Gerald. It's something I'd like to know, too."

Jussy whirled at the sound of the deep voice coming from behind her. A broad-shouldered man with a very menacing expression was approaching from the drive.

"None of your business, Baker," Gerald snapped.

Sam folded his arms across his chest. There was something decidedly threatening in the movement. He didn't glance once in Jussy's direction, but he had made a point of placing himself between her and her brother.

"You're wrong," he said coldly. "It is my business. And I'll give you exactly one minute to explain yourself before I cram you into that suitcase of yours and drive you back to the airport. Understood?"

Chapter Eighteen

"Lord a mercy! I can't believe all that was goin' on right under my nose!" Regretfully, Ella shook her head. "Most excitin' thing ever happened in Waccamaw and I had to be upstairs sewin' curtains!"

"Believe me, Ella, you were lucky to have missed it."

Ella threw Jussy a worried glance. Poor thing had been sitting there at the kitchen table pale as a ghost practically all afternoon. With Sam back in town, she should've been turning cartwheels.

"Want some chicken?"

"No, thanks. I'm not hungry."

"It's almost three o'clock, darlin'. You ain't had a bite since breakfast."

"I know."

Ella planted her hands on her ample hips. "And you better snap outta that funk before Sam gets back. He'll think you blame him for hauling your brother off as a trespasser, 'stead of bein' grateful to him for showin' up when he did.''

"I know I should be grateful. I *am* grateful. I just wish..." Jussy rubbed her burning eyes. Of all the thousands of ways she had dreamed of Sam's return, this ugly scenario hadn't been one of them.

Ella looked worried all of a sudden. "You don't think he'll have your brother tossed in jail, do you? I mean, he deserves it, threatenin' to take Ashley away and all, but how would it look? Ashley's daddy with a record—"

"I don't think that's what Sam had in mind." But Jussy couldn't be sure. She'd never before seen the expression Sam had had on his face when he'd tossed her brother into the car after Gerald had dropped his suitcases and taken a swing at him.

Gerald had looked nearly as stunned as Jussy had when Sam had deflected the blow easily and grabbed him in some kind of a wrestler's hold. Then he had easily manhandled Gerald into the car and slipped into the driver's seat.

"I'll be right back," he had called to Jussy through the window, but he hadn't said where he was going.

That had been more than two hours ago.

In the meantime, Jussy had tried to make some sense of what had happened. Part of her was filled with a bubbling joy because Sam was back, while the other part of her sore, battered heart grieved for her brother, whose irrational behavior went beyond her understanding.

But more than anything, she was afraid. Her fear for Ashley overshadowed even the breathless happiness she felt at Sam's return. She didn't doubt for a minute that Gerald would use Ashley to get what he wanted. And he was right about one thing: judges didn't always settle custody cases in terms of a child's best interests.

Gerald was Ashley's biological father. Jussy was merely the little girl's aunt, a single woman embarking on an uncertain career. She had little money, and even less to offer her niece in the way of a nurturing family environment.

In fact, she had nothing to offer Ashley except love. And if newspaper headlines were any indication, that wasn't always enough.

"He's back."

Ella was peeking through the kitchen curtains.

Jussy felt her heart contract. "Is he alone?"

"Looks like it. Oops. I'm wrong. He's got Joey Ritter with him."

Jussy sprang to the window. Sure enough, the gray-haired man in the dark blue uniform was getting out of the passenger's side of Sam's car. Gerald wasn't with them.

"Oh, Ella! What do you suppose happened?"

"Got me, honey. I think we're about to find out, though."

Male voices could be heard, then the door creaked open. Jussy turned. Her eyes found Sam's. He looked back, grim and unsmiling.

"Afternoon, Miss Waring, Ella."

Both women greeted the police chief warily.

"Y'all have a seat," Ella invited, because Jussy was too nervous to remember her manners. "How about some iced tea?"

"That'd be great."

Both men pulled up chairs. Desperate to keep busy, Jussy cut them each a slice of lemon pound cake. She could feel Sam's gaze upon her, but she couldn't bring herself to glance at him again. She'd never known him to look so cold.

Silence fell.

Then Sam said quietly, "Sit down, Jussy."

She did so, truly apprehensive now.

"I've asked Chief Ritter over to see if you want to press charges."

"What? Against who? Gerald?"

"Him or Tod Slater, or both." It was the police chief who answered. "We got plenty on Slater already. Not just what happened here at your place. I'd like to see him in court, Ms. Waring."

Jussy knotted her hands together. Her throat ached with tears of betrayal. How could Sam possibly expect her to press charges against her own brother? Granted, what he'd done was unforgivable, but he was still a Waring—and Ashley's father.

She threw Sam a look of scorn, and was glad for the anger that surged through her.

Sam understood the look clearly enough; Jussy could tell by the way the muscles in his jaw started to clench. Had she hurt him? Good! Let him know what it felt like for a change!

She turned back to Chief Ritter. "What about my brother? Where is he? Did you arrest him?"

"Nope. Mr. Baker here convinced me to let him go back to California."

"Excuse me?"

"I took him to the airport," Sam answered. He wouldn't look at her, and that muscle in his jaw was still working in and out.

"B-but why?"

"I figured you wouldn't want to press charges against your own brother. I figured you'd want to find some other way of helping him. So I convinced him to enroll in a self-help program for alcoholics instead."

The way he said that left no doubt in Jussy's mind that Sam's way of convincing her brother hadn't been pleasant. She looked helplessly back at the police chief.

"You want me to press charges against Tod Slater? You know I can't do that without involving my brother."

The police chief looked unhappy. "I know. Mr. Baker told me as much, but I was sort of hopin' I could change your mind. I've managed to build up a mighty good case on him for some other stuff, you see. Especially in this last week, since Mr. Baker came to see me about the break-in."

"What do you mean?" Jussy's eyes clung to the police chief's, if only to keep herself from looking at Sam. "He's known about this since last week?"

"Yup. In fact, Mr. Baker's the one who found out who done it. Spent two whole days askin' questions, wantin' to know if folks had seen anybody headin' down the road to your place on the mornin' your birds was let loose. Jasper Oley finally remembered he'd seen a gray pickup truck before the sun come up, when he was out walkin' Beauregard."

"Who's Beauregard?" breathed Ella.

"His hound," said Sam and Jussy in unison.

"Tod Slater has a gray pickup truck," Jussy added quietly.

Sam nodded. "As soon as I found out, I confronted him about the break-in. He told me your brother had put him up to it. There wasn't time to come back and let you know. I barely caught the last flight to Los Angeles."

"You went to Los Angeles?" Jussy's eyes were wide. "Why? To see Gerald?"

Sam nodded grimly. Jussy didn't know it, but those grief stricken eyes of hers were cutting him to the quick. "Turned out I was too late. By the time I got there, he was already on his way here. Ironic, isn't it?"

And she'd accused him of running out on her. Had thought he'd hightailed it home to Boston. Had called him a coward.

Wearily, Jussy put her face in her hands. All she wanted to do at the moment was crawl into Sam's lap and lay her head against his shoulder and tell him how sorry she was. She'd never needed him more, wanted him more, than she did right now.

And at the same time she was trying hard to convince herself that it was enough just to have him here.

It had to be enough. She didn't dare expect more. Not when it seemed so unlikely she'd ever get it. Sam might have been a total stranger, sitting there across from her so distant and calm. And she'd been unfair to him just now, so totally unfair.

"So what happens now?" she asked in a muffled voice, not looking at anyone.

"We can't do anything if you decide you don't want to get involved, Miss Waring. Our hands are tied."

"I'm sorry, Chief Ritter." Jussy's voice trembled. "I'd really like to help out, but I can't. I just can't."

"Because of Ashley?" Sam asked quietly.

Jussy bit her lip and nodded.

He sighed heavily. "I can understand that. I just wish you'd think about the . . . Jussy?"

Her heart skipped a beat. "What?"

"Will you look at me, please?"

Slowly, unwillingly, she lifted her head. She saw that Sam's mouth was no longer hard, but soft and compelling. His eyes caressed hers like a physical touch. She bowed her head quickly and stared at her feet.

"Oh, no, Juss," Sam said softly. "I want you to look at me. I want to know what you're thinking."

Jussy's jaw clenched. Didn't he realize that it took the starch clear out of her backbone when he talked to her like that? When she was desperate to keep some distance between them, his voice alone seemed to be pulling her closer, commanding her to drop the tenuous hold she had on her feelings—and her heart.

Sweet Lord, she wasn't going to let him hurt her again. She was going to accept very calmly his announcement that he was taking the next flight back to Boston. Why shouldn't he, now that everything had been resolved?

Only it hadn't been. Not for Jussy. Not for Sam.

And certainly not for Ella Reid. "Hold on a minute, there!" the older woman hollered.

Her bark startled all of them, especially Joey Ritter, who stared at her openmouthed, as though he'd never seen her before.

"How can we be sure Juss and Ashley are gonna be safe from now on? If Tod Slater done a favor like this for her brother once, what's to keep him from doin' it again? Maybe somethin' worse this time, like kidnapping our baby?"

Jussy sucked in her breath. The thought had never occurred to her. She turned a beseeching gaze on Sam. "Oh, Sam, no!"

Her plea struck to the very core of him, to that primitive part of every man's soul that decreed he must protect to the death what lay closest to his heart.

And Sam knew suddenly, without the shadow of a doubt, that what lay closest to his heart was Jussy. How else could he explain the way the gnawing emptiness in his heart was filled merely by lifting his head and looking at her? Why else would he have fooled himself into believing that he was doing a mad, impulsive thing like chasing her brother clear across the country only because he was worried about the welfare of the Oleander Inn?

Unlike Jussy, he had at first refused to believe that love, true love, could hit a person so quickly, and wholly without warning. But now he could no longer deny the obvious. He had been in love with this courageous, whiskey-haired woman from the very first.

He cleared his throat. "Nothing's going to happen to Ashley."

Jussy's frightened eyes latched onto his face, wanting so hard to believe that. "But you were there, Sam. Gerald said—"

"I heard what he said."

Sam's feelings for Ashley were there in his voice, in the way his hands clenched slowly into fists on the table in front of him.

Watching him, Jussy could feel the uncontrolled beating of her heart begin to slow down. Loving someone meant trusting them, she realized with a sudden sense of shock. Trusting them without question or doubt or a moment's hesitation. And she trusted Sam to look after Ashley. Everything in his manner said that he would.

"You can always fight him in court," Chief Ritter was saying soothingly.

"I'd be too scared of losing," Jussy confessed.

"Who says you'd lose? Got a mighty good case, if you ask me. Your sister-in-law named you guardian. Your brother never had custody, and rarely saw Ashley anyway. And if you got yourself a husband like this one, your chances would be even better." The big policeman gave Sam a hearty slap on the back. "No judge in his right mind'd rule against such a fine couple!"

For a second you could have heard a pin drop in the kitchen. Jussy's face turned chilly red. Sam stared off into the distance.

"Lord a mercy!" Ella exclaimed briskly. "Will y'all look at the time? I gotta be in Litchfield 'fore the fabric store closes! You suppose I could use your car, Sam? Oh, and let me give you a lift, Chief Ritter. We'll take some pound cake home to your wife."

"I ain't got no wife."

"No? Now ain't that interestin'. All this time I was sure a handsome feller like you was firmly hooked." Ella paused, the wheels in her head turning furiously. "Tell you what. I'll throw in a strawberry cobbler, too. Strawberries ain't the best this time of year, comin' from California the way they do, but the cobbler's mighty tasty, if I do say so myself."

"You made that pound cake, Mrs. Reid?" The admiration was clear in Joey Ritter's voice as he hungrily watched her wrap up an enormous wedge.

Ella, preening, nodded vigorously.

"Well, I'll be. It's about the best I've ever had."

She blushed bright red.

Sam got slowly to his feet. His expression might have been carved of stone. "Let me walk you both to the car. We'll decide what to do about Slater in the morning."

"Mighty kind of you."

They all trooped down the back steps, leaving Jussy alone at the table. She heard their animated voices and Chief Ritter's rumbling belly laugh in response to something Ella said.

A few minutes later the sound of car doors slamming was accompanied by the grinding of gears as Ella shifted the transmission with a heavy hand. Then Sam's familiar steps could be heard crossing the back porch.

Quickly Jussy sat up, wiping away the tears and combing her fingers through her hair.

Sam appeared in the doorway. Heaven knows why— maybe because she was so tired and discouraged—but it seemed that all she could think about when she turned her head to look at him was the way it had felt to make love with him.

She had tried so hard to forget him. The inn, the carriage house, the fate of her birds and Ashley—into each of these she had poured all of her energy only to end up making the awful discovery that everything in her life—except Ashley—was meaningless without Sam.

Worse, he had only to show up in her kitchen door and she felt herself coming instantly to life. Shock and heartache slipped away like mist over the marshes the moment their eyes met, and the knowledge that she loved him so much, needed him so much, was scarier than anything she'd ever known.

Sam, too, found himself overwhelmed by something totally unexpected when he came through the door and saw Jussy sitting there alone in the kitchen. He hadn't noticed until now how small and fragile she looked. Her skin was pale, almost translucent, and there were shadows beneath her beautiful eyes—eyes that gave every evidence of having spilled recent tears.

"Oh, Jussy," he said.

Her throat closed up. She breathed deeply, willing herself to stay in control.

Crossing to the table, Sam reached out his hand to her. "Come on. You need a nap. You're exhausted."

Although Jussy knew it was true, she couldn't bring herself to touch Sam at the moment, no matter how brisk and impersonal he sounded. She looked up into his face, then down at his outstretched hand, hesitating.

"What's the matter?" he taunted. "Scared?"

She set her jaw at a mulish angle, the way he knew she would.

Hiding a grin, he leaned closer, his hand reaching out to her.

As she took it, almost mindlessly, he pulled her upright and reeled her in. Before she knew what he intended to do, he had wrapped his arms tightly around her. His free hand threaded through her hair. Splaying his fingers across the back of her skull, he brought her head against his chest.

Jussy could feel his heart thundering beneath her cheek, or was that merely her own pounding pulse? She felt his warmth flowing through her, and her eyes drifted shut.

Oh, God, she thought. *It really was like coming home.*

"My poor Jussy." Sam's breath stirred her hair.

"Oh, Sam." She leaned into the hollow beneath his chin and swallowed hard. "I just don't know what to say anymore."

"Then don't say anything. Get some sleep. Things always look better after a nap, don't they?"

"I wouldn't know. I don't usually sleep during the day." Her voice was barely audible.

"That's half the problem. Ella told me you've been pushing yourself too hard."

Opening the back door, Sam led her down the stairs and across the lawn. "Whose idea was it to move into the carriage house?"

"Mine and Ashley's." Jussy shivered against him. "Oh, Sam, what's going to—"

"Shh," he interrupted. "Don't think about that now. I'll take care of everything, I promise."

Oh, it felt heavenly to believe him, to lay such an impossibly heavy burden on his shoulders and know she didn't have to worry about it anymore!

In the carriage house, Sam noted with approval how tidy and welcoming Jussy kept the place. Ella's influence was clearly rubbing off. He fetched a glass of iced tea from the refrigerator, added a lemon wedge and a sprig of mint and brought it back to Jussy.

He found her standing in the bedroom door where he'd left her, arms hanging at her sides, slim shoulders bowed.

Crossing to her, he tipped up her chin and smiled into her tired eyes. "Poor Juss," he said again.

It was his gentleness that undid her. Jussy tried to remind herself why she couldn't possibly let her heart be moved, but her will seemed to have left her completely.

"I thought you'd gone back to Boston," she said in a choked voice.

A spark of anger flared in his eyes. "How could you think that? Did you honestly believe I'd just up and leave, without knowing who vandalized your aviary, without knowing whether you or Ashley might be in some kind of danger?''

"I thought—I was sure you'd decided you'd had enough of us—of me.''

"Oh, Jussy!'' Sam put down the drink and turned back to her, not sure whether he wanted to laugh or weep. "You were right. I did try to put you out of my mind. I told myself I was going after your brother simply for the sake of my money and the welfare of the inn. I spent most of this week chasing down Tod Slater and flying out to L.A. and back, and trying to convince myself I didn't miss you, didn't need you, wasn't absolutely miserable without you. I told myself that I'd get over you if I gave it enough time.''

"I see.''

He caught her arm when she tried to turn away and pulled her toward him, gently, deliberately. "Do you know, I've never done anything more futile in my entire life.''

"Neither have I,'' Jussy confessed, without looking at him.

Sam grew still, as though he could scarcely believe she had just said what he'd been wanting so badly to hear. Then he smiled at her and held out his arms in a tempting promise of ever after.

Jussy shook her head through a blur of tears. "I can't, Sam.''

His arms dropped to his sides.

"When you leave again, it'll only make things harder to bear.''

"Who said I was leaving?''

She could only stand and gape.

"Jussy...''

But even as he started to speak, he realized that words weren't enough. Not for what he saw in her eyes, not for what he felt in his heart.

Without another word, he turned and moved toward her. He pulled her roughly into his arms and into a kiss of shattering possession.

It turned Jussy inside out. All the pain and doubts and fears melted away into glory.

"Oh, Juss," Sam breathed against her willing mouth, while his heart thundered and desire seeped slowly and deliciously through every rejoicing fiber of his being.

He kissed her again, deeply, so that her vision blurred and the bones of her body turned to liquid as she melted against him. Jussy wasn't sure if he carried her to the bed or if they walked. She wasn't aware of anything but the moment Sam laid her back against the pillows and leaned down to deepen the kiss. Its joyous intent gave way to more elemental needs. His lips were teasing torment. His tongue plundered and coaxed, tasted and tortured.

"So good," he murmured against her mouth. "Like coming home."

Her eyes were like stars as he told her that. He knew, because he opened his own to look at her.

Rolling onto his side, he took Jussy over with him. Slow warmth gave way to quickening desire. Jussy could feel the throbbing heat of him through the fabric of their clothes. Her hands reached boldly for his jeans, and Sam sucked in his breath as she unfastened his belt and his swollen flesh sprang free to her touch.

"Oh, Juss," he said hoarsely.

But that was all. Shuddering with pleasure, he closed his eyes as she caressed him.

They helped each other undress. It was a slow, magical dance, without the urgency that had gripped them a moment ago. Sam found himself filled with unbearable tenderness as he drew back Jussy's shirt and kissed the narrow slimness of her naked shoulders. Though he burned for her, he would atone for all the pain he had caused her.

He slipped his hand into the waistband of her panties and slowly drew them off. He caressed her flat stomach and the curve of her hip.

She was beautiful. Hard work and years of swimming in the creek had honed her muscles, made them sleek and indescribably sexy.

He lifted his head to look at her, running his fingers through the silky richness of her hair. "Do you know how beautiful you are?"

Jussy's lips curved as she brushed her own fingers across his wonderfully sexy mouth. "Do you know how beautiful *you* are?"

Sam chuckled and caught her to him. She fit so well against his heart that he wondered fleetingly if she hadn't been molded solely for the purpose of being there. The thought made him chuckle again.

Smiling at him in response, Jussy slipped her arms around his neck and brought his lips down to hers. "There's nothing funny about this, Sam Baker," she whispered. "Come here and let me show you."

Arching, she wrapped herself around him and their legs tangled. Heated, aching, their bodies came together.

Rising on one elbow once the drugging kiss was over, Sam moved his mouth slowly to her breasts, loving first one rosebud nipple, then the other. Jussy's head fell back as liquid fire poured through her.

Trailing kisses along her stomach, Sam went lower, slowly and deliberately making his intent clear.

Instantly Jussy's muscles tensed and she moved sharply beneath him.

"No, Juss, no," Sam murmured gently, knowing this was new to her. "Trust me."

"I do," she whispered, and she relaxed beneath him.

In response, his kisses became more gentle as he proceeded ever closer to the core of her femininity. He wanted

his moment to be Jussy's alone, and he took his time
bringing her to the edge of her own passion.

Tenderly he stoked the fire within her until the heat of it
thrilled her being. She was fire and ice, quivering on the
edge of an explosion, and still the exquisite torment continued.

The pleasure built and Jussy burned, whispering his name
in a rush of tremulous wonder. She could wait no longer.

Neither could Sam. In giving Jussy pleasure, he found
that he had fanned his own desire to heated torment. When
she moaned and arched beneath him, he, too, could hold
back no longer. Rearing up, he poised himself above her,
aching with need.

"Oh, Juss..."

Murmuring his name again, she drew him to her. Her
thighs parted and he entered her swiftly, urgently.

It took only a few fierce thrusts to bring them both to a
shattering climax. Shuddering, gasping, Sam wrapped her
tightly in his embrace, while Jussy gave a groan of stunned
delight as her body convulsed beneath his.

Clinging fiercely, they flowed together into waves of
shimmering release.

Too long. It had been too long for both of them.

Never enough, and more than enough.

There was no turning back now, and both of them knew
it. And neither cared.

Chapter Nineteen

Slowly Jussy lifted her head from Sam's chest and took a long, possessive look at him.

He opened his eyes and did the same.

As their sated gazes met, they laughed. It was spontaneous laughter, rich and exulting, a celebration that healed and bound.

"Ah, Jussy," Sam said in a tender voice she'd never heard before. "I love you. I knew it the moment you accused me of it that last night we were together. That's why I ran, like a coward. I thought loving you was the last thing I wanted. I know now that it's the only thing I do want."

She'd waited so long to hear him say it. But now that he had, the feeling was more wonderful than anything she'd imagined. The whole world seemed filled with new promise. She wanted to tell him that, but she couldn't find the right words.

It didn't matter. Sam had something else on his mind.

"I want you, Juss." The laughter had died away, replaced by an earnestness that was reflected in the burning blue of his eyes.

"Wh-what?"

He reached for her hand, lacing her fingers through his. "I want you for always, do you understand? I thought I had my life all worked out. My apartment in Boston, my work, my friends—they seemed like enough. Hell, they *were* enough! I had no desire to change anything—but only because I'd never met the one woman who could show me there was so much more."

Jussy had grown still. Her heart teetered on the brink of eternity and shattering pain. She had to make sure. She would give him a final out if he wanted it. After that, it would be too late. She would never let him go.

"Like going to oyster roasts with beer-swilling rednecks, enduring days of breathing plaster dust and taking thirty-mile drives to the nearest pizza parlor?"

"Oh, Juss—"

The answer was there, in the way Sam's voice broke with emotion when he said her name, and his mouth quirked in that wonderful way he had of grinning at her whenever something all but overwhelmed him.

"None of that matters. I love you. And I want to hear you say it back. Say it," he urged roughly. "Say it now."

"I love you," Jussy whispered, and the thrill of saying it aloud after dreaming about it for so long spread through her with slow-burning delight.

"Say it again," he commanded softly.

"I love you, Sam."

Then he was holding her fiercely and kissing her in away that made her senses swim.

"I can turn most of my work over to my partner," Sam said, drawing back just enough to look into her eyes. "Set up an office here in the carriage house and take care of special projects without having to spend a lot of time in Boston. You'll come with me whenever I do have to go, won't you?''

Jussy cupped his cheek with her hand. She had to make sure he was real, that what he was telling her wasn't a dream. She was shaking just a little. "I— Do you want me to?''

Sam's answer was a throaty laugh. Taking her hand, he kissed the tip of each slim finger, then tucked it comfortably against his chest, right above his heart. "Always. And in the summer, when it's too hot to stick around, we'll go diving in the Caymans or the Great Barrier Reef. Ella should have everything under control up at the house, and I'm sure you can find someone to take care of your birds while we're gone, right?''

Jussy's eyes were like stars. Then her gaze faltered. "What about Ashley?''

"She'll come with us, of course. The sooner she gets certified as a diver, the better. You, too, Juss. How soon can you start lessons?''

"I—I don't know.''

This exuberant Sam was going to take some getting used to.

"Great. We can drive down to Charleston tomorrow and visit the dive shops. I'll have extra equipment sent down from Boston. You can use it until we can outfit you with your own.''

Smiling, he took Jussy's face in his hands and made as if to kiss her, but she resisted. He drew back, his expression puzzled.

"You make it sound so easy,'' she breathed, afraid she was going to cry.

"Oh, sweetheart. That's because it is.''

"What about Tod Slater?''

"We'll leave him to Joey Ritter. He's got enough on the man to run him out of town without involving your brother or your birds."

Her brother. Jussy could feel her happiness seeping away. The warmth of Sam's body, still wrapped around hers, was suddenly not enough. She shivered.

"Talk to me, Juss," Sam whispered, gathering her close.

She turned her face into his shoulder. "If Gerald tries to take Ashley—"

"He won't."

"How do you know? Supposing he does?"

"He can't. There isn't a judge in the country who'd award him custody. Not with everything we have to offer her. A stable home. A real family. A mother and father in every sense but the biological one. Of course, she can have a relationship with her father if she wants to. We won't deny her that. But only if Gerald cleans up his act. And I have a feeling he will."

But Jussy suddenly didn't care about Gerald anymore. She'd latched on to the other thing Sam had said—the thing that was making her head spin and leaving her feeling senseless with joy.

"Is this—are you saying we're getting married, Sam?"

Instead of answering right away, he rolled her onto her back. Coming up on his elbows he tangled his legs with hers and took her face in his hands. His expression, his words, were intense.

"I am, Juss," he said roughly. "Are you willing to give me a try?"

Her heart, her answer, were there in her eyes as she drew in breath to tell him so.

"Say it," Sam urged. "I want to hear you say it out loud. Tell me that you'll marry me."

Her eyes went all dewy and her vision blurred. "Oh, Sam—"

But she was interrupted by a sharp tug on the sheets, which were still tangled around their legs.

"What the—?" Sam twisted around abruptly.

They were both startled to see a small gray parrot climbing toward them from the floor, in the only way a parrot with clipped wings knows how—by grasping the sheets with his nails and his great, curved beak.

Mr. Binks, resentful at having been neglected, had left the T-stand in the kitchen and come into the bedroom to join them.

"Oh, no," Sam groaned, as the beady-eyed bird waddled toward them. There wasn't time to ease away from Jussy and dive for cover. Not before that powerful beak took a healthy chunk right out of him! How like the miniature monster to plot an ambush!

"Jussy!" he yelled, but it was too late. Mr. Binks lunged.

Wincing, Sam closed his eyes.

The painful bite didn't come.

Cautiously, he opened one eye. To his utter astonishment, he felt the soft brush of feathers against his skin. Holding himself perfectly still, he looked down and saw the gray parrot actually nuzzling his shoulder with every evidence of affection.

"What the—?"

"Sam," Mr. Binks said lovingly.

Sam's startled eyes swept up to Jussy's. "What in hell is going on? Has he had a lobotomy or something?"

She was trying hard to hold on to her laughter. "I'm not sure. I mentioned your name a lot after you left. Maybe it helped change his mind."

"It couldn't have! It's a trick."

"I don't think so. He's never devious—at least not in that way."

"Then tell me quick, before he changes his mind again and takes a chomp out of me," Sam said urgently. "Will you marry me, Jussy Waring?"

"Oh, God, I—"

"Sam stay!" crowed Mr. Binks. "Sam stay, now!"

"Well?"

"Kiss Inks! Kiss Inks now, please!"

Jussy's arms tightened around Sam's neck. "I think that qualifies as an answer, don't you?"

"No. I want to hear you say it. Say it, Jussy."

"Yes," she said with a sigh, above the thundering of his heart, above her own. "Yes, I'll marry you."

And just in case, she brought his head down to hers and kissed him, before Mr. Binks had a chance to.

* * * * *

COMING NEXT MONTH

**#979 SUNSHINE AND THE SHADOWMASTER—
Christine Rimmer**
That Special Woman!/The Jones Gang

From the moment they were thrown together, Heather Conley and
Lucas Drury were instantly drawn to each other. Giving in to that
passion made them expectant parents—but would Heather believe in
Lucas's love and stick around for the wedding?

#980 A HOME FOR ADAM—Gina Ferris Wilkins
The Family Way

Dr. Adam Stone never expected to make a house call at his own
secluded vacation cabin. But then the very pregnant Jenny Newcomb
showed up on his doorstep. And one baby later, they were on their way to
an instant family!

#981 KISSES AND KIDS—Andrea Edwards
Congratulations!

Confusion over his name unexpectedly placed practical businessman
Patrick Stuart amongst Trisha Stewart and her cute kids. Pat *swore* he
was not the daddy type, but he couldn't resist sweet Trisha and her
brood for long....

#982 JOYRIDE—Patricia Coughlin
Congratulations!

Being thrown together on a cross-country drive was *not* the best way
to find a mate, Cat Bandini soon discovered. Bolton Hunter was her
complete opposite in every way—but with every passing mile, they
couldn't slow down their attraction!

#983 A DATE WITH DR. FRANKENSTEIN—Leanne Banks
Congratulations!

Andie Reynolds had spent her life taking care of others, and she'd
had it. Then sexy Eli Masters moved in next door. The neighbors
were convinced he was some sort of mad scientist. But Andie sensed
he was a single dad in need....

#984 THE AVENGER—Diana Whitney
The Blackthorn Brotherhood

Federal prosecutor Robert Arroya had time for little else but the pursuit
of justice. Then Erica Mallory and her adorable children showed him
how to trust again. But could their love survive a severe test?

PRIZE SURPRISE SWEEPSTAKES!

This month's prize:

BEAUTIFUL WEDGWOOD CHINA!

This month, as a special surprise, we're giving away a bone china dinner service for eight by Wedgwood**, one of England's most prestigious manufacturers!

Think how beautiful your table will look, set with lovely Wedgwood china in the casual Countryware pattern! Each five-piece place setting includes dinner plate, salad plate, soup bowl and cup and saucer.

The facing page contains two Entry Coupons (as does every book you received this shipment). Complete and return *all* the entry coupons; **the more times you enter, the better your chances of winning!**

Then keep your fingers crossed, because you'll find out by September 15, 1995 if you're the winner!

Remember: The more times you enter, the better your chances of winning!*

*NO PURCHASE OR OBLIGATION TO CONTINUE BEING A SUBSCRIBER NECESSARY TO ENTER. SEE THE REVERSE SIDE OF ANY ENTRY COUPON FOR ALTERNATE MEANS OF ENTRY.

**THE PROPRIETORS OF THE TRADEMARK ARE NOT ASSOCIATED WITH THIS PROMOTION.

PWW KAL